PROBABLY
YESTERDAY

PROBABLY YESTERDAY

Twelfth in the Prairie Preacher Series

PJ Hoge

iUniverse, Inc.
Bloomington

Probably Yesterday
Twelfth in the Prairie Preacher Series

iUniverse books may be ordered through booksellers or by contacting:

iUniverse
1663 Liberty Drive
Bloomington, IN 47403
www.iuniverse.com
1-800-Authors (1-800-288-4677)

ISBN: 978-1-4759-5813-3 (sc)
ISBN: 978-1-4759-5814-0 (ebk)

Library of Congress Control Number: 2012920037

Printed in the United States of America

iUniverse rev. date: 10/26/2012

In memory of my dear friend, Sister Carmel.

With special thanks to Mike H.

PROLOGUE

The bullwhip cracked the frigid air and its end tore across her back leaving huge welts and bruising the muscle below. The whipping did not stop until at least thirteen swaths of pain had been laid. The young girl managed to stumble her way into a small log shed behind the piles of stacked firewood. She pulled the door closed behind her and the whipping ceased.

She heard her father ranting outside, but he did not open the door, for which she was grateful. However, she heard him wedge something against the outside of the door and then he shouted, "You will stay there until you decide to obey your father or you will no longer share a place at his table!"

She had never seen this rage before in her father and was shocked to the point the pain of the whipping did not fully set in until she was alone. Leisel was not certain what had precipitated his violent anger. Her father had always been strict, but never this way. Her mother watched the whole thing, but never made a move to come to her aid. Maybe she was frightened herself.

It was late afternoon and below freezing already. It would be very cold that night. For some time, Leisel stayed curled up, whimpering and trying to think of what to do. She was thankful that she had her woolen coat on, or the whipping would have been worse. As it was, she could feel blood oozing from a lash across her neck and throat. She wadded her shirt to stop the bleeding. The longer she stayed there, curled in the corner, the colder she became.

It seemed an eternity before she heard her father and her brothers come out to milk cows. She was certain her father would come to let her out, but he did not. When she heard them leave the barn and go back into the house, she became extremely worried and in fear she may not survive.

She moved inside the dark shed from memory and found a bag of flax straw that she pulled over herself to keep warm. She was very grateful that she had her winter leggings and mittens on. She lay there alone in the dark listening to the wind howl through the trees. Leisel didn't know that a person could ever feel so desolate.

T he freezing sleet stuck on the windshield wherever the windshield wipers did not clear. It was wet and bleak, but not windy as Jeff pulled up in front of St. John's rectory in Merton, North Dakota that night in mid-April 1971. Kincaid's new Mercury came to rest in the drive in front of the detached garage and Jeff Wilson turned it off.

The lights were on in the kitchen as he approached the door and reached out to knock. Father Landers opened the door immediately, startling them both. "Come on in. We were watching for you! Nasty weather, huh?"

"That is an understatement. There is a fine layer of ice on everything. Don't know how the highway will be! The gravel roads were even slippery," Jeff acknowledged as he carefully stood on the carpet by the door. "Your steps are life-threatening."

"Keeps out the intruders," Father Vicaro quipped as he came into the kitchen. He was the senior priest in Merton and had been there for years. He was slightly balding and wore bi-focals, usually pushed up on his forehead. Looking like the older Italian gentleman that he was, he was in his mid-sixties and just recuperating from breaking his thigh earlier that fall while scraping ice off the parking lot. He was well-known as a down to earth, slightly cantankerous tease. He was very devout, but had a warped sense of humor. "I tried to get these two whippersnappers to go out and clear it off, but to no avail. They seem to think that I'm the only one with experience at cleaning ice."

"Yah, yah," Father Bart patted his head. "We saw you at work last fall. No need for a rerun. I'll put some salt on the ice before we pack the car."

PJ Hoge

"Salt? What happened to shoveling?" the old priest squawked. "It will deteriorate the concrete and we'll have to put in new steps."

Father Landers looked at him with his big smile, "You dingbat. We aren't going to soak the steps in salt! Are you certain you don't need to go back to bed? Maybe more sleep would make you compatible."

"I don't need more sleep and leaving you and Slick alone to run this joint would be a disaster," Vicaro grumped.

"You are right about one thing, sleep won't help your personality," Father Bart poked. The thin, fair-haired young priest chuckled. "I'm going to put salt on it anyway, and if you don't like it, you're welcome to wash it off."

Vicaro looked at Jeff for support, "I can't believe the diocese sent me these two! Landers is slower than molasses and Slick is . . . . well, Slick."

Jeff smiled, "Sounds like you guys get along very well."

"Hurrumph," Vicaro groaned. "Well Wilson, you better take good care of our girl. Sister is the only person that can keep a lid on these two and make my life tolerable."

"She keeps a lid on you, Frank Vicaro!" Landers pointed out. "But yes, take care of our girl. We need her! We got her a bottle of sipping rye and I want to give it to you. Keep it for her if she needs it. Then tell her it is because we love her. Okay?"

Jeff smiled as he took the bottle, "I will do that. Nice of you guys. How is she doing? Were she and her mother very close?"

Vicaro got serious, "Not at all. That is why this is really bothering her. I hope you make it out there in time for Sister to see her before she passes. It would be worthwhile for her to do that. Her family life was . . . well, peculiar. I'm glad you'll be with her."

Bart came back in and added, "One of us would gladly have gone, but this week is insane. It was a blessing that you stepped forward and offered to take her. She actually considered taking a train! Can you believe that?"

"Is there train service to her hometown?"

"No closer than sixty miles! But she would have done it," Landers explained. "Sister has more grit than most but she needs someone to tend to her soft heart also. She'd never ask. We feel good that you'll be there for her."

"You guys don't even know me," Jeff grinned.

"We do," Vicaro disagreed. "You are Matt's friend. Carl Kincaid thinks you are a good soul! If those guys think you're okay, then you're okay."

2

"Thanks," Jeff said seriously. "How long has it been since Sister saw her family last?"

"Long time. I think she saw a brother a few years back but that was it." Vicaro explained. "He was traveling through and they spent some time together. Anyway, we can't survive without her, so we are entrusting you with our very survival!"

Jeff laughed, "Not putting on much pressure there, are you Vicaro?"

"That's our Frank," Landers chuckled. "I put together some food in this basket."

"So did Kincaids and Schroeders. Good night, we'll have enough food to feed a small army!" Jeff went on, "And of course, Schroeders packed chains, shovels and gravel in the trunk in case we run into bad roads! Elton even lent us his huge coffee thermos!"

"Then you'll be in good shape," Vicaro gave a satisfied nod. "Heavy clothes, boots, blankets, food. You may need all of it. The prairies are bad enough in this weather, but the mountains can be treacherous. I forced Sister to pack some Carhartt's and overshoes in case you get stuck. She fussed about it, but relented. She knows that habits are not conducive to climbing over mountain snow drifts!"

"Yea gads," Jeff shook his brown hair. He was a nice looking man who had kind, soft brown eyes, "You folks are making me wonder if we should even go."

"Ah, you'll make it." Vicaro broke into a huge devilish grin. "You might not, but Sister can take care of you!"

Sister Abigail came into the kitchen lugging a suitcase and a large bag, "Sister will do what?"

The younger priests ran to take her load, "We can put that in the car for you. You relax a minute and have some toast before you take off. You haven't had a bite to eat."

"It is three in the morning! My stomach isn't ready for food. However, a swig of that coffee would be much appreciated. Top of the Morning, Jeff. It is so kind of you to offer to take me out there."

"I had nothing pressing and I've never seen the Rocky Mountains. It works out beautifully. Besides, I wasn't looking forward to Kincaid's plans of yard work!" Jeff shook his head. "My word, he is digging up his entire place! The man is possessed."

3

"Yah," Vicaro grinned. "He never goes half way with anything, but even I think he is going a bit overboard with his yard. Believe me, he'll keep you hopping and you will more than pay for your room and board!"

"It sounds like it," Jeff finished his coffee. "So, Hwy 2 is the best way?"

"Yes, shortest. No roads are good in this sleet, but when the sun comes up, it should thaw off. The forecast here is for it to get warm. Don't know about out in Dahlgren," Landers said.

"We'll know when we get there," Sister said. "Jeff, I want you to know that I can drive so you don't need to do it all yourself. It is a long haul out there and this weather will make it longer. If we hit bad weather, we're holding up until it passes. No need to compound the problems. Okay?"

"Yes, Ma'am," Jeff nodded. "We won't take any unnecessary risks. These guys have told me they need you!"

Sister beamed, "They're only worried about their bellies. Well, I left food in the freezer and the fridge. You should survive until we return, if you behave to each other! No squabbling, hear?"

"Yah, we hear," they all grumbled.

Father Vicaro led them in a word of prayer and they left. Sister called out, "I will miss you boys and keep you in my prayers. We might be back unless Jeff and I can find something better to do!"

"No, you just come back," Father Bart said emphatically. "We know you can find something better to do."

So, the thirty-two-year-old ex-priest and the fifty-nine-year-old nun pulled out of the drive in a borrowed 1970 Mercury Marquis headed to a tiny, western Montana village about six hundred and fifty miles away.

t wasn't until they were heading north on the highway that either of them realized they hardly knew each other. Silence flooded the car with only the rhythmic sound of the windshield wipers and the blowing of the heater challenging it.

They only met at Christmas time when Jeff came up to visit Matt Harrington, but he stayed at Kincaids. Matt's mother, Maureen Harrington had married Carl Kincaid only a few months before. Kincaids and Harringtons were great friends with Schroeders and they are all part of the loose but firmly knit group known as the Engelmann Clan. Sister and the Fathers were also part of the clan. Jeff and Sister met at all the functions of the group over the holidays.

About ten minutes later, Sister asked, "Would you care for some coffee from the thermos?"

Jeff smiled, "Not yet. If I drink any more, we'll be looking for a rest area in a few miles."

"I need another cup, but you're right. We can't stop along the road any old place in this weather, can we?"

"At least, it isn't windy."

"True enough," Sister looked at the young man. "Jeff, I know you got swindled into driving me. I hope that you don't feel you have to care for me."

Jeff chuckled, "I allowed myself to be swindled. This trip sounded exciting, though the reasons are unpleasant. And I do have to take care of you. I would expect that you'd take care of me if the situation was reversed."

Sister smiled broadly, "Thank you for that. You know, I think the world and all of Matt. I know he had a very rough time in his decision to leave the priesthood. It was a difficult situation. How was it for you?"

"Difficult. Matt was kinder about it than I was. I just got angry. Why that Bishop thought that pedophile should be allowed to continue with his behavior while Matt and I had to shut up about it, is still beyond me! I didn't understand it then and I don't understand it now! Matt took it all in and thought about it. I was just straight-out hot-headed furious, and I still am. I told the Bishop I was resigning when he put us on suspension. Matt spent the time thinking about it before he decided."

"Do you think his way was better? I watched him struggle for months before he decided."

"I decided, and then struggled," Jeff laughed. "I still am struggling about some things. So I guess it is about the same difference."

"Are you excited about your new job? Where is it, at the state reform school?"

"Yes, in Mandan. A counselor and teacher. I think I will like it. I have always enjoyed teenagers and I liked the similar job I had in New Mexico after I left the church."

"You really did leave the church. Matt is still a Catholic. Do you think you will ever come back to the Catholic church?"

"Don't know. I went to the Episcopalian church with my father in New Mexico and up here, I go with Schroeders to the Lutheran church. I have such a difficult time when I get inside a Catholic church. It makes me sick. Maybe someday I will."

"Maybe."

"Do you think it matters?" Jeff asked.

"Not to me and I doubt if it does to God. If going to church makes you feel sick, you probably shouldn't go. You still believe in God and live a decent life. I think that is where the bear gets into the buckwheat. But then again, I am a merely nun; not a priest."

Jeff laughed until he had tears, "Merely a nun? I have never met a nun I would say was merely anything! And especially not someone who can take care of the crew you have at St. Johns!"

"You're already my favorite fella!" Sister laughed, "Truthfully, my menfolk are a good bunch. I have been with Frank so long that I don't even hear his bluster! He is a wise old soul and doesn't take life too seriously. Landers is a doll and of course, Bart is like a son to me. We had quite a time when he first came to help while Frank was hospitalized. He had his hands full and tried so hard to do a good job."

"May I ask, does Father Landers have a first name? I have heard the other guys, but he is only called Landers."

"His name is Benjamin, but he doesn't look like a Ben or act like one. He is definitely a Landers. Now Bart, he is definitely a Slick."

"What a nickname! He must have really looked funny that day he went horseback riding with Matt," Jeff shook his head.

"You should have seen him!" Sister laughed, "He had on stiff new blue jeans and brand new cowboy boots. His cowboy hat was spanking new without a single crease in it. Then he put that red kerchief around his neck and he looked for all the world like Howdy Doody! I tried to warn him, but he was so nervous about riding a horse for the first time, I didn't want to say too much. You know, he loves his nickname! What a kid! So, when do you start in Mandan?"

"First week in May. I have three weeks left before I start. I liked working in New Mexico. The National Guard guy I was filling in for got back a couple weeks early. So, now I get to see the Rocky Mountains!"

"I hope the weather is nice so you can enjoy them," Sister Abigail said. "The high mountain forests are one of the grandest things a soul can ever see."

"So that being true, if I'm not prying, why are you in the middle of the prairies?"

"The good Lord must have figured I spent enough time in the mountains and needed to see something else. I have been in Merton now almost thirty years! It is amazing when I think of it. I love the prairies too, but the mountains are my home."

Silence fell over the two for a while again. Jeff asked for some coffee and Sister poured it for him. When he took it, he nodded a thank you. She pulled out the ashtray on the dash so he could put his cup in it so it wouldn't spill. He smiled at his passenger. She was about five two. She had a wisp of grayish hair that seemed to sneak out under her bandeau (headband). She had bright sparkling blue eyes and rosy cheeks nearly always drawn up in a smile. She was quick and unpretentious.

She noticed him watching her and asked, "What is it? Have I toothpaste on my face?"

"No," he chuckled. "I was just hoping you're nice as you look!"

"Right back at you!"

Jeff was about five-ten and of medium build. He had a very tanned complexion. He was good natured and out-going, but had a strong, silent side to him.

"I guess we need to stop in Minot to fill up with gas. Carl, Elton and Frank all hammered that into me. I don't think we'll use that much gas getting to Minot," Jeff pointed out.

"No, but they all believe it is better to drive on the top half the tank—"

Jeff finished it, "As the bottom. I know, they all said it. I guess it makes sense."

"It does. Sometime, that last ounce of gasoline could be what saves you." Sister explained, "However, young man, I think we'll be in fine shape."

Jeff smiled, "Hope so. You can take a nap if you want. I'm wide awake."

"I'm not tired a bit. I guess I'm a bit churned up about the trip and all," Sister confided.

"Has your mother been ill long?"

"I guess. She is simply weakening. At eighty-five, she has outlived most of her generation who settled in the Purcell Mountain range. They all seemed to marry early and die young. It is rough terrain and that carried over to the folks who made their lives there."

"Were they mostly farmers?"

"No. It is timber and mining country. Folks kept livestock for food and transportation. They farmed only enough to feed the livestock. Many of the people who settled there were either on their way to the Canadian gold fields or on their way back. It wasn't very civilized when I was a girl. Most of our medicines were old wives' remedies or some Indian medicine. Some was actually very good. Church was mostly by itinerate preacher or whatever folks practiced in the home. Having said that, there was faith. Strong faith, but little in the way of organized religion."

"So you must have grown up in a Catholic home," Jeff guessed.

"Not at all. My family was a smattering of religion picked up here and there, superstition and common sense. None of which would fly in any mainstream church. God was mostly who you blamed when things went wrong."

"I've heard of that religion before." Jeff chuckled, "So, how may I ask did you end up as a Catholic nun?"

"I won't like to think I have ended up until I shuck these mortal coils," Sister pointed out. "But to this time in my life, it is the only place I feel comfortable. I'm content with my life and reconciled to the circumstances that got me here."

Jeff thought about that for quite a while and wondered what she meant. He decided not to say any more about it, since he didn't know her very well, but it did make him curious.

After a time, he fiddled with the radio station and then finally gave up. As he turned off the radio, he asked, "Could I convince you to sing to me?"

"Not if you want to keep your sanity. My singing is not enjoyment for man or beast. I envy folks with a good voice. My music ability goes as far as tapping my foot."

"Oh." Jeff thought a bit, "So what does your mother have?"

"From what my oldest sister, Svanhild, said, she has pneumonia. That is not uncommon near the end of most final diseases. Jeff, I haven't had much contact with my family, so I really know very little."

"I'm sorry. Many families are like that. Father Frank said you visited with your brother not many years ago."

"Yes, Cap. He was always my friend. He and his wife were traveling through and stopped to visit. It was grand to see him. You know, visiting with him put me instantly back the four decades since I had lived at home. Cap grew up to be a fine man."

"Was Cap his given name?"

Sister grinned, "His given name is Copernicus! The only times I ever heard it used was when he was in trouble and my parents would use his entire name—Copernicus Olaf Haldorson! I would imagine they felt he had been adequately punished with all that!"

"You must have been a youngster when you left home?"

"Nowadays it would be considered so, but then it wasn't. I was born in 1913. I left home when I was fourteen. That was considered grown in those days in our neighborhood. I had completed all the school that was available. My sister married just a month after she turned fifteen."

"That's true. People grew up a lot faster then."

"It was time for me to leave, for everyone's sake. I never came back to live there. My visits home have been extremely sparse over the years. Cap and I kept in touch with letters. My next younger brother Birger and I kept in touch until he was mortally wounded in the war. I didn't leave under good circumstances and from what the boys said, my name was not to be mentioned in the family home. That is why I was surprised that my mother asked Cap to see if I could come to see her now. She said she needed to make peace. So, I came. I wouldn't have otherwise."

"Did you go to your father's funeral?"

"No. I received a letter from Cap saying he passed over. He asked Cap to send me a message. He did, but I didn't receive it until after he was gone. Having said that, I don't know if I would have gone back to see him if I had heard from him earlier."

"You are so cryptic," Jeff said. "I don't want to be intrusive, but I'm curious about it. Why did you leave?"

"Tell you what? If you allow me to buy you breakfast at the truck stop after you fill gas in Minot, I'll tell you the entire story!"

After a light breakfast, filling gas and cleaning the layers of accumulated ice off the windshield, the pair was back on the road. They turned onto Hwy 2 and were now heading west out of Minot. It was still not daylight, being only about four-thirty in the morning. The talk at the truck stop was about how treacherous it would be when the sun melted the first layer off the ice and turned it to water, deeming the entire highway as slippery as grease. The pair decided to take a break for about an hour when the sun first came up.

They headed out onto the flat prairies, with nothing but white landscape, icy highway and low gray clouds in a sky beginning to filter in the morning sun. They settled into their seats and got comfortable. Then Sister Abigail had a great yawn.

Jeff looked at her and shook his head no, "You aren't going to get away with that, little Miss! I waited patiently all this while to hear your story, so you get no nap!"

Sister giggled, "I'm wasn't going to take a nap. I was just getting my jaw all limbered up. Want some coffee?"

After pouring them each a cup of coffee and put it on the console, she arranged her skirt and cleared her throat. "Where was I?"

Jeff chuckled, "Killing time."

"You certainly are a curious one. I don't think my life is that interesting or exciting."

"Not to you. I have never known anyone that left home at fourteen. Well, maybe I have but I never knew it."

"I certainly hope you won't be disappointed, young man. You know it was a different time. The 1920's in the mountainous regions of Montana were not much different than the 1890's. Progress didn't come fast up there. It was definitely more pioneer than modern. Lives were centered on mining, lumbering and mostly surviving."

"What did your father do?"

"He built wagons and wagon wheels and sold them at the Mercantile in Dahlgren. Mostly made to order as he had to fall the trees and cut the wood for each one. He was rather busy. My brothers helped him."

"What was the population there?"

"Don't know if anyone ever counted us! I guess it was named for Stafford Dahl who built the Mercantile. Later a blacksmith moved in and opened his shop nearby. Then his brother built a mill there by the river. He ground flour and feed for the neighborhood and the lumberyards around. Eventually, another fellow opened a boarding house, bar and café. I don't know how many ever stayed in the boarding house, but the bar did a good business.

"Mr. Dahl got himself a mail-order bride and she was a schoolteacher. That is when the school opened. When I was in first grade, we met in a room over the Mercantile. Later, the community built a small, log schoolhouse. We started in March and went until Christmas. No one thought it wise to have children wandering around in the winter weather of January or February. Besides, I doubt that Mrs. Dahl wanted us all snowed in with her!"

"How many kids were in your class?"

"There were seventeen in the entire school, all nine grades. There was only one other person in my grade, Johann Lofgren. He and I were the same age and he was Cap's best friend. We were like the Three Musketeers and did everything together. We climbed trees, caught frogs, snakes and gophers, had a huge rock collection and were always busy. When we were quiet, we would look at the sky and plan traveling to Mars someday. We just knew it was all mountains and lakes."

"I bet you were disappointed when man landed on the moon and it was so barren," Jeff suggested.

"No. I thought it was just the first step. Maybe they will find our Mars someday, huh? Back to Dahlgren. The population of the actual town was about fifteen souls, but in the surrounding area there were maybe a hundred.

And that covered at least a thirty mile radius from the town. Dalhgren sat in the foothills of the Purcell Mountain range."

Jeff frowned, "I thought we were going to the Rocky Mountains."

"West of Glacier National Park is the Whitefish Range and then the Purcell Mountains, but they are all part of the Rocky Mountains. We were skirted to the north and west by the Yaak River, to the east by the long, skinny Lake Koocanusa, which feeds into the Kootenai River."

"Sounds like Indian names, uh?"

"They are. Yaak means arrow and Kootenai means bow. Neat, huh?"

"It is." Jeff nodded, "How do you say Yaak?"

"It is pronounced 'Yahk'. Anyway, north of the Yaak River is British Columbia and to the west is Idaho. The biggest town nearby was Yaak, and it still isn't very large. Maybe a few hundred souls!"

"So you were rather isolated."

"Most folks were happy that way. There were miners and lumbermen that came in and out, but no one paid much mind to them. Mr. Dahl got the newspaper every time he went to Yaak for supplies. He would post the already aged news on the wall of the Mercantile to share with everyone. Svanhild would read it and tell my parents the news."

"Your family must have been Scandinavian?"

"Mixed with German, Russian and French. I doubt if the folks really knew. Mother named Cap—Copernicus because of some book she read, and Father liked the name Svanhild because he thought swans were the most beautiful birds in the world. In fact, we usually call her Swan. After me, there was Birger, Brigit and Oliver. My father's name was Olaf and mother was Frida."

"Was your name always Abigail?"

Sister shook her head no, almost sadly. "In those days, I was known by Leisel. You know, like diesel but with an L. My hair was pure white blond and I was an athletic tomboy. Swan was a delicate, graceful lady and I was the one who probably had a pocket full of dirty angleworms. I had freckles and her skin was the color of porcelain. She was beautiful and I was a rowdy."

Jeff grinned, "I think I would have liked Leisel better."

"Thanks. She would have liked you, too. So, if you promise not to get so bored you fall asleep and drive us in the ditch, I'll tell you the tale of Leisel Haldoran."

"I already know I won't be bored," Jeff said as he took a drink of his coffee.

Leisel Haldoran's home was not in Dahlgren hamlet, but up in the rugged mountains between Grizzly Peak and Lost Horse Mountain in the Purcell Range. It was a small log cabin where she lived with her parents and siblings. They lived in a log cabin that had two rooms. One was the living area and the other was their parent's room. Up in the loft is where the kids slept. Since heat rises, it was always warm up there. Father had straw on the floor Mother covered with blankets stuffed with feathers called feather ticks. Mother raised geese and used their down. The family was very fortunate to have down ticks since they are warmer and softer than feathers.

Leisel was five when she started school. She walked the six miles with her older brother and sister to the upstairs classroom in Dalhgren. Leisel's father paid for the education of his children by trading Mr. Dahl a four-horse wagon for each of his children's schooling. Dahl's had four wagons when Leisel started school and was awaiting delivery on the fifth, for little Oliver's schooling. The word in the community was that Dahl has as many wagons as Haldoran has kids!

Leisel liked school and loved her classmate, Johann Lofgren. He also had freckles and was tow-headed with blue eyes. He was taller than Leisel, but only by a couple inches. They got along very well. So much so, that Leisel hated the winter breaks from school because they didn't get to see each other then. Lofgrens lived next closest to Haldorans, but they were upstream and up a very steep path. The winter snows often filled in the passes and so they two families rarely saw each other.

When Leisel was in the second grade, Cap broke his arm. He missed school for some time and ended up in the same grade with Leisel. They didn't mind and it made their Three Musketeers even more fun.

Later on, some new folks moved in to the east. The Haldorans visited a lot with the Amundsen family. Sometimes Otto worked with Father on the wagons for extra supplies. Otto was the man of the family and he usually reeked of stale tobacco and old booze. His wife, Merta, was a nice lady, but often had bruises. She rarely spoke, but mostly just tended to their four children. Otto was a lot older than Merta, but younger than Father. Leisel had heard her mother and Swan whisper that Otto beat her. Leisel wasn't surprised. He wasn't a nice person and she didn't like it that he passed gas whenever or wherever he felt like it. Her father would never have allowed any of his family to do that! Otto never helped and he never talked to children unless he was ordering them about.

When Leisel was twelve, Merta Amundsen died while giving birth to their fifth child. There were whispers in the neighborhood when Edna Metzger came to care for the children. The community seemed convinced that they would marry, but after the long winter weather broke, Edna Metzger left town and moved to Butte. So, Otto was alone with his children. He spent a lot of time hanging around Leisel's father and moaning that he had no wife. He would drop his children off at the house for Mother to watch while he went out to visit with Father. When Mother noticed how he was looking at Swan, she talked to Father and soon Otto wasn't around so much.

Swan finished school when she was fourteen and she turned fifteen that spring. She was sweet on a local fellow Albert Nystrom from across the valley. He was a nice guy just seventeen. He had built a small cabin a few miles from Dahlgren. After the cabin was finished, he and Swan married. He worked with the blacksmith. Before their Christopher was born, Al was starting to build his livery in Dahlgren.

By now, the sun was beginning to rise and the roads were become very slippery. The pair pulled in Williston to refuel and decided to have a short break. This time, Jeff sprang for the apple pie and coffee.

4

The roads were hazardous enough so the pair didn't talk much at all for the next fifty miles. Finally, the sun and traffic had burned off most the ice and things were safer. Then they relaxed. Their plan was to stop again at Wolf Point.

After a time of silence, or listening to the car radio, Jeff turned off the radio and asked, "How did Swan and Albert's business do?"

"Very well," Sister smiled. "From what Cap says their four children all graduated college and Albert, who was quite ambitious, has transformed his livery into a trucking company keeping up with the times. He does very well for his family. He and Swan are very content with their lives."

"That's good," Jeff nodded. "I like happy endings."

Sister giggled, "Then Swan's story should be yours."

"But I still like Leisel. What is the rest of her story?"

Leisel's day that December began in a grand way. It was the day that she and Cap had both honorably completed their classes. There was no graduation, but they received diplomas signed by the County Superintendent. Children considered it a privilege to be able to attend any school, so they were grateful to have completed their studies. It was very special because Mrs. Dahl said, "These Three Musketeers were my best class ever!"

At noon break, Cap went to the mill to get some feed for Father. Johann and Leisel shared their lunch and then went out for a walk. While they were walking, Johann took her hand and asked her to marry him. She said yes and even gave him a peck on the cheek. He said he had wanted to marry her for a long time, but even more when he realized that he wouldn't get to see her every day at school anymore. She was in total agreement. He was going to work for the summer at one of the mines and then would have enough money to build a cabin and get married. They had picked out a clearing on the mountainside years before. It was the Musketeer's favorite place to play or picnic. Leisel could hardly wait to tell her parents.

When Cap returned, the couple told him and he was ecstatic. He was going to ask fourteen-year old Virginia Lange's father for her hand in marriage and already knew she would say yes. He was going to work at a lumber camp and then build a cabin at the other end of the clearing. It was all settled. It would be the dream they had all shared for years.

On the way home, Cap and Leisel were probably the two happiest people on the planet. The day was cold and crisp, but it was sunny. Clouds were forming over the mountains however and it looked like the weather could change soon. They couldn't wait to get to the cabin nestled inside the tall evergreen forest. To the back of their yard was a tall rocky cliff and to the west a rock path that curved upward and around to the higher mountains. The tree branches were covered with snow and fragrant from the dampness. The small cabin with its few outbuildings was like the cover of a scenic Christmas card.

Inside the cabin, it was toasty warm and Mother had a great dinner to celebrate the completion of studies of her children. She had roasted a big turkey and baked an apple pie. It was going to be a big dinner. The family had hoped Swan and Al could join them, but baby Christopher had a cough. So, they were staying home to tend to him.

Birger, Brigit and Oliver were picking at the apple pie when Father came in. He hugged his wife and congratulated his children on their diplomas. He seemed in a good mood as he sat down with his mug of coffee. "So Cap, what are your plans for the future?"

Cap stood tall and proud when he told his father that he had already signed up for the lumber camp, would take the money to buy a bit of land in the clearing and dig a well. Then he would build the cabin and ask Virginia to marry him.

Father stirred some cream into his coffee, "I'm certain that Birger, Oliver and I would be proud to help with the well and cabin. Virginia is a fine girl."

Cap grinned and then Mother hugged him. "Do you plan to be a logger?"

"Not for long, just to get a start. Johann and I want to build a sawmill in the valley."

"Sounds like a fine plan. Dahlgren could use one. I know I would be a good customer," Father said. "I'm getting too old to hew those logs into wagons."

"We can help you, Father," Birger and Oliver volunteered.

"I know boys, but this will be a grand idea." Then Father stirred his coffee some more, "And Leisel, what about you? What plans do you have?"

"Johann and I are getting married as soon as our cabin is finished. It will be at the other end of the clearing from Cap. I will have a fine life."

Father stopped stirring and he repeated, "Johann? Johann Lofgren?"

Mother gasped and a strange expression fell over Father's face. Everyone in the room looked to him waiting for his next word. It was a few minutes before he said, "He has not asked for your hand."

"He will be by tomorrow," Cap explained. "He had to help his Pa fortress the cave-in of their well."

Father grunted and continued to stir his coffee. Leisel stared at the cup worried that he might wear the bottom clear through. Then he shuffled his feet. "No. You will not marry Johann Lofgren. I will not hear of it. Do you understand? I will hear no more about the matter. It is absolutely forbidden!"

Leisel's heart rose in her throat and she nearly threw it up. She felt faint and was unable to move. Surely, her ears were playing tricks on her. She stood motionless staring at her father.

Cap was shaking his head no, "But Father, Johann is a fine fellow. I thought you always liked him. You said he came from good stock. Why not? Why can't he marry our Leisel?"

Father glared at him, "I have spoken. I will not be defied. If you continue to argue for your sister, you will not be allowed to marry Virginia. That is my final word."

Silence settled over the room and Cap looked at Leisel. She knew his look and that he was ready to battle for her, but she shook her head no. She didn't want Cap to be in trouble.

"Father," she said quietly, "Can you tell me a reason why?"

He became angrier than she had ever seen and he jumped to his feet, "Because I am your Father and I have forbidden it." Then he looked around the room like he was grasping for an excuse, "You shall marry Otto Amundsen. I have promised you to him and I will not have my word broken."

Mother dropped the dish she was holding and Cap almost choked. Even Birger yelled no. Leisel jammed her diploma in her skirt pocket and grabbed her coat. "I would rather die than become his wife. I will not marry him! He is despicable and he beat Merta! How could you promise me to him? Do you not care about me at all?"

He was now screaming, "You will marry Otto, as I said."

"I will drown myself in the Yaak first!" She pulled her coat on and reached in the pockets for her mittens. "I will never marry that man! I will marry Johann!"

Father grabbed his bullwhip and everyone else scattered. Leisel ran for the door but Father caught up with her just outside. The beating began. He whipped her back and only one lash caught her around the neck. Blood flowed generously from the wound. Leisel staggered as fast as she could away from her father who was ranting with profanity that she had never heard before. She pulled herself into the larder, a small log shed built to store supplies in. She managed to pull the door closed behind her and her father did not try to open it. She fell to the ground. After a bit, she crawled over to a corner and curled up behind a stack of wooden crates. She was there when she heard her father wedge something on the outside of the door. Then he shouted, "You will stay there until you decide to obey me or you will no longer share a place at my table!"

It was late afternoon and below freezing already. It would freeze that night. For some time, Leisel stayed curled up on the cold, dirt floor, whimpering and trying to think of what to do. She was thankful that she had her woolen coat on, or the whipping would have been worse. The whipping had not stopped until at least thirteen swaths of pain were laid. As it was, she could feel blood oozing from the lash across her neck and throat. She wadded her shirt to stop the bleeding. The longer she stayed there, curled in the corner, the colder she became.

She had never seen this rage before in her father and was shocked to the point the pain of the whipping did not set in until she was alone. Leisel was not certain what had precipitated his violent anger. Her father had always been strict, but never this way. Her mother watched the whole thing, but never made a move to come to her aid. Maybe she was frightened herself.

She did not understand what had happened. He was happy when Swan and Al were going to marry. She knew that Otto had wanted to wed Swan, but Father didn't force her to marry him. He seemed proud and glad for Cap. What had she done? She had mostly been a good girl, even though a tomboy. He had rarely had to discipline her about anything. She didn't understand.

Cap was right, Father had always said what a fine lad Johann was and that he must have come from a fine bloodline. Why wouldn't he want him to be his son-in-law? Had he had a falling out with the Lohgren family? Had he really made a promise to Otto because he was somehow indebted to him? Leisel couldn't believe any reason important enough to force her to marry him. He was foul, stinky and mean. Even Father had said so on occasion.

It seemed an eternity before she heard her father and her brothers come out to the small barn to milk cows. She couldn't see out because there was no window in the larder, made of simply rough-hewn logs. She was certain someone would come to let her out, but no one did. When she heard the men leave the barn and go back to the house, she became extremely worried and feared she may not survive.

She moved inside the dark shed from memory and found a bag of flax straw in a gunnysack that she pulled over herself to keep warm. She was very grateful that she had her winter leggings and mittens. She lay there alone in the dark listening to the wind howl through the trees. Leisel didn't know that a person could ever feel so desolate.

Sister became quiet as if she was reliving that very painful time in her life. Jeff reached over and squeezed her hand, but never said anything for some time. Finally, he asked, "Is this the turnoff to Wolf Point?"

Sister snapped out of her daze and looked at the passing sign, "I believe it is the next turn, five miles up. Looks like the sun is doing it's work. I wasn't paying any attention. How have the roads been?"

"Getting better, but I still think we need to take a break after we fill up with gas."

"If I remember correctly, Glasgow has a really good place to eat by the highway. I would suggest we eat there and only have a break here."

"I would like a break and walk around a bit. No more coffee for a while! I think I could use a soda," Jeff smiled at his passenger. "Are you okay? I'm sorry this was so painful for you. You should have told me to mind my own business."

Sister smiled at him, "Ah, I needed to remind myself. I don't dwell on it and so I often forget how it was. It is good to not forget. I have long since forgiven everyone, but I should not forget. I had been building myself up to a big guilt trip after I spoke with Swan on the phone about Mother. I felt I should have been with her all these years. I am glad I remembered that there was really no choice when I left."

W ithin twenty minutes, the pair was back in the Mercury and heading out onto the highway. "I actually feel quite rejuvenated," Jeff smiled. "I think I may survive to Glasgow."

"I hope so," Sister giggled. "Folks can usually stand a lot more than they are aware they can, if push comes to shove."

"Sister, if you don't want to tell me anymore, I understand, but I need to know, how did Leisel survive in the cold?"

Sister nodded and continued, "The bag of flax straw helped a lot. Before long, Leisel whimpered herself to sleep. She woke later when she heard rummaging at the door. She was at first frightened, not knowing if it was a critter or Father returning in anger. She crouched further back in the corner, but when the door opened, she was relieved to see Cap.

He ran to her and asked how she was. She embraced him and broke down in tears while he comforted her. Finally, she asked, "Do you know why Father was so angry?"

Cap sat down cross-legged on the ground and said, "No, I don't. I thought and thought and I can't think of a thing. It must be something because I have never seen him like that in my life."

"Did he say anything about me?"

Cap put his arm around his sister who had now sat next to him, "Brigit was crying before we went to bed and Father said that your name was not to be mentioned in his presence until you married Otto. Brigit cried harder and

Father told her to stop or he would send her to the shed, too. She went up to the loft then and only cried very quietly. After that we all went to bed right away and only after we knew he was asleep, did we talk."

Cap turned to Leisel very seriously, "We don't know why, but none of us think that you'll be able to change Father's mind. Will you marry Otto?"

Leisel shook her head with determination, "I meant it, Cap. I would rather die. I want to marry Johann. Otto is like a huge bore pig. I would not bed with him for anything. I will run away."

Cap tightened his arm around her, "I thought as much. I don't blame you. If you would have said you'd marry him, I think I would've had to sock you!"

Leisel giggled for the first time, "You are such a rowdy, Cap."

"We kids thought about it and decided. Brigit gathered your things and put in a few of her own clothes. Oliver gave you his secret stash of biscuits that he always keeps under his feather tick in case he gets hungry. He said that should hold you until you can get some food. I tied it all up in this thin blanket for you to carry. You should be able to put it over your back."

Leisel winced, "I don't know, Cap. My back really hurts."

"Let me look," he said as he moved the candle.

She took off her coat and pulled up her camisole. He gulped in anger. "There is no call for this! I'm going in and giving Father some of his own medicine!"

Leisel grabbed his arm, "No Cap. Promise me you won't do that! You need Father's help with your well and cabin. You cannot leave, too! You must be a good son. I already know you are the best brother in the world. Promise?"

Cap thought a while, "It is wrong. He had no business doing this to you—to anyone. He is wrong. He should just have said what his problem is. This is wrong."

"Cap, please?" Leisel begged.

The muscles in Caps' jaw moved back and forth as he thought it over. "Okay, I will; but remember, I'm only doing it because you asked me to. Otherwise, I would not. I promise."

"Thank you Cap and thank the other kids. I don't want anyone to get into trouble on my account. Did Mother say anything?"

"No," Cap said, "But she probably doesn't have anything she can say."

Leisel shrugged but her tears gave her away, "I guess I just thought she might beg for him to let me come into the house."

Cap hugged her, "Here are some matches, a flint and a few candles. I have an address of the boss from the lumber camp just across the Yaak River. I have a couple dollars I saved up and you can buy your passage on the ferry. When I was looking for a job, they needed a flunkey."

"What is a flunkey?"

"That is a cook's helper who also helps keep the bunkhouses cleaned up at the lumber camp. They hire men or boys usually, but they will hire girls for that job. It isn't a fancy job, Leisel, but the pay is good and you'll have a place to stay with food to eat. I brought my old boots and put new leather strips in the bottoms for you. I know they are too big, but with all your socks on, they should be okay. You need to remember to keep your feet warm or you will be sunk. Brigit gave you her favorite neck scarf, and you must wear it; especially with that horrid cut on your neck. Go find this man at that lumber camp. When you can, write to me at the Great Northern Lumber Office. I will answer as soon as I get it. You must promise to keep in touch with me. I love you so much. You are the best sister in the world."

"Is that the same company you will be working for? Cap, I cannot take your money. You need it."

"You need it more and I won't argue. Your job will be with the Yaak Lumber Company while my job is with Great Northern. That is really very good, because there would be less chance Father would find you."

"I'll pay you back as soon as I can. Promise. You don't think Father will look for me, do you?"

"No, but I never imagined he'd do this!"

"I love you too, Cap. Will you tell Johann?"

"I will as soon as I can," Cap said. "And I will transfer messages to him if I can."

Leisel put her head on his shoulder and the two sat in the dark shed for some time. Finally, she said, "I must go now before daylight so you don't get caught."

Cap helped her to her feet and then put the pack on her back, adjusting it so it was the least painful. Then he gave her the address and directions to the lumber camp. "Maybe we will meet again before long."

"I hope so. I will miss you so much," Leisel answered as she hugged him.

Cap patted his pocket, "I nearly forgot. Birger wants you to have his compass."

Leisel started to cry again, "But Cap, he worked all last winter to save money to order it. He loves it so."

"He said he loves you more. He doesn't want you to get lost." Cap put it in her hand and said, "Now make us proud of you, Leisel. We will always love you. Let me walk with you to the edge of the high path. Then I can brush the tracks away so Father won't know where you went."

Cap walked with her in the moonlight and reminded her of every survival rule he had ever heard. When they got to the rocky edge of the high path, called so because it led to the higher country, Cap gave her a final hug. They both trembled in fear and then they shrugged goodbye. There are things that words cannot convey.

Leisel stood watching him as he returned to the yard, brushing every footstep away. He replaced the log his father had wedged against the door and then went to the house. As he went behind the side of the house, he waved to Leisel and she waved back. She stood there sobbing but soon gathered her senses. She needed to get out of sight of the cabin before Father found her. He would surely punish her siblings severely if he saw what they had done. So she hurried up the path, being careful to step only on the bare rocks so her tracks could not be seen."

Jeff wiped his tears on the back of his hand and sniffed, "That is so sad."

"Maybe," Sister agreed. "However, it is a memory that I shall always cherish. I can close my eyes anytime and see my brother in the moonlight, sweeping over my tracks. It was a wonderful thing."

6

A fter filling their gas tank again in Glasgow and having a good meal, the couple got back on the road. They had bought some soda pop to drink while they decided to travel as far as Havre before they stopped again. They would refill at any gas station on the way however. This time, Sister Abigail placed the sodas in the console and settled back. She continued with her story without Jeff asking.

During her life until then, Leisel had always thought that hobos were bad people, somehow deserving of their fate. She was taught to avoid them as they may do her harm and to never to offer them food or water because they might steal from her. This December while considering her current fate, she thought differently about it. She wondered if some of them had been handed a situation like hers that they could not overcome. What she would have given to come across a hobo, or even Otto! He would at least have food. She remembered the large turkey that Mother had prepared. She hoped her Father gagged on every bite.

They had always gotten along well, shared jokes and stories and had very few harsh words. She was unable to understand what had happened that he couldn't have explained his reason to her. She was certain that he had to have one. Angry as she was at him, she did not believe he would act that way on a whim. It must have been something very important. It made her sick to think that he wouldn't even allow the other kids to speak of her. What had she done?

She climbed over the pass before the sun was high in the sky and then moved toward the west, by Birger's compass. She was now on a path toward Yaak, following a direction she had never gone before. That was the only place that she could get a ferry across the river. Fortunately, chances were slim that anyone would know her there.

The liners Cap had put inside her boots moved up and wrapped over her toes. It did offer protection from the holes in the boots, but made her toes cramp. Her ankles rubbed on the back heel of the boots. Before long, she had large blisters on both feet.

Her neck was very painful and swollen. Swallowing was difficult, but she did eat some of Oliver's biscuits. She giggled at how he had squirrelled them away. They were dried out and crumbly, but she had to agree, it did keep hunger at bay.

The load on her back was not that heavy, but it rubbed against her bruised back. She had put on her turtleneck sweater over her camisole because her shirt was all bloody.

By nightfall, she was worn out, thirsty and hungry. More importantly, she was very frightened and worried. She was beginning to realize that her childhood was over and she would likely never again see her family. The only thing that kept her going was the knowledge that Cap would keep in touch and the hope that Johann would come for her. Maybe he would ask her to run away with him. They could still have a good life, although not the one they'd planned. It would turn out okay. She could work as this flunkey and save her money. With that and Johann's money, they would be able to build their cabin. It would be okay. Probably it would turn out better than it would have with yesterday's plan. Yes, probably yesterday's idea wasn't the best. This could be better.

She found a small idyllic clearing near a frozen stream with clear running water under the ice, surrounded by tall evergreen and fir trees. She decided to camp there for the night and let her feet rest. She was worn out and beginning to run a fever. Leisel was tempted to just sit down and rest, but she knew that if she did that, she wouldn't get up again. She forced herself to gather some sticks and rocks to make a fire pit. She found some sappy pine needles to put on the sticks so that the fire could start. Pitch, pine sap, was as good as any petroleum for starting a fire and she had to be careful with her six matches.

She started the fire and then opened the blanket. Her love and respect for her brother grew as she looked at what he had packed for her. He had given her a small hand axe, his pocketknife that he was so proud of, a large eyed needle, thread and a small pot that held about two cups of liquid. It was perfect for water or food, not that she had anything besides Oliver's biscuits.

She took the axe, went back from the clearing and trimmed some boughs of cedar. She got enough to lay on the ground as a thick mat so she could sleep on it. Then she found some longer sticks to craft a slip-shod lean-to over the mat and sided the fire. It would hold only if there was no wind, but there wasn't any now. She covered it with cedar boughs and then sat under it. She stirred the fire to get it hotter and sat on her mat. By then, the last of the sun was gone and night was closing in.

She ate another biscuit and drank some water from her little pot. It was pretty out and the moon was bright. She watched as some deer came down to the far end of the clearing to drink from the stream and then move on. Then she started to cry. She curled up on mat and covered herself with the thin blanket. She was so homesick and missed Cap something awful. She cried herself to sleep.

She had no problem remembering to fix the fire, because as soon as it burned down she became very cold. She was also afraid of wolves, and she knew they would not bother if she had a fire. Her night was a tortured, painful sleep punctuated with feeding the ravenous fire. It wasn't long before she realized how fast the wood burned and promised herself the next night, she would find more wood when she made camp.

The young girl woke up with the sun streaming across her face. Her fire was smoldering embers and she was hungry. She hurt much worse today then she had the day before. Leisel knew she had better move around or she would be in even worse shape. She heated a bit of water on the coals and wiped her face and neck. Then she felt her shirt that she had rinsed out the night before. It was frozen solid, but she thought that maybe it would be dry in another day. She packed up her things and tied the blanket's corners together. Then she checked her feet.

She wrapped her feet tightly with strips she tore from an old petticoat that Brigit had put in her bag. Then she put her socks over the wrapping and her feet felt better. Before long, she was on her way.

The routine repeated a couple days and she became more adept building a camp and banking a fire. She was becoming very hungry and had only two biscuits left. Her fever was high and her lips were cracked. She felt awful, but was determined to get to some form of civilization.

That day, she walked down a path that led to Yaak. She was aware that folks were staring at her. Probably some did because she was a stranger and probably some did because she looked like a hobo. No one spoke to her but a few crossed the street to walk away from her. She easily found her way to the ferry and purchased a crossing. The man who took her money said it would be about over an hour before it left, so she asked where she could buy some food. He told her to go to the corner and knock at the blue door. That was the back of the Bed and Breakfast, and they were known to give soup to the needy. She nodded and followed his directions.

It made her angry at first that he would think she was needy and a beggar, but before she told him she could afford to pay, she decided against it. He didn't need to know and probably didn't care. Maybe, just maybe, she was needy

She knocked at the blue door and a round, aproned lady with her hair tied in a bun opened the door. "Hello, come on in. Angus, come see the fine girl who is here for a bite to eat."

A tall man with wild gray hair and bushy eyebrows came in wiping his hands on his apron, "Well, greetings to you! Would you like to have bean soup or chicken noodle?"

"Whichever you can spare. I can pay you some for it."

"Not to worry, little Lassie. We have more than we need of both. How long do you have to eat?"

"I have a ticket on the ferry and the ferry man said it would leave in about an hour."

"Well, then we may just want to fix you up with a meal. Would you be interested in that?"

"Yes, please."

The man grinned and as he headed back to the kitchen, he said to the woman, "Elizabeth, I think you might want to tend to her injuries."

She nodded and said, "I was of a same mind."

The lady took her by the hand and into a nearby, small room with a cot and a wash basin. She never asked what happened, but she dressed her neck and then asked if she had any other areas that needed tending. Leisel showed her back and feet and the lady wrapped her wounds. "I think I can get a pair of Angus' large socks to fill those boots for you, if you don't mind his big feet! I washed most the smell out!"

Leisel's eyes filled with tears and she smiled, "I think I would love them."

When they returned to the kitchen, Angus had a huge meal set up at the table for her. "Sit and eat," he motioned to the heaping bowl of beef stew and fresh bread. "I noticed your baggage and was thinking I have a spare carpetbag that you might want to take ownership of. I think it would be easier to lug than your blanket, since it is ripped and might not last long. That is if you have far to go."

"I don't know how far it is. I'm heading to the Yaak Lumber Camp. I guess it is on the other side of the river to the west."

"I believe it is north by northwest of the ferry. I can go check at the assayer's office if you give me a minute. You eat and I'll find the way for you. Please think about changing your things to the carpetbag. It has yearned to go on a jaunt and tired of collecting dust in my cupboard. Elizabeth can help you."

"Angus, I was having the thought we should send some of that healing salve for her neck. It is very infected."

"Good idea. Follow Elizabeth's directions for using it and try not to smell it! It will make your eyes water! However, it heals the worst of infections."

Angus returned in a few minutes with the directions written on a paper. "Do you read?"

"Yes, sir. I finished the ninth grade."

"Isn't that wonderful, Angus!" Elizabeth smiled. "I have a small gift for you then, my girl."

"Oh no," Leisel objected, "You have been way too kind."

"There is no such thing, girl," Angus said with his hands on his hips. "Kindness is one of the few things with no limit."

"I must repay you. I have two dollars."

"You have a bigger need of that than we. You just be kind to someone else. That is all the repayment we ever want. You give your sacred promise?" He demanded an answer with his look.

"I do, sir. Thank you so much."

"Now eat up and I'll pack you a lunch to carry. You drink coffee? I can tie some in a bit of muslin and you can throw it into a cup of boiling water and you will have a dandy cup of coffee," the older man beamed. "Can I tie it for you?"

Leisel giggled, "I would like that."

Angus laughed and told Elizabeth as she came back into the kitchen, "This Lassie has a wonderful smile. I was lucky to see it."

"Well, that is good," the lady said as she handed a small book to Leisel. "You may find some pleasure in reading this while you are traveling. Then you will be reminded you are never truly alone."

Leisel looked at the small book. It was the King James Version of the New Testament. She had never had a Bible or any book for that matter of her own before. She beamed and clutched it, "Thank you ever so much. I will keep it nice forever."

"Read it and wear it out," Elizabeth ordered. "That is the only way it is any good!"

Leisel forgot herself and gave them both a big hug! "I will remember you forever. Someday, I shall come back to see you."

"You do that, and remember what I said, There is never such a thing as too much kindness."

Leisel made it to the ferry in time and was the happiest she had been in days! The food was wonderful and civilization was great, but the kindness; that was the best.

Jeff had to ask for a tissue to wipe his eyes, "Gee Sister, you are tearing me up with your story! I have to know, did you ever see Angus and Elizabeth again?"

"I did. Over the years, we became very close. I stopped to see them every time I was in Yaak I would stop and knock on the blue door. I wrote to them and before Angus passed on, he knew I was going into the convent. They were some of the kindest folks I have ever met. I still carry the little Testament they gave me."

She reached in her pocket and pulled out the small worn book with the black leather cover. It was about three inches by four inches.

Jeff looked at her, "How could you even read it? The words must be miniscule!"

"I was younger then and my eyes were better!" Sister giggled. "They were the best people I have ever met and they weren't Catholic. However, I learned more about Christian kindness from them than in any old convent anywhere."

"Well, we are here. Havre, Montana. Where is this good place to eat? I have developed quite a hunger!"

The couple had decided to start looking for a motel anywhere from Shelby to Cutbank. It had been a long day and there were now snow flurries. "We don't want to be driving around the mountains in a snow storm if we can help it," Sister stated. "I'm not worried," Jeff smiled, "I'm with a world class mountain woman! I feel very secure."

Sister chuckled, "I was much younger then, and I still almost didn't make it. Once I got off the ferry and looked at the tall mountain range before me, my discouragement returned. I knew it would be thirty or forty miles to the camp, mostly uphill. I was one scared little girl."

"Don't doubt that a bit."

Leisel was thankful for the carpetbag that was not like a suitcase, but rather a backpack. It fit over both her shoulders and carried a lot. There were small belts on the sides where she put her axe and water pot. It evened the load and made the walk easier.

She began climbing and at first followed a cart trail to the north. That was easy walking. By that night when she made camp near a waterfall, she had covered quite a bit of territory but felt her body failing her. She heated up the covered tin bucket of stew that Angus had sent and then realized that the bucket could become a kettle because there was a handle attached to the side of it. He had also given her a spoon, which she cherished.

The next morning, it was snowing and windy. It made walking more difficult, but she managed to get to the end of the road before darkness set in. From the directions Angus had given her, she figured she was about fifteen miles further up the road. Before she turned off on the rugged trail, she debated. Angus had told her she could stay on the road. It would be further by ten or more miles, but easier walking. However, about five miles up, it would turn into a logging road. There might be some lumberjack traffic on there and it could be dangerous to camp or walk around where men were moving sleighs of heavy logs. When a teamster drove a team to the landing (place where logs were stacked for the spring drive where they were shoved into high running steams on their way to the lumber mills), it could be dangerous. They had little chance of stopping a sleigh filled with tons of logs going downhill. Sometimes, the teamsters would lose control and the teams were overrun by the momentum of the sleigh. That was called sluicing and it usually ended with a dead team and maybe driver, too. Once past that, she would still have to travel west to find the camp.

She debated. There would be more chance of seeing humans if she stayed on the road, but a longer and more dangerous way. Besides, she had no way of knowing where the loggers were working presently. This camp was semi-permanent, but where the crews worked from it varied. She chose to take the more isolated path to the camp.

That night a storm came up and she decided she had made a mistake. It blew so hard that she could barely keep her lean-to standing and her fire going. The next day, the storm continued and it was colder. She managed to gather enough wood so she could keep warm throughout the night, but she was now almost out of food again.

Her neck was even more swollen and she could hardly swallow. The third day, the weather subsided, but Leisel paid little attention. She was so ill. She had a headache, muscle aches, sore back, throat and feet and now an upset stomach. She shivered from the chills but felt so hot, she wanted to tear her coat off and roll in the snow.

She no longer cried or even thought very much. She only wanted to curl up and sleep. She did sleep. It was a fevered sleep and she was tormented by nightmares. She had difficulty keeping drinking water thawed. She was now coughing so hard she could hardly stand. It was painful to take a deep breath.

By the end of the third day, she just lay in her lean-to and waited to die. She didn't care anymore about anything. She only wanted it all to stop. She turned over on her cedar mat and covered herself with the thin blanket.

The following morning, Leisel opened her eyes when she felt her shoulder being shaken. She weakly opened her eyes and saw a fair-haired young man. "You alive?" he asked.

She tried to answer but it was only a moan. Then he yelled, "Bring Pendergast and come quick. We need help!"

Leisel couldn't see who he was calling to, but she didn't care. She looked at him and tried to smile. Then she fell back to sleep.

When she woke again, she was being carried through the forest in the arms of a giant. She felt the size of a newborn in his arms. She decided she must have become mad from the fever. She turned a little in his arms and she heard a non-melodic, however very comforting, hum from the man. It reminded her of a cat's purr. She looked up at his enormous beard and went back to sleep.

When she woke the next time, she realized that she was in a bed. She looked around in wonder and the first thing she saw was four bearded men in red-plaid flannel shirts staring back at her. They were lined around the bed and apparently had been there for some time. It made her smile.

When she did, one of the men shouted toward the door, "Call Rudner. She is coming out of it!"

Then the young man looked at her and asked anxiously, "You are, aren't you?"

She gave him a puzzled look, "Are what?"

"Coming around! You are the first person we've tended to and we don't want to lose you. We won't, will we?"

She had to smile, "I hope not. I think I was lost."

One of the other men asked, "Where were you headed?"

"Yaak Lumber Camp. My brother said they needed a helper. A funky or something!"

The large man with an apron broke into a big belly laugh, "A flunkey? Then you must want to talk to me and the bull of the camp. He is the foreman, Boss Rudner. This is Yaak Camp and I'm the cook, so my word goes in the cookhouse. I have never had anyone walk through a storm to be my flunkey, so I say you have the job! But you need to heal up first! Were you kidnapped by some renegades? You look in tough shape!"

"No, I wasn't kidnapped." Leisel looked around at the men who had not moved from their stations surrounding her bed. "I heard you had a job."

The young man laughed, "I'm glad I came upon you then. You got here just in time for dinner!"

"Did you find me?" Leisel asked, trying to piece together the missing time.

"Yah, me and Booker here, were heading over to the new strip when we saw your lean-to all blown down. We almost thought there was no one about, but I saw a bit of your scarf blowing and decided to have a look. And there you were!"

Booker nodded like crazy, "Yup, there you were! Freezing with old man death coming up the doorsteps, but Slim and me got to you in time. A bit of thing like you shouldn't be trotting about in a winter storm! You should be more careful."

"Yes, I should," Leisel agreed and then she coughed. "I may have made it to the camp if I hadn't gotten sick."

"Might have," the cook agreed, "But might not have, either."

She smiled and then noticed the giant who had carried her, standing at the foot of her bed. "Hello," she said. "Thank you for bringing me here."

The large man smiled, but said nothing. Booker explained, "Pendergast don't hear or talk, but he has a kind heart. That is good because he is the strongest man in the mountains. Why, the next tallest man might come up to his chin! He is so strong that he came and picked you up like a little kitten."

"How can I thank him for carrying me here?"

The young man Slim leaned down and said, "Just look at him and smile. He will understand."

Leisel looked at Pendergast in tears and held her hand out to him, "Thank you so much for saving my life!"

Pendergast came over beside her and took her little hand in his large, callused one and then took his other hand, made it into a fist and patted his chest. He looked at her and gave her a bit of that hum he had done on the trail and then stepped back with a huge smile. Although not a word was spoken, everyone in the room knew an unbreakable bond had been forged.

He stepped back and the 'bull of the camp' came in. That dark haired man with a Ranger hat came over to the bed, and peered at her, "So you'll make it. Good. These guys aren't earning their salt. If we'd had to hang your boots, I wouldn't have gotten a log cut by any of them."

She looked at him trying to figure him out what he said. The cook explained that she had come up to get the flunkey job. The boss looked at her and shook his head. "Why on God's green earth would you want to do that?"

"I need work," she answered simply.

He looked her over with a deadpan expression and then broke into a grin, "Best reason I ever did hear. Well, if Cook wants you, you got the job. But you have to get these other guys back to work, or you'll get sacked right away!"

Slim smiled, "We'll head out right away, Boss. Just take care of Pendergast's girl."

"What is your name, Pendergast's girl?"

"My name is Leisel," she answered.

"I don't like that," Boss Rudner stated, "I say we call you Little Pendergast."

Booker frowned, "That's too big a mouthful. How 'bout Half Pendergast?"

Cook shook his head, "I'm calling her Half Pint, and you guys will too if you know where your next meal is coming from."

Sister smiled, as she remembered that, "The others all went back to work and Boss Rudner told me to get well and rest. He would settle up with the hiring papers when I got well. Then he welcomed me to the camp. I went from almost dead to a flunkey called Half Pint. I was in a warm bed and I knew I had found a home, at least for a while."

The next few days Leisel, now known as Half Pint, spent in her room. Cook only allowed her to be up a little each day. He wanted her to get over her cough before he let her move around too much. She was allowed visitors in the evenings. Every day after dinner, Slim, Booker and Pendergast came by. After knocking, they would come in with some stools and sit around her bed. They told stories of their day and asked if she was getting better. Then Cook would knock and tell them to clear out. The older man watched over her like an eagle.

Her room was small and held a single bed with a log bedstead. It had a nice mattress on springs and fresh blankets. Inside the room was a chair and a four-drawer chest. A small, curtainless window looked out into a big tree. It did let in some light, but no one could see in or out.

It was a fine room to Leisel's notion, never having had a room of her own, but she wondered when she would have to return it soon to the rightful resident. She knew she was getting stronger and sometimes when it was daylight, she read from the New Testament that Elizabeth had given her. She had never read or heard about some of those things before.

On the fourth morning, Cook came in and sat at on the wooden chair after breakfast. "I've been thinking it is about time that you came out into the world, if you feel up to it. Your cough seems better, but mark my words; if it comes back I am sending you back into quarantine."

"Oh, am I contagious?" the young girl asked innocently.

"Don't think so; but then, you sure could be. However, I can't be having you hacking up all over the fella's vittles or they'd be mighty cantankerous. Meals are part of their pay and those men work hard, so we can't be messing with it. Now, if you do okay this morning, maybe tomorrow you can be up all day. Ready to try?"

"Yes sir," Leisel answered. "I'm getting restless and want to start earning my keep."

"I want you to do that too, but you need to heal up good. Like Slim said, you are our first patient and we have a stake in you. We want to make certain you heal the right way. Put on some clothes and come out for breakfast."

Leisel was excited as she put on her clothes. She noticed they were washed and even her shirt looked fairly good. Most of the bloodstains were gone. She was weaker than she thought she would be, but was very glad to get moving around again.

She opened the wooden latch on the door and came out into the large dining room. The walls were built of chinked logs, as was her room. Chinked logs were ones that the cracks between them were filled with a mixture of mud and chopped straw to make them secure and sound. The room was enormous and filled with rows of long, tables hewn from logs, covered with oilcloths. The benches were 'Deacon seats'; seats made of halved logs with the flat sides up for sitting.

One end of the huge room was open cupboards filled with blue enameled tin ware for the men. On the other side was the row of cook stoves and kettles where the meals were created. There was a pump with a pail near the outside door, next to a few washbasins, apparently for the men to wash when they came in to eat.

Cook motioned for her to sit down and he brought her a plate filled with flapjacks and a mug of coffee. He sat down across from her and motioned to a woman who was putting some plates back in the cupboards. He introduced her, "This here is Lana Isaacson, the wife of a Cat Skinner. Lana, this here is Half Pint and she'll be our flunkey. Say hi."

Lana smiled and held out her hand, "Hello, Half Pint. You are a bit of a celebrity here. The boys are very proud of your recovery and take all the credit for it. For me, I am glad to have another woman in camp. Sure enough, there is Mrs. Rudner and her little girl but they don't mingle much with us lowly folk. It will be fine to have you around."

"Thank you, Lana," Leisel said as she studied the woman. She seemed to be in her twenties and very friendly. Leisel quite liked her. "I hope we can be friends."

"I'm certain we can," Lana answered and then went back to the kitchen.

Cook watched Half Pint as she ate the stack of pancakes. After a minute he said, "I think your clothes will do fine, but you should see Ink Slinger about getting some good-fit boots! The ones you have are ill-fitting and will damage your feet."

Half Pint nodded, "Who is Ink Slinger?"

"He is the camp clerk. He does the payroll, is the timekeeper and runs the van."

"What is the van?"

Cook chuckled, "It is from an Indian name *wangan*, and is like the camp store that sells boots, some clothes and necessities, like tobacco plug. You don't chew, do you?"

Leisel giggled and shook her head no. Cook grinned at his joke, "Didn't think you did, but thought you might. They sell that, too. Ink Slinger writes it down and will take the money out of your check."

"Is his name Ink Slinger?"

"Not likely, but that is what he's known by. I'll walk over with you when you are ready, okay?"

"Okay," Leisel answered. "Can I stay up the rest of the day and maybe wander around outside?"

"No. You get to be up now and then go rest. This afternoon after second lunch, you can stay up so we can walk over to the van. Then you need to rest. If you do okay today, you can stay up longer tomorrow."

"Are there two lunches?"

"Yes. Breakfast starts at five in the morning. Then there is first lunch at ten, and second lunch at two. Dinner is at seven. Two sittings of men each meal. Meals are part of the men's pay and they need good meals because they work hard. Feeding these two hundred men keeps us hopping. If they can't come in from where they are working in a decent time, we take them a nosebag show."

Leisel shook her head, "Mr. Cook, I don't know what that is either! I hardly understand anything! What is a nosebag show?"

Cook had a big belly laugh, "Half Pint, I'm not Mr. Cook. I am Cook. Plain old Cook. You will understand it all soon enough. A nosebag show is taking food in pails to the men where they work. They don't like it much, because it often freezes."

Leisel nodded, "Okay. I will try to remember all this. How will I know where to find them?"

"I will go with you at first so you know how to do it. You'll do just fine. You have to be fine. Slim, Booker and Pendergast are counting on it. Oh, before I forget I need you to promise me something."

"What is it? I will try," Leisel said earnestly.

"I want you to always treat Pendergast with respect and courtesy. He is a fine man but his mind is a bit slow. He is huge and many folks foster fear because of his size. He was the best-hearted person in the mountains. If I ever find that you are funning with him, I'll send you packing within the breath."

"I promise. I'd never do that to Pendergast. He saved my life and carried me from the forest. I could never treat him badly. Do you know how tall he is?"

"I heard once about seven foot nine. He is big all over, but it is muscle, not a bit of lard. A kinder person you'll never find. Treat him good and he will be your ally forever."

"I will, Cook. You have my word."

"Oh, and while we are on the subject, you need to be careful around all these men. Most are very respectful and will treat you proper. There are a few who are wild as the woods. Steer clear of them. Be careful not to flirt or play one man off against another. That breeds frightful discontent. I will not scrape a knuckle to save you if you do. If you have any questions about a man, ask me and no one else. There is no room to bend that rule. Hear?"

"Yes sir." Leisel looked at him, "Can I be friends with Slim and Booker?"

"I thought you already were, girl! Of course. They are fine men."

"Good." Then she got a worried frown, "Cook, can I ask you about a bother?"

"Shoot."

"I was asleep a long time and woke up in a night gown. How did I get it on? Who washed me and all that?"

"Your friends, Slim, Booker and Pendergast took turns watching over you for the four days you were so sick. One of them was always by your side. Lana and I bathed you and the nightgown is hers. Don't worry. None of us will tell anyone about it and we don't go yakking about other folk's past lives. We all saw your lashes from the whipping and know that something awful must have happened. You can tell us if you want or keep it to yourself. Remember

Half Pint, whenever you tell someone about your past, you are giving them a tool to cause hurt. So think long and hard about it."

Leisel's eyes reddened with tears, "Thank you, Cook. I think you are a great friend"

Cook stared at the floor and his face carried an odd look, then he cleared his throat, "Looks to me like breakfast is taking the wind out of your sails. You get back to bed and rest some for this afternoon."

"When will Boss Rudner want me to sign up to work?"

"Likely after the Christmas break."

"Oh my, I forgot all about Christmas! When is it?"

"Next week. We will be closed down for most of the next couple weeks. The boys get paid out Friday. They collect their pay twice a year unless there is an emergency or they pull up stakes. They get paid out before Fourth of July, too. Many take off to the nearest skid row to blow it all. Then they come back broke, tired and ready to work again."

"You mean there will be no one here for two weeks. Will I have to leave?"

"No way, Half Pint! Some of us will be here. I will be and so will Pendergast. Some of the other stragglers will be around. You can be right here in your place."

"Cook, whose room am I in? Someone is probably anxious for me to give them their room back."

"No, Trautman was a short-staker and never intended to be here for a long time. He worked as flunkey for me only until he could get paid out and on to his next job. You took no one's room. That is yours, but you need to keep it clean."

"I would have liked to meet your friends. They sound like some fine people," Jeff said as the Mercury pulled off the highway and turned toward Cutbank. "Hope we can find a good motel. I think I'm tired."

"You should be," Sister nodded. "You drove all the way and all I did was talk like a chatterbox. You are right. My friends were fine folks, and if you are interested I will tell you more about them over dinner."

"Does this mean that you are giving me a tool I could hurt you with?"

"I guess I am, but I think you are trustworthy. Besides, I think I could take you," Sister giggled.

"My, you are a rowdy," Jeff laughed. "This place looks good and there is a café across the street. What more could we ask for?"

T he couple checked into a motel that was across the road from a café. The rooms were modest, but clean. Jeff carried Sister's bag to her room and then said, "I'll be by as soon as I wash off some of the road dust."

"Okay. I'm quite hungry myself, so I'll be ready."

A few minutes later, he knocked on her door and the two walked out into the crisp night. It was a beautiful evening. Even though it was gently snowing, the moon still was lighting the sky and even a few stars were peeking through. There was no wind and it was so quiet one could almost hear the snowflakes as they dropped onto the fresh mounds already on the ground. The air was pungent with the aroma of wet pine and Jeff took a deep breath. "This is wonderful. I see why you love the mountains so much."

"This is just the foothills. But there is no sound like the whistle of a gentle breeze through pine needles. It always makes me homesick."

"May I ask, where do you miss when you say home?"

Sister broke into a big smile, "Depends. Now I would have to say St. John's, but when I'm at St. Johns, I mean the mountains. Anywhere in these old Rockies. My roots are as much in that old lumber camp as in the place where I was born."

"I get that. I get as homesick for my parish in Boston as the home where I grew up. I guess it being homesick is more for a part of your past than geography."

"I agree," Sister smiled as she opened the menu. "Oh look, they have Rainbow Trout! I think I will have that. I love a good trout."

"I was looking at the steak," Jeff chuckled. "At least they never got the idea to put the beef's head on my plate like they do with fish. What is with that anyway?"

Sister laughed, "Maybe because a fish never gets a chance to kick you when it is alive!"

Jeff shook his head, "You are truly weird."

After their food arrived, Jeff asked, "How was Half Pint's first Christmas away from her family?"

"It was sad, but remember, her family was not very religious. They had a Christmas tree, exchanged gifts and ate a big meal. That was the extent of it. So, Christmas at the lumber camp was very different. The lumber camps were noted for not being religious. Of course, the names of all deity were mentioned often, usually in every sentence, but not in reverence! The men talked boisterously and very profanely, but they were not anti-religion. They had standards. Decent women, all children and anyone's religious belief were off-limits. Even if they didn't agree, they never said anything."

"Did they have any religious customs?"

"No, when a co-worker was killed, which happened with some regularity because it is dangerous work, the custom was to hang their boots in a nearby tree on a nail. No one ever touched it. It is said that in the mountains of Maine there are still boots hanging on very rusty nails in the forest. The religious men sometimes said a word or prayer and everyone was silent during it, but there was no talk of it. In time, I learned that some men were very religious, but they never made any bones about it."

"I heard out East that they were all drunkards," Jeff pointed out.

"No, but then most folks didn't see them except when they were paid out and hitting the saloons. They had been storing up for almost six months, and were ready to party. Some were alcoholics but many did not drink at all between pay outs. They would take their pay, go to a saloon and hit a brothel. Some spent the entire two weeks in an alcoholic fog. Few had families to visit and years back, there were no women in the camps. Cook was right, they would be hung over and broke when they came back to camp. Their lives were very uncluttered, but many were wounded souls."

"It would have been a hard life."

"Yes and in earlier times, they worked seven days a week for fourteen hours a day. When Half Pint was there, they worked six days a week and only twelve hours a day. Most the time, they were off on Sunday. They spent their time on Sundays relaxing and catching up on their sleep, sharpening their axes or saws and things like that."

"So what was your Christmas like?"

Half Pint was all dressed and waiting for her friend's knock. That night, she opened the door herself instead of calling to come in. The men were all surprised when she did and were pleased. "Come in, I have been waiting."

Booker nodded and said, "Pleasure to see you with your clothes on." The second the words left his lips, he turned beet red. He stammered, "I didn't mean that."

Leisel smiled and said, "I know what you mean. Come in, I have so much to tell you all."

They came in and each sat on the stool they brought with them, except Half Pint. She sat on the chair. "I had such a fine day! Cook let me get up to eat in the dining room and then he walked over to the van so Ink Slinger could fit me with these boots."

Her guests all praised her fine pair of boots and then she said, "Ink Slinger said if I take good care of them, I can trade them in when I outgrow them. Isn't that nice?"

"It really is," Slim said. "Have you ever taken care of leather boots before?"

"No, is it hard?"

"We will show you how to oil the leather and such. Right boys?" Slim offered.

The other two nodded and Pendergast made a rubbing motion and pointed to her. She looked at him, "Thank you. You have been so good to me, all of you. Cook said I shouldn't thank you, but I need to live so you aren't sorry you saved me."

The men looked uncomfortable and Leisel was sorry she had said it. Then Booker saved the day by saying, "Well, I already am glad we saved yah. I would've hated to hang those old boots of yours on a tree!"

Slim punched him, "You are really an idiot!"

Booker took that as a compliment. He was a middle-aged fellow with brown hair and a full, thick beard. He had a good medium build and wore the ugliest hat in camp. It even had holes in it! He always got grief about it, but never bought a new one. "I love this hat and will never part with it. In fact, if I meet my maker in these mountains, I want my hat hung with my boots!"

Slim chuckled, "I was looking forward to burying it deep!"

Now Booker punched him.

Half Pint told the men about Ink Slinger's offer to lend her some books. "Isn't that the best news?"

"We guys don't read much, so I suppose it doesn't matter much to us," Slim said and then added, "But I am happy for you."

Half Pint got an idea, "How about I find a good book and I could read it to you at night when we visit?"

"That would be okay, right Booker?"

"It would be better than listening to you brag all the time!"

"I think it would be good," Slim confirmed. "I think Pendergast would even like it, especially if has pictures."

Half Pint was excited, "I will ask Ink Slinger if he has some with pictures. So, what are your plans for Christmas?"

Booker slapped his knee, "I have big plans. I am taking the river to Eureka to spend my money. I know a saloon there that has some fine ladies. I'll be there until my money runs out. I thought Slim was coming along, but I guess his plans changed."

"Yah, I'm going into Yaak. I will spend some money in their saloon no doubt, but I thought I might come back to camp and work on my gear."

"Right." Booker shook his head. "I don't think anyone believes that."

"Well, that is what I'm going to do," Slim protested. "Just watch."

Booker went into a fit of laughter, "Yah, but I know your motives."

"What motives are that?" Half Pint asked innocently.

Booker turned red again, "He wants to fix his gear, but he also wants to keep an eye on you."

"You don't need to do that. Cook will be here and he said Pendergast will be, too. You go have a good time," Half Pint said, still missing the point.

"I don't want to go off to get drunk, okay?" Slim said sternly. "Is that okay with you?"

47

"Fine with me," Booker said while Pendergast just smiled.

"Me, too," Half Pint said. "I'm happy you will be here. That will be fun. Maybe we can visit."

Slim gave a self-conscious nod, "I better hit the muzzle loader. I'm tired."

Half Pint frowned, "Isn't that a gun?"

Booker answered, "Nah, it's a bunk that you have to crawl into from the foot, like Slim's."

"Okay," Half Pint smiled. "Good night. I guess I have to get some rest too, because Cook says I can be up most of the day tomorrow."

Slim gave her a funny look, "Half Pint, we men are not allowed to talk when we eat because it wastes too much time. We'll get fired if we talk about anything that isn't necessary. So, don't think we are ignoring you."

Half Pint nodded, "I'm glad you told me. I'll only talk biscuits to you at mealtime."

As the men went out the door, Pendergast looked at her and patted his heart as he did every night. Booker waved and Slim looked very uncomfortable. "See you tomorrow."

That night Leisel thought about how Slim had acted. She liked him and hoped that she had not somehow upset him. The lumber camp had many little rules she didn't understand.

The rest of the week, all two days, were busy. Half Pint started to help Cook and Lana. She watched as rows of men came in and chowed down without a word. A few nodded to her but other than that, they could have been so many cows eating oats. She was disappointed that none of her friends, except Pendergast even acknowledged her. Pendergast came over to her and patted his chest over his heart before he sat down. He seemed so proud of her.

That evening, Booker and Pendergast came to visit with Half Pint. When she asked after Slim, Booker replied he wasn't feeling very chipper, so went straight to bed. Booker told her that he was teaching Pendergast how to play checkers and asked if she would keep the board and play with him while he was gone. She agreed and thought it would be fun.

The next day, Slim seemed well enough. Of course, he said nothing to her or even looked in her direction, but she was bothered. She knew something was amiss. She didn't know if she should talk to Cook about it, or just give it time. That night, he did not come by again and this time, she said something to Booker.

"Could you please tell Slim that I know he isn't sick. I'm sorry I somehow offended him, but I'd like him to tell me about it in person. I only have a couple friends here, and he is one of them."

"I'll tell him, Half Pint. I don't know if he will listen. It wasn't your fault, but mine. I should have kept my trap shut. He is embarrassed that I told you he wanted to stay here to keep an eye on you."

"Is it the truth? Then no one should be embarrassed. I like to have him keep an eye on me."

"I'll tell him," Booker said, seriously. "I know that will please him."

The next day at first lunch, Ink Slinger and the Bull of the Camp, Boss Rudner, handed out the pay vouchers to the men after they ate. There was a lot of whooping and hollering. The men started clearing out in minutes. Soon the teams of horses and oxen were hitched to wagons and filled with loggers; heading to civilization to uncivilize it!

Half Pint had not seen Slim all morning and was becoming very worried. Booker came over to her room to tell her good-bye and give her the checker board. He never mentioned Slim.

By noon, there was only a handful of people around. The Rudner family was going to San Francisco for the holidays and even Lana and Bert, her husband, were leaving. They were going to Potlatch, Idaho to be with her family.

When Half Pint returned the nightgown after laundering it, Lana said, "You can keep it. It is my Christmas gift to you. I noticed that you didn't have one."

"But I didn't mean to take it," Leisel began.

"Shh! Accept it and say thanks. That's all," Lana interrupted. "You're going to make this a nice place to be. That is a good present for me."

Half Pint hugged her goodbye.

About an hour later, Cook knocked on her door. "Me and Pendergast are going to Yaak with the cat skinner. He is also giving Ink Slinger a ride. That old tractor isn't fast, but it will get us there before dark. We'll be back tomorrow with some supplies for the rest of the two weeks. There is some meat cut up and bread for sandwiches to set out. Could I ask you to put that out and then clean up after? There are only about five men still here. I'm sure you will be okay."

Half Pint nodded, "I can make some eggs and side pork for breakfast tomorrow. It needs to be ready at six, right?"

"It doesn't matter that much, but their stomachs will be growling by then. Can you do it alone? If not, I can stay."

"I can do it. Could I ask you a favor? If I write a note to my brother, could you post it for me in Yaak?"

"Sure can. Hurry and write it."

Leisel jotted a short note telling Cap that she had arrived and was now working in the Yaak camp. She thanked him for all his help and said she would write more later. Then she gave her love to him, her siblings and Johann.

She ran out to hand the envelope to Cook as he climbed on the tractor and then stood back to wave while the noisy machine puffed and cranked its way out of camp. As she turned to go back into the cookhouse, she noticed Slim watching the tractor leave from the front of his bunkhouse. He looked her way and she gave him a big wave. He looked and then returned a small wave back.

About five, a couple of the men who had stayed behind came up to the cookhouse. They had been imbibing liberally from their stash of home brew and were feeling very frisky. They came up to the porch of the cookhouse and loudly demanded they be fed.

Leisel got nervous, but she had most of the sliced meat ready for them. She quickly sliced some sourdough bread. They slopped that all up and then Franz turned to her. "I think we need some dessert, huh Top Hat? We have a pot of honey right here. No one else is around, so what do you say?" a big rough logger spat.

"We could get in big trouble, Franz. You better forget it."

"Do I see a streak of yellow? Top Hat, I thought you were a man!"

"I prefer being a living man to a dead one. You should, too. It will lead to no good. You were so reckless in Yaak, we can't go back there anymore. I'll knock you out with your peavey if you keep it up!"

Just then, two of the other men came to the cookhouse. One gave Franz a dirty look and he asked, "Are they giving you trouble, Miss Half Pint?"

Leisel shook her head no, but her tear-filled eyes gave it away that she was terrified. "They are just feeling their oats."

"I'll explain it to them," one of the other men said.

When he went over to where Franz and Top Hat were sitting, Slim came in. One look pretty much explained the situation. He came right over to Half Pint. "You okay?"

"I'm fine," Leisel answered as she busied herself slicing more bread.

Slim watched her a minute, but she didn't look at him. Then he went to sit with the other two men. She knew they were talking about the first two guys. She hated that. Cook had only been gone a little while and she had a problem. He would never trust her alone again. She wondered if she had been too friendly to those guys or something.

By the time the latecomers had their sandwiches, the other two had bored of the whole thing and went back to scrape the bottom of their hooch bottles. It wasn't until she had picked up their plates that the tears began to roll silently down her cheeks. She was so afraid that Cook would send her away.

She filled the washbasin with water and started to wash up their plates. She didn't notice that the other men were finished and had now left. When she turned around to put the rest of the dinner things away, it was only Slim there. He was clearing off the table.

She never said a word, but nodded to him when he brought over the plates to the washbasin. She turned to wash them, but he stood there. She was almost finished washing the plates when he finally spoke, "It wasn't right for me to ignore you. I was wrong."

"If I gave you an offense, you should have told me so I had a chance to repair it. But you don't have to visit with me every night. I was spoiled, and I know it. You don't owe your spare time to me."

Slim cleared his throat, "What if I want to?"

"Then do."

He smiled for the first time and then said, "Where's the dishtowel? I'll help you."

She pointed to the towel and they finished the dishes and put them away. They did not talk at all. When he hung up the towel he asked, "Want to do something?"

"I'd love to take a walk, but I don't know my way around these woods very well. Could you go with me?"

"We shouldn't go very far because it is dark, but maybe we could walk over to the lake."

"There's a lake?"

Slim flashed his winning smile, "Not much more than a pond, really."

"I'd like to see that."

"Grab your coat." Slim pulled his mackinaw on and buttoned it. "I need to keep you warm. You get sick again, I'll be in trouble."

When Half Pint returned from her room, she had her wool coat on and her mittens and scarf. She noticed Slim who was wiping off the cupboard where she had sliced the meat. He was a good looking man; fair hair, blue eyes and a big smile. He was about five-ten with broad shoulders and lived up to his name of Slim. He was about nineteen or twenty from what she knew and seemed to have good manners. She was so glad that they were talking again.

She went over to him, "Did I leave a mess? Cook will dip me in hot lard."

When Slim smiled, the corners of his eyes wrinkled, "No, he won't. He'll never know. Besides, if he heard what Franz said tonight, he would be too busy sharpening his knife." Now his smile was gone and he looked directly at her, "Those men are bad, Half Pint. They have been in the hoosegow every town they've ever been in. Promise me that you'll keep yourself safe. If you need me, just holler, I'll be here for you. In fact, I might bunk in the cookhouse tonight, just in case they get any ideas."

"I think I'll be okay," Leisel stammered.

"No, me and the other guys worried about it. I'll put out my bed roll back by your door. So, if you get up at night, don't step on me!"

"Slim, do you think that is necessary?"

"I do. No arguments."

"Will you be comfortable there?"

"Have you ever seen my muzzleloader? Rolling my bindle out here will likely be more comfortable."

"If you insist. Can I ask you something that is a bother to me? If Cook was here, I would ask him, but he's not."

"What is it?"

"Was it something I did or said that made them act that way?"

Slim shook his head, "Not at all, except maybe being a pretty girl. Most their ideas come out of a bottle. You were fine. Why?"

"Cook said I should be careful and if I was a trouble, he would send me off."

"I have watched you, Half Pint. You are nice to them all, but give no one any reason to think that it is anything more than that."

"Good. If I do, will you tell me?"

Slim grinned with a tease, "Only if you are making eyes at someone else. If it is me, I won't say a word."

Half Pint giggled, "You are such a rowdy."

They walked over to the lake and it wasn't very big, but it was pretty. They sat on a big rock and watched the moon reflect off the water. They were very quiet but simply sat and enjoyed the quiet. Slim touched her arm and then pointed to a big moose who came down to drink. They watched him until he left.

"I suppose we should go back in. If you get too cold, Cook and Pendergast will have my hide."

"You guys don't have to be responsible for me every minute," Half Pint objected. "I'm a big girl and can stand up on my own."

Slim put his arm around her shoulder, "I remember. That's how come you were sleeping in a snow bank when I came upon you. If it's all the same to you, we'll keep watch. Not because we think that you are incapable, but because we worry for you."

She looked at him and for an instant, they eyes met. Neither moved, but she felt that she became a part of his soul. She had never felt that way about anyone before in her life. She thought he might have felt that way, too.

They got up and walked back to the cookhouse. They stopped first at Slim's chinked-log bunkhouse so he could get his things. It was the first time Half Pint ever went into one. In some places, bunkhouses were called ram pastures. One sniff would explain why. On one side was a row of bunk beds jammed next to each other. On the other were cots jammed next to each other. It was no wonder they were muzzle-loaders, because there wasn't room to walk between the beds. It smelled like dirty socks and old chewing tobacco, but it must have slept thirty men. In the middle were a couple pot-bellied stoves for heat.

Slim gathered his things and then pulled the door closed. "Everyone left from my bunkhouse. It would be spooky to sleep in there without all the snoring!"

Half Pint giggled, "I used to sleep in the loft with my brothers and sisters. Only Oliver snored but Brigit talked in her sleep!"

"How many brothers and sisters do you have, if you don't mind me asking?"

"Three brothers and two sisters. I'm smack in the middle. My oldest sister married two years ago. We had feather ticks over the straw that Father put in. It was very comfortable and since it was in the loft, it was always warm. How about you? Do you have brothers and sisters?"

"I had a twin sister, but she died before I could remember. Then there were my two older brothers."

"Were they twins, also?"

"No, but they looked alike. All us kids did." Slim went on, "My mom died with the same Influenza that took my sister. So, it was just dad and us boys. We all went out on our own as soon as we could."

Half Pint nodded, "I'll try to keep in touch with Cap, my older brother. He is my best friend in the world."

"That is nice. I didn't know my brothers that well. They were quite a bit older than me. I mean they were fine, but I just didn't know them."

When they got to the cookhouse, they fixed the fires and then Half Pint had an idea. "How about we move a couple Deacon benches together and you can make your bed on that? Then you won't have to sleep on the floor."

"That is no matter."

"It could be, if I step on you!"

Slim laughed, "I guess so. It would be like Pendergast stepping on me!"

"Just for that, I'm not going to help you move the benches!"

But she did. Before long, they had three benches moved together and Slim rolled out his bedding. Then they said good night.

It was about two in the morning when there was a ruckus at the door of the cookhouse. Sure enough, there was Franz. Apparently, Top Hat had no interest in accompanying him on his venture. Franz was very drunk. He quickly turned away when he saw Slim stationed by her door. No one even had to say a word before he left.

Jeff smiled at Sister, "I think they want us to leave. They are all standing there with their coats over their arms. Shall we go?"

"Oh yes, I forgot myself. You should have told me to hush up."

"Not at all. I'm worried though," he said after he left a big tip for the café workers.

"What is it?"

"Are we going to get to our destination before we finish the story?"

"I hope so. The story will not be over until you hang my habit in the woods!" `

Jeff cracked up, "I can just see me nailing a habit to a tree. I would spend my golden years in an institution!"

T he next morning was dreary and the gray, heavy clouds were so low one could almost wear them. Jeff put the motel curtain back in place and thought seriously about going back to bed. He stared at it, but didn't give in to the temptation. It wasn't that he wanted to get back on the road, but he wanted to hear more about Half Pint. Over breakfast and a few minutes discussing the weather ahead with the waiter, Sister returned to her story.

Leisel's alarm clock went off at four-thirty. Leisel came out of her room, dressed and ready to start her day, She was shaking down the coals in the cook stoves, when Slim joined her. "I forgot you got up earlier than us."

"You can go back to sleep. I'll try to be more quiet."

"No matter. I just need coffee."

"I set the pot to boil so as soon as the stove heats up there will be some."

Slim looked at her and smiled a big smile. She looked at him and asked, "What was that for?"

"Nothing. I just felt like smiling."

Half Pint giggled, "Good. You are a good smiler. I think we should have scrambled eggs, fried potatoes and beans with our ham. Does that sound okay?"

"Biscuits?"

"There are some left-over ones. Or do you want fresh?"

"Those will do fine," Slim shook his head, "Don't make too many. I doubt Franz and Top Hat will be eating much."

"I need to cook for them regardless."

"I know, but it seems a waste." Slim watched her as she brought a bowl of boiled potatoes out of the back pantry. "Did you hear Franz last night?"

"I did." Leisel nodded, "Thank you for watching over me."

No more was mentioned.

Before long, breakfast was ready and Half Pint went out to bang on the Gut Hammer (the term for a triangle or horn used to call the men to eat). She came in and suggested they fill their plates. "We can all serve ourselves, right?"

"I think so," Slim said as he scooped some scrambled eggs onto his plate.

Within a few minutes about ten men showed up to eat. Top Hat came in alone, but asked if he could take a plate back for Franz, who was feeling poorly. Leisel said he could, but reminded him he had to bring the plate back or Cook would be after him.

By seven, Slim and Half Pint had cleaned up the cookhouse and folded up Slim's 'bed'. As he went to take his bedding to his bunkhouse, he said, "Think of what you'd like to do today. We still have time before Cook and Pendergast get back to do something."

Half Pint sat down and rested her chin on both her hands, "What would you like to do?"

"Have no idea."

Half Pint got a big grin, "How about we gather some berries!"

"Berries? Would they even be good? They're probably frozen!"

"I don't mean to eat. I mean for decorating a Christmas tree. Tomorrow is Christmas Eve. We need to have a tree."

"Where would we get a tree?"

Half Pint got the giggles, "We are in a forest, you loony bird! Where would we get a tree, indeed!"

Slim laughed, "Oh, I forgot."

"Come on. Let's get a bucket to put our berries in."

As the two headed off to the woods, Slim told one of the men who was sitting on the porch of his bunkhouse what they were going to do. He got an odd look on his face. "I haven't had a Christmas trees in years! When I was a kid, we used to make popcorn strings. Do you think Cook has any corn we can pop?"

"I don't know, but you can ask him when he gets back. He should be back by noon. What we really need is a star for the top," Half Pint suggested.

"That's what we will do then. I will round up some of these sweatbags and we will fix up a star. You got the tree?"

"Not yet." Slim answered. "How big do you think it should be?"

"Only big enough to fit in the cookhouse, with room for the big star. Me and some boys will get us a beauty. You go get some berries."

They had a great time and visited a lot. Neither asked any questions about the other's personal life, but both volunteered some. They laughed, teased and even managed to gather a half a pail of berries. When they returned, they found some of the men over at the machine shop. They were working on the star. Even Top Hat was helping. He was crafting the big star for the top of the tree.

Next to the cookhouse, stood a neat fir tree, perfectly shaped and pounded into a homebuilt stand. Half Pint got tears and said, "I have never seen such a pretty tree"

Slim teased her. "Now who forgot they were in a forest? Goodness girl, you are surrounded by trees!"

"I know, but this is our Christmas tree!"

"You are funny."

By the time Cook, Ink Slinger and Pendergast got back, all the men except Franz, were sitting in the cookhouse. They were popping and threading corn onto string or making strings of blue, purple and red berries for their tree. All the while, they told tall tales and joshed one another. On one of the tables, there were several small stars displayed along with one very large shiny star for the top.

Cook started to laugh, "I guess you are planning a Christmas gala? What are the vittles for this event?"

The elves of Yaak Camp had not thought that far ahead, but within minutes, they all had ideas. It was decided that they would have baked goose for Christmas Eve. Then they would have a big ham for Christmas dinner.

Cook rummaged around in his larder and drug out all sorts of ingredients. "Okay, you folks think we need this—you all can help. I will bake three pumpkins, but you all plan on helping turn them into pies!"

By that evening, everyone had helped. Even a sullen Franz came over and stayed to chop cabbage. He seemed to be relieved that no one had reported his behavior to Cook. A couple men decided that they should have trout for breakfast on Christmas morning and Cook said he would cook them, if they caught them. After conning a bag of sandwiches out of Cook, they headed off to a nearby stream.

Excitedly, Half Pint helped Cook make the sweet and sour red cabbage to eat with the goose, which they stuffed with apples and onions. It was a lot of fun and everyone seemed in a good mood.

While they were cooking, Half Pint said, "I feel bad because I have nothing to give anyone for Christmas."

Cook turned to her in shock, "Girl, this whole Christmas is because of you! You gave this all to us."

"Christmas is for everybody. I mean I don't have presents."

"Well, why don't you mix up some cookies for all the guys that are here. They will all like that. No one will have presents."

"May I do that?"

"I'm ordering you to," Cook said gruffly, and then grinned. "There are some raisins over there, so get with it."

"Yes sir." Then she gave hugged his arm, "You are the best."

"I would like to say I was, but I think I surely am not."

Christmas Eve morning, it was snowing but rather pleasant. After breakfast, the fisherman asked Cook for a nosebag, so they could fish most of the day. "We'll be back early for our goose dinner. After that is when we are decorating the tree, right?"

"I thought that we were going to do that this afternoon."

"Nope, us guys decided we should all get to help. It is our Christmas, too."

Cook watched the man and then broke into a huge grin, "You're right for certain. We will wait until after dinner and dishes are washed."

"Dishes?" the old logger groaned. "Never signed up for that."

"Don't worry," Cook said. "I got it covered."

"You do the dishes and we'll clean the fish."

"Hey Cook, we hanging up stockings?" a cat skinner called out.

"No way. I refuse to have anyone's old stinky socks hanging around my cookhouse!"

Even though they all agreed, there was a lot of teasing going on about it.

After the one lunch served that day, some of the men asked if they could heat enough water for baths. Cook said they could and lent his two boilers to the men so they could heat up water in one of the bunkhouses. After they left with the boilers, he asked Half Pint if she had planned to wash up, too.

"Guess that means I can't to be the only one to stink tonight. That wouldn't be good, would it?"

Cook looked at her cockeyed, "Don't think you would stink, but I imagine you might. Guess I could scrape a layer off, too."

By five o'clock, dinner smelled magnificent. Half Pint was wearing the only dress that Brigit had packed and had braided her hair nicely. She looked great and even Cook was wearing a clean shirt.

One of the men came in with some small cedar boughs and placed them on the tables. He asked Cook for some candles to set them on the long table they were going to use. It looked very pretty.

Some of the men brought the tree in and it was set in the corner, waiting to be decorated. Then Half Pint went out and banged the Gut Hammer. Men started appearing from their bunkhouses and headed toward the cookhouse. They all were cleaned up and some had even shaved! It was amazing to see.

When they came into the cookhouse, most took off their hats and nodded at Half Pint. She smiled and noticed that Cook shook each man's hand before he took his seat.

They passed the big goose, fruit stuffing, boiled potatoes with creamed corn gravy. There was also rice pudding for dessert. A meal at the cookhouse had never been so cordial and the conversation so pleasant, even the bragging was low key!

Slim brought his plate over and made it a point to sit by Half Pint. Even Cook sat down to eat with the men, and that *never* happened. Pendergast sat on the other side of Half Pint and looked wonderful. He had trimmed his beard and slicked his hair back. Leisel thought he was a fine looking man. Slim was very good-looking without his beard. While they all visited, he was very polite to everyone. She decided she really liked him.

After dinner, one of the men brought out his harmonica and started playing Christmas music. He only knew three Christmas Carols, so soon had to fill in with other music. The fisherman brought in their fish, which they had cleaned before dinner, and put them the coldest spot in the larder. The rest cleared the table, while Slim, Half Pint, Pendergast, Ink Slinger and Cook did the dishes and put them away.

Then they all turned to the tree. Everyone, including Franz, helped decorate. There was a lot of friendly banter and everyone had an idea of how it should be done. Pendergast was given the honor of putting the star on top, and he beamed with pride when they all clapped. Cook brought out his bottle of brandy and gave everyone a little shot. Then they all sang Silent Night. It wasn't pretty, but it was wonderful.

Ink Slinger and Cook sat with Pendergast over another bowl of rice pudding and Slim asked Half Pint if she wanted to go for a short walk. When she went to get her coat, Cook said, "Don't let our girl get too cold. You keep watch over her."

"I will, sir."

"I figured you would, but thought you might forget."

Slim smiled, "I won't forget.

While he and Half Pint went for their walk, they could hear the harmonica player still playing his three carols. It was still and white outside. As they walked down the trail padded with fallen pine needles covered with snow, Half Pint took Slim's hand. "Cook said that most the time, no one does anything for Christmas here."

"Don't imagine they do. Most folks are gone and the rest are too lazy. This is your Christmas, Leisel."

She turned and looked at him, "You have never called me by my given name before! What is yours? I don't even know your name!"

"My name is Arthur Carl Peterson."

She studied him for a minute and then smiled while she repeated it. "I can see that."

"But I like Slim better."

Leisel giggled, "I do, too."

"May I ask what your whole name is?"

"Leisel Hildegard Haldoran."

Slim chuckled, "Okay if I stick with Half Pint?"

"Fine by me."

They walked in silence for a while and then she said, "Slim, thank you for staying in the cookhouse last night. I think you saved me from a terrible fate."

Slim grinned, "As Cook would say, 'might have or might not have'."

Half Pint started to laugh.

C hristmas morning, Leisel got out of bed before the alarm even went off. She got dressed and was excited, but also felt very sad. She wondered what was going on at home and if anyone even missed her. She and Mother had worked on a winter coat for Brigit. She had been anxious to see how it fit her and if she liked it. Without realizing it, she started to cry. She put her head into her pillow so no one would hear, but had a good cry. Then she got up and decided to make the best of her day. It had been fun so far, and the fishermen were proud for everyone to taste their catch.

She had the table set before the fishermen arrived. They were more excited than she had ever seen anyone over some fish! Cook sent her off to get her cookies. She had written everyone's name on one with blueberry syrup. He told her to put one on each man's plate. He would tell them it was from her.

The names were a little difficult to read because the syrup had soaked in a bit, but after the men came in to the ringing of the Gut Hammer, they were all pleased. Half Pint served the fish while Cook kept frying them, so they did not sit with the men. After breakfast, many men came up to her and thanked her for their cookie. Slim was standing by her, when Franz came up carrying his hat in front of him, "Mighty kind of you to give me a sweet. I didn't 'spect there would be one for me."

"Of course there would be! Have a Merry Christmas," Half Pint smiled.

Then the man asked Slim, "If I offered you a hand, would you see fit to shake it?"

Slim grinned and held out his hand, "Have a good Christmas, Franz."

Cook had been watching it from across the room and came up to them. "In my whole life, I never saw the beat. What was that about?"

Slim looked after the man and said, "Oh earlier he had his mouth flapping booze and I think he apologized."

"My God! A Christmas Miracle!"

Slim and Pendergast stayed around to help with dishes and then Slim asked if he could take Half Pint for a walk. Cook thought, "Only a quick one. We need to get to work on dinner."

"I promise I'll help you when I get back."

"I expect you will, or I think you might not," Cook grinned.

As the two left the yard, Slim was walking very fast and Half Pint had to run to keep up. Finally, she quit and stood her ground, "Slim, when he said a quick walk, I don't think this is what he meant."

Slim stopped and looked, "Oh, I'm sorry, I just wanted to get you alone so I could give you my present."

"If you keep dragging me, I may not have the breath to open it." Then a realization came over her, "Slim, I didn't get you anything."

Slim said "I know. This is just a thing I whittled. I am not a very good whittler, so it isn't much. Here."

She opened the handkerchief wrapped gift he handed her, "Oh it is a pretty—horse?"

He chuckled, "It is sort of a short-necked horse. I told you I didn't do a good job. You don't need to keep it if you don't want it around. I know it is junk."

"No, I love it. I'll keep it on my chest of drawers. It is very fine. Thank you so much," she gave him a sweet kiss on the cheek.

Half Pint looked at the horse and then wrapped it in the handkerchief again. She looked up to see him chewing his bottom lip.

"What's wrong?"

"Ah, could I have my hanky back? It is the only one I have."

She giggled, "Yes, but can you wait until I get back to my room and put General in his place?"

"Who is General?"

"My famous short-necked steed!"

That time, Slim kissed Half Pint on the cheek, "Let's get back to help Cook."

"Please don't run!"

That afternoon was great. The ham dinner and pumpkin pies were wonderful and everyone was mellow. After the pies, they all sat around and played cards or checkers. It was a nice day.

The next days were quiet but never again as mellow as that Christmas holiday. Those who stayed for Christmas at Yaak Camp seemed to all feel that they shared a very special time. Pendergast took a lot of time teaching Half Pint how to keep her boots oiled, patiently showing her how to keep the leather soft.

The Mercury was packed and breakfast was out of the way, so the pair were ready to head west on Highway 2. They intended to make it to West Glacier for their next meal, but of course, had to stop at every gas pump along the way. They were losing their good weather, but they wanted to see how far they could get before the threatened storm set in.

Once settled in the car, Jeff asked, "When did the men all come back from their break?"

"Oh, they dribbled in depending on how soon they ran out of money and sobered up. Leisel was getting more and more homesick as time went on, especially over the four days that Slim went into Yaak with a cat skinner. He was picking up some things for Ink Slinger and Cook. Half Pint missed him terribly and that's probably why she was so homesick."

New Year's Eve the men who were at the camp moved the tables in the cook house and had a dance. The floor was pocked and splintered from the calks in their boots. Calks were short spikes the loggers needed to climb around the lumber. However, they all danced with each other, Leisel or broom or handy mop. They had a good time. Half Pint especially enjoyed her dance with Pendergast, but when he twirled her, he picked her right off the ground.

By the end of the following week, everyone was back and work started in earnest. She and her friends had little time to visit like before, but when they did, she read them *The Three Musketeers*. Even Pendergast seemed to enjoy it.

By the end of January, Leisel was finding it hard to keep going without having heard from Cap. He had promised he would write. She worried. What if Father had banished him, too? Why had Johann not come to find her? She tried to keep her happy demeanor, but Lana who was now a good friend, and Cook knew she was hurting.

It was Cook who took things in hand. He called Half Pint aside one day and asked her what was the matter. She hemmed, hawed and tried to not say much but that she was homesick. He didn't buy it.

Then he went to Slim. "I need to talk to you about Half Pint. She is hurting real bad and won't talk about it. Do you know what's eating at her?"

Slim shook his head slowly, "No, I have been worried about her, but she won't tell me anything either. Just that she is homesick."

"I know, but I think it is more than that. I want you to talk to her and find out. Okay? If anyone can find out, you can."

"I'll try, but I don't know how far I'll get. Cook, that little girl means a lot to me."

"I see that, Slim. That is why it is important that you find out. If she can't cheer up, she may become sickly or move on. We don't want that, do we?"

"No, I don't want her to leave."

That Sunday after breakfast, Slim came over to her room and knocked on the door. She was in her room darning socks. She answered the door, "Hello. I thought you were going to spend the day with Pasqual at the machine shop."

"I decided I want to talk to you instead. Can we go for a walk?"

"It is awful cold out."

"It won't be warmer for months, and I want to talk to you before then," Slim said with conviction.

"Of course, I'll get my coat."

Before long, they were sitting on a log watching the frozen lake. "I have to ask you some things, Half Pint. I don't mean to pry, but we are worried about you."

She frowned, "Who is we?"

"Cook, Booker, Ink Slinger and Lana mentioned that you seem so sad these days."

"I don't think it is very nice to talk about me behind my back," she stood up.

Slim jumped to his feet and grabbed her, "Look Leisel, it is not like that. I worry for you. You know that. You may not realize it, but because you have taken a huge part of my heart, I don't want you to be one bit unhappy if I can help it." Slim said seriously, "So, tell me."

Then she started to cry. Slim held her in his arms while she cried out all her fears, doubts and worries. All the while, he patted her back and smoothed her hair.

Finally, she took a deep breath and told him what happened when she left home, "Slim, I still don't know why Father was so angry. Now I worry why Johann never came for me and I haven't heard from Cap. It all happened so fast, the only one I ever said goodbye to was Cap. It makes me feel horrible. I don't even know if Brigit's coat fit!" Then she started to cry afresh. Slim gave her a hug and took her back to sit down. "Let's see. I'll go to Yaak with Cook next week for supplies. I can check around to see if there is a letter for you at the Yaak office. I will nose around the Great Northern Office and see what I can find out about Cap. Leisel, I know it seems like it has been forever, but it takes a long time for information to travel between the log camps. If he said he would keep in contact, I sure he will. It seems to me that he stuck his neck out for you before and I don't reckon he would forget you very soon. I know we aren't your family and I'm not Johann, but please give everything time. Try to smile and remember we each only get so many days to be alive. Every one that we waste being sad is gone forever. We can't someday say we want that time back. We can't say if I had known about this yesterday, I would have probably done differently. We are where we are at. You have to live each day without thinking of what you may have missed. If you do, you will miss it all. Don't leave a pile of probably yesterdays."

She watched him as he talked and knew she was becoming very fond of him. She certainly deserved no better friend. Then she started to cry again, and he put his arm around her.

"Slim, is there something wrong with me?"

He laughed real hard, "You silly thing. There is not a thing wrong with you! Don't you think that Booker, Cook and I would have told you? You know us! Whatever happened is not your fault. Now listen to me about this."

"Okay. But how can I be happy when I don't know?"

"We can always be happy if we make up our minds to be. Don't look for the bad stuff. When you start thinking of it, put your head on a different road. Of course you will be sad sometimes, that happens. But you don't need to follow that trail."

"What makes you sad, Arthur?"

He grinned when she called him that, "Oh, when I think of how it was after Mom and my sister died. Dad was very upset and stayed away a lot. My brothers were stuck with me and didn't want me around, so I was alone most of the time. But I loved seeing my Grandma. So when I get down, I think about her. I don't even know where my brothers are and I hear from Dad once a year on my birthday. But Leisel, he always remembers my birthday! Isn't that nice?"

She gave him a hug and said, "You are such a good person."

"Well, if you come back to the cookhouse all cold and sick, Cook won't think so. And if Pendergast finds out I let you get sick, he will turn me to mush!"

Half Pint raised her eyebrows, "He could too, you know."

"Yes'm, I do know."

The weather turned ugly, so Cat Skinner didn't go for supplies the following week, but when he went the next week, Slim was his passenger. He not only carried another letter to Cap with the two dollars he had lent Half Pint, he had promised to stop by the folks at the blue door and tell them Half Pint was doing well.

When he got to the Yaak Lumber office, he had the clerk rummage around. The clerk found a letter there for Leisel from her brother. He was so thankful and hoped that it would bring her some cheer. He had half a notion to take the ferry upstream to Dahlgren and talk to Mr. Haldoran himself, but decided that he shouldn't do that without her permission. He had very mixed feelings about it. He didn't want Johann to come for her, but if that would bring her happiness; he figured it would be best.

He went to the ferry and asked about the blue door. The ferryman frowned and said, "You don't seem down on your luck."

"I'm not, but I'm carrying a message from someone they helped."

"I guess it is alright then."

Slim knocked on the door and waited. The lady with her hair in a bun opened it with a cheerful smile, "Welcome young man. What can I help you with?"

"I don't need any help but I came to deliver a message. May I come in to speak to you and Angus? You are Elizabeth, I presume."

"I am at that. Come in and sit. I have some coffee if you would like and maybe a cookie to go with it."

Slim smiled, "Thank you Ma'am. That sounds very nice."

After she called Angus, she refilled her cup and sat across from him. "You don't sound like you were reared around these parts. Where are your roots?"

"I'm from Indiana. I have worked up at the Yaak Lumber Company for near four years."

"Hello!" the burly Angus said as he offered his hand. "A logger then?"

"Yes, I'm a tree topper. I shimmy up the tall spar trees and trim them on the way. We set a pulley up there, so we can lift other trees out."

"My," Elizabeth gasped, "That sounds scary!"

"It isn't so bad, I check my rigging and the other boys watch out for me."

"It is still a long fall, no matter who is watching!"

Slim grinned, "Now I am scared."

"What be your need, son?" Angus asked as he poured himself some coffee.

"I came to deliver a message from a little lady that you helped. Her name is Leisel and she now works with our camp cook. We call her Half Pint.'

"I remember her, was she carrying a carpet bag?"

"She was. It is a fine Kennebecker,' Slim nodded.

"Kennebecker?"

"Oh that's what the guys from the eastern lumber camps call them and I guess I picked up the expression. We have a few Easterners who migrated west and bunk with us."

Then Slim went on to explain how Leisel arrived in the camp and how she was now doing. After several questions and comments, Elizabeth and Angus gave their blessings to the arrangement.

"She was in a frightful state when she was here," Angus said. "She had taken a hell of a beating. Do you know who wielded it?"

"I guess her father, but she doesn't know what made him so angry," Slim explained.'

"I wonder why the good Lord allows some folks to have children. I'm glad that I don't have to be their judge."

Slim had a nice visit with those folks and then returned to help Cat Skinner load the supplies. He was anxious to return to camp, but was worried about the news he carried.

When they got to camp, Half Pint was in the kitchen mixing up a batch of sourdough bread. She looked up when they were carrying boxes into the pantry. Slim smiled at her, "I have a letter from Cap in my pocket."

She started to tear up, and Slim grinned at her, "Don't cry, Half Pint. You will ruin the dough! I'll bring it to you when we get the supplies unpacked."

"Thank you, I'm so excited!"

It was a half an hour later when the two went to her room and he gave her the letter. "Would you like me to stay or leave?"

"Could you sit and wait? I might want to go for a walk after I read it. Cook said I could take a break."

Slim sat on the chair while Half Pint sat on the bed. She read the letter and then stopped to cry a few times. Slim watched her with concern, but never said anything. Finally, she put the letter in her lap and covered her face with her hands. She tried at first to stifle her sobs, but when Slim came over to sit beside her, she turned to him and cried. After a couple minutes, she said, "I still don't understand. In fact, I even understand less now."

"Do you want to talk about it?"

She shrugged and then picked up the letter. She summed it up: Cap says he is well and so are the other kids. Mother and Father seem okay. They have never mentioned my name again or that I was gone. Nothing. The day after I left, Cap went over to see Johann. His brother said that he and his father had a huge row the night before, Johann took his horse and left. No one has seen him since. He did leave a note for Cap though, which just said, 'I'm sorry. Tell Leisel I am so very sorry.'

Cap said when he asked around, no one knew that Johann had left or had any idea of where he had gone. Cap had dropped off the letter on his way to the Great Northern camp. He said he would keep in touch.

"Slim, I know nothing! You must have been wrong, I must be truly horrible!"

Slim put his arm around her, "Don't say that. You know better. I think there must be something else afoot. You may still hear from Johann. Be a bit patient. Come on now, I will go for a long walk with you before dinner."

Jeff frowned, "Did you ever find out?"

"Don't be impatient my little friend," Sister smiled. "There is a nice little café over there. After we fill with gas, I will buy you a soda pop. Sound good?"

"Only if you keep talking."

They sat in the blue vinyl booth to enjoy their Coca Colas. Sister took a drink and continued.

That spring, the lumber was stacking high, but the weather didn't look like it was going to break soon. The Bull of the Camp, Boss Rudner, hired some short-stakers to help feed the sawmill in the valley. They would run some loads down to the mill with the sleighs. It was hard work and they were a rough group with no long-term stake in Yaak Camp. Some of these fellows were troublemakers. A dozen of them decided to give Lana and Half Pint a bad time. Boss Rudner and Cook both told them to shape up or drag up, but it made little difference. They were warned; the next infraction and they would all be paid out. Some of the old guard took turns keeping an eye out for the girls, even to walking Lana back and forth to her cabin and waiting until her husband came in. Three men watched Rudner's home, his wife and daughter.

Of course, Slim, Booker and Pendergast kept a close eye on Half Pint's situation. One of the old guard (long time employees of the company) usually slept the night in the cookhouse since Cook slept at the other end of the building from Half Pint's room to make certain there was almost always someone nearby for her.

One night, while Pendergast was sleeping at the cookhouse, one of the meanest of the short-stakers came in, all boozed up. Of course, Pendergast being deaf, he couldn't hear him as he crept by. The man went into Half Pint's room and jumped on top of her. Something woke Pendergast and he flew into the room in a wild rage. He grabbed the man off her and smashed him down to the floor. He busted a couple of his ribs and his arm. Cook came running in when he heard the ruckus and they threw the man out of the cookhouse. Pendergast was so upset that he had let the man get by him, that he hit his fists on his own head. Half Pint consoled him and finally Cook got him convinced that he did a best job anyone could do.

After a bit, folks settled down and hoped to get some rest before morning. However, Pendergast spent his time pacing the floor. Shortly before the sun rose, friends of that short-staker came back with their pistol. They rushed the door and shot Pendergast three times in the chest. Then the six of them took off on horseback.

The cookhouse turned to chaos. Cook tended to Pendergast, while Half Pint frantically clanged the Gut Hammer. Folks came running from all over. Rudner sent a gang of men to follow the short-stakers, and if nothing else, keep them out of camp. They were to report the incident to the Sheriff in Yaak.

Meanwhile, Ink Slinger, Half Pint and Lana helped try to save Pendergast. Slim and Booker came to the cookhouse and kept vigil for their dear friend. He had lost a lot of blood. They were able to quell the bleeding, but eventually, the man with the big heart weakened to the point he could no longer breathe evenly.

As he lay on Half Pint's bed surrounded by his friends, he looked around. He smiled weakly and then patted his chest as he looked at Half Pint. He died minutes later while holding her hand.

It wasn't only Half Pint who was heartbroken. The whole camp took the death of their beloved giant very hard. Everyone figured a way to blame themselves for his death, while they also mourned his loss.

Boss Rudner was furious with himself for not firing those men earlier. He said he would try to contact his family and pay to have his body sent back to them. Cook explained, "He had no other family, Boss. We were it. I think he would like to be buried here in Yaak Camp. This was his home."

"Then he shall be," Boss Rudner said. "We'll give him a fine burial. I'd like some boys to build him a coffin. We'll need a big one and use the best wood."

Before the sun began to set, a grave was dug under a lone pine that stood to the back of the yard. A grand coffin had been built and some men carved his name in bold letters on the top. Others formed a cross for him and still others built a short fence around the single-grave cemetery, pounding thin stakes into the frozen earth. One of Pendergast's friends, a teamster, swept out a wagon and hitched up the gray team that were the giant's favorite, to carry his body to the gravesite.

Lana and Half Pint went through his few things, found his best clothes and readied him for burial. They found the cookie that Half Pint had given him on Christmas. They put it in his shirt pocket. Cook and Ink Slinger helped them dress him.

At three o'clock, the whole camp gathered to bid him farewell. His coffin was loaded into the wagon and taken to his resting place. Booker and Slim hung his boots on a nail on the big old pine tree. Ink Slinger read some words from his Bible and Cook said a few words to tell him goodbye. They all stood in silence. Some men filled his grave in and a lone harmonica droned out the tune of *Old Rugged Cross*. After that, Boss Rudner said a few words before he said that work would resume the next day like usual. Then the crowd dispersed.

That night, Slim took Half Pint for a walk. Slim said that was the biggest funeral he had ever seen for a logger. Usually there wasn't much. But then, little would never do for Pendergast.

The couple walked a long time, took turns crying over their loss and spent a lot a time holding each other. Slim had been friends with Pendergast since he came to Yaak camp when he was fifteen. Pendergast watched over him 'because I was a puny runt,' Slim explained.

"No doubt he cared for you, Slim. He knew you felt that way, too," Half Pint pointed out.

"Half Pint, do you know what he meant when he thumped his heart to you?"

"That he cared for me; we were friends?"

"He loved you with his whole big heart. That's what he was saying. He would have never asked you to marry him or anything like that, but you were the only girl I ever knew him to love. You should be honored."

"I thought he was my friend and I tried to be good to him."

"You always were," Slim gave her a hug. "You were always very good to him. He enjoyed being around you. He was so proud when you polished your boots the way he'd taught you. You made him happy when you played checkers with him. Although, he wasn't very happy when you trimmed his beard!"

"He let me do it!"

"I know, but it was a real act of love. He couldn't wait for it to grow back," Slim chuckled. "We better get back now. Tomorrow will be a busy day."

Before they got to the cookhouse, Slim took her in his arms, "I don't want another day to go by without telling you how much you mean to me. You have given me a whole reason for living I never had before. I know you're still waiting to hear from Johann, but I want you to know if you ever decide to quit waiting, I'd be pleased if you would be my wife. You don't need to say anything. Just know it."

Then he kissed her cheek and left her at the cookhouse door. Dumbfounded, she went in her room, lit the lamp and noticed someone had made up her bed. She looked at the bed where one of her dearest friends had died just hours earlier. But somehow, it didn't make her sad. It made her feel very comforted. She put on the nightgown from her friend Lana and crawled into the bed. Curled up, she remembered how she felt when she being carried to the camp by the goliath who hummed soothingly to her.

"You're killing me, Sister! "Jeff wiped his eyes, "Do you think Pendergast's grave is still there? If we have time, could we go visit it?"

"I would like that, but I don't know what is still there. Maybe we can find out."

"I'd really like to see that camp, too!" Then Jeff looked out the window, "It is snowing harder now. We better get on our way if we hope to get to West Glacier."

"Maybe we should check with the some of the truckers."

"Good idea."

After they checked with some truckers, they thought they could make it at least as far as West Glacier, but might have to stay the night there. Some roads further west were closing in.

As the pair drove out onto the highway, they could see that the conditions had deteriorated from the night before. "Maybe we should just bunk in here," Jeff suggested.

"The truckers said we can make it to West Glacier, so I think we should try. I would hate to come this far and have Mother pass away before I ever got to say goodbye."

"I agree. Let's go. After all, that is the reason we came," Jeff nodded. "Sister, did you ever see Johann again?"

"No, but I did come to understand more about it." Sister poured the driver some coffee, "I will continue, okay?"

"I don't understand something. What did you mean about 'feeding the mills'?"

"Oh, see how it worked then was the lumber camp was separate from the sawmills. The lumber camp would cut the timber, stack it and when the rivers thawed in the spring and the water was running high, the loggers would have a drive. They called it 'bringing her in'. The boys had accumulated huge stacks of forty-foot logs from their entire winter's work. It was an exciting time when they rolled the logs into the fast running streams and floated down to a lower bay. There the logs would be pulled out of the water and sent to the sawmills. The loggers did not have anything to do with the mills except 'feed' them the raw timber. Hopefully, they could stack up enough to keep them sawing until the next drive. In that era, the demand for wood was growing, and it was almost impossible to keep up."

Jeff frowned, "Did all the lumber companies use the same rivers and streams? How did they keep from getting the logs from getting mixed up?"

"All the logging companies, of course, had to use the same waterways. We all tried to get our timber into the water before the others. In those times, we were so snoosed up that it would have been impossible to add any more juice. The men used a branding axe to mark each log on the end. The brands were registered like cattle brands and there were state inspectors at the mills. Stealing raw lumber was a serious crime. The logs had to be sorted at the end of the drive. It must have been a lousy job."

"What language do you talk?" Jeff teased. "When you say snoosed, what do you mean? Did those guys drink, smoke and chew?"

"A few drank in camp; but it was stupid and dangerous. Boss Rudner didn't like it none. Most men chewed tobacco, because no real logger ever smoked cigarettes. Too dangerous around the timber and sap, (pitch from the evergreens) is like lighter fluid and quite explosive. Some smoked pipes or cigars at night in the bunkhouse, but not outside."

"Makes good sense."

"When they gave something the juice or snoosed it up, that meant they speeded it up or added power to it. Those boys worked hard and long hours. They lived for bringing her in, and took a lot of pride in bringing in their year's work. That was the pay out and the beginning of their summer break. Then they would come back for the next go round,"

"I can see the lure of it. It must have been a fantastic experience."

"It was. Except for the short-stakers who moved around a lot, many of the men had strong bonds with each other, but not very sentimental. Many times, they knew someone for years and never knew their real name or where they came from. They knew them simply by their occupation and the person they were at that time. Then there were some they came to know more about than real family."

"I can see that. There must have been some freedom in that."

"There was. I'm certain it was therapy for many a wounded soul. Although with all the blasphemous profanity flying around, one would never think so on the face of it." Sister giggled. "The different jobs even vied for the title of the worst language! The teamsters, bullwhackers and river hogs seemed locked in competition of who could use the foulest tongues, but even Cook could spew a mouthful! He was determined to not be known as the boiler of a hardtack outfit and would yell his head off if you messed up some food."

"Boiler of a hardtack outfit?"

"Yes, a boiler was the nickname for a lousy camp cook and a hardtack outfit was a camp known for its bad food. It was hard to recruit workers to a hardtack outfit. Those boys were rather fussy about their beans. I can tell you that!"

"I imagine. They didn't have much else to look forward to!"

Then Sister put her cup back in the console and continued.

That spring was very cold and the rivers didn't break clear of the ice for the drive until late. That is why the short-stakers were been brought in to drag sleighs to the mill. After losing Pendergast, Rudner refused to find another crew. He told the owners that he would drag up rather than do that again. They were unhappy, but knew Rudner ran a good camp, so they relented.

The landing (place where the logs where stacked waiting for their watery trip) was filled to overflowing. During those couple late springs months, Booker, Slim and Half Pint didn't get much time together except some on Sundays. Much discussion went into Booker's summer break. He was going to spend it in Yakima and knew of a certain lady that he wanted to spend time with. He had met her in Eureka, but she had moved and was setting up her own business in Yakima. He took a good deal of ribbing about it, but seemed to enjoy the teasing. It was the jolliest anyone had ever seen Booker.

Slim and Half Pint had made no plans for their break.

While Cook stayed in camp over the Christmas break, he usually was gone on the summer one. He would move the van (a cook tent rigged on a wagon) down the river with the drive to provide food and supplies for the workers along the river, as they kept the timber flowing on the river smoothly. Then he ended up at the mill. There he would take some time off, buy supplies and rest up. He was always back in camp before anyone else. He usually went with Pendergast but this time, Ink Slinger was going with him.

The Rudner family was going to take the train to San Francisco over the break. Lana and her husband were staying because Lana was now in a family way. A new Iron Burner (blacksmith) had joined up and was going to bring his wife up at the beginning of break and move her into his newly built cabin. It stood next to Bert and Lana's cabin. The men laughed about it and called it 'the village'. Blacky's wife was a teacher from out in New Hampshire and she would be tutoring Rudner's little girl in the fall.

In late April, Half Pint got an invitation to ride down to Yaak with Cat Skinner when he picked up supplies. Excited at the prospect, she still seemed on edge about it. Slim soon figured that she was afraid. On one of their walks, he asked her, "Why don't you want to go to Yaak? Cat Skinner will watch out for you and I imagined you'd have a nice time."

"Slim, what would I do? I only know Elizabeth and Angus. I have no money and I know Cat Skinner wants to hit the saloon. It would be a fright."

Slim listened and then shook his head. He never said anymore, but came back a couple days later and said, "I talked to Boss. I'm hitching a ride into Yaak with Cat Skinner and he okayed a small draw from Ink Slinger. You can have a small draw too, if you come to Yaak."

Half Pint was shocked, "You mean you and me? To Yaak? For two overnights?"

"Yup, interested?"

"What about Cook?"

"He wants you to get out of here to see the other world for a bit. He thinks it is a good idea."

"Oh Slim, that would be—I don't know, really something!"

Slim chuckled, "I'll take that as a yes."

"What did Cat Skinner say?

"He was snoosed up cause he won't have to load the supplies alone."

"I would have helped."

"You weren't going to go!"

Half Pint kissed his cheek, "You are the very best!"

Four mornings later, Half Pint threw her Kennebecker to Cat Skinner, who caught it and acted as if it weighed a ton! "What you got in there, rocks?"

"Yes sir. As big as I could carry!"

"Well, climb aboard and mind your skirt. I don't want it to catch on the mechanics."

"What mechanics?"

"It is an expression, Half Pint," Slim chuckled. "Just sit down and let me on."

It was a neat trip though very cold. Half Pint loved seeing the forest from the bounce of the corduroy road, so called because of the logs partially buried horizontally to offer support from the mud and snow. Slim pointed out where the different plots (also known as strips) were and how logs were moved to the landing on skid roads. The logs on the bottoms of these roads were the same direction of the road and made to be watered down, iced or covered with straw. They would make the loads very slippery and increase the velocity as it moved. He pointed out another tree topper who was working high up a forty-foot tree. These men were also known as high climbers or high riggers. Half Pint frowned, "That's awful dangerous, Slim. I don't think I like you doing that! What would I do if something happened to you?"

"I feel as safe up a tree as anywhere," the young tree topper answered. "You could get burned working over the bean pot."

"That's different and you know it."

"I promise you, I'll be safe. I'm very careful because I have a girl I have to watch out for," then he squeezed her hand.

It was dark when they finally arrived in Yaak. Cat Skinner turned his keys over to the clerk and headed out to the saloon. The keys to any machinery had to be checked into the Yaak Office before the boys went out drinking. Then there was no worry of them getting lost or someone driving his caterpillar through town during a drunken adventure! "Meet you back here tomorrow afternoon to load supplies. We'll be heading out at daybreak the next morning."

"Have a nice time," Half Pint waved.

The clerk read the instructions from Rudner and Ink Slinger. "I'll have the supplies here by two tomorrow. Here is your draw. Now know this, we won't bail you out of the hoosegow. You get in trouble; you get yourself out. If you don't help load tomorrow; it will be docked from your pay. If you aren't here when Cat Skinner leaves, we'll figure you drug up. No bend on that!"

"Okay, sir," Slim nodded. "We'll be here."

The two took off down the street with Slim carrying her Kennebecker while his bindle was over his shoulder and holding her hand. He was walking fast and Half Pint finally stood her ground, "Why do you never remember my legs are only half as long as yours? Please slow down."

Slim broke out in a laugh, "Guess I should remember. After all, you are my Half Pint!"

Leisel was more pleased that she could imagine. She beamed all the way down the street. She had never felt so good in her life.

They passed the Rooming House and even a flop-house, but Slim kept going. When they arrived at the Bed and Breakfast with the blue roof, Slim started up the steps.

Half Pint pulled on his arm, "I can't afford anything this nice."

"Who said you have to? I'll pay for it."

"That isn't right. I should pay for my own."

"Look dumbbell, I'm getting your room. I planned to do it and I have the money for it. I want you to have a nice, safe room and maybe even a hot bath with fresh towels."

"Do I stink?"

"There is no way in Hell I'm answering that question!" he chuckled. "I'll check you in and then I'm going over to the Rooming House."

She started to object and he interrupted, "I promise to take a hot bath there myself and I'll be back here to have breakfast with you. Now, I can carry your Kennebecker up to your room. Here is your key. Don't lose it."

Half Pint followed him up the steps and waited while he unlocked the door, "The guy from the desk said he'll bring up water in a couple minutes for your bath. He will knock, so let him in. Check the peephole before you open the door! Hear me?"

Half Pint nodded, "How will I find you in the morning?"

"I'll be in the lobby at six. If something should happen and you need me before, I told the clerk where to find me. Okay?"

"Slim, you paid. You should be staying here."

"No Half Pint. I don't want to tempt fate," then he gave her a real kiss goodnight.

The next morning, Half Pint nervously descended the steps to the lobby. Walking down the hallway, she became very aware of the noise the calks in her boots made. The calks were noisy and damaged floors In the log camp, it didn't matter because all the floors were covered in 'calk pox'. Boots with smooth soles would have been dangerous.

She was worried she might miss Slim and was so relieved when she saw him sitting there waiting. It was well before six, so he must have come early. She came up to him with a big grin, "I see you took a bath."

Slim pretended to sniff the air, "You, too!"

They went into the dining room arm in arm. They sat at a round table and soon, Elizabeth approached them. "God in all His Mercies! I must tell Angus! It is our friends from Yaak Camp! Come see for yourself!"

The door to the kitchen opened and Angus strolled over to the table extending his large hand to Slim. Then he gave Half Pint a kiss on the cheek, "A fine sight for sore eyes! Slim told us you were doing well."

"It is good to see you and to thank you in person for the wonderful kindness you showed me," Leisel smiled. "I would've never made it without your help."

"I hear that this lad and his friends get some of the credit, too!" Elizabeth added.

"They did. They were wonderful," Half Pint beamed.

"I'm delighted to hear that." Angus smiled, "What can I feed you? I have some venison sausage and potato-eggs. Could I bring you some?"

Slim grinned, "What are potato-eggs?"

"Eggs fried over onions and boiled spuds. They are my favorite."

"If you say so, that will be fine with me," Slim nodded. "What about you, Half Pint?"

"That sounds good, but I also saw that sign for cinnamon bread," Half Pint said. "I would like to try that."

"I'll fix you up with both." Angus chuckled and went off to the kitchen.

Elizabeth brought them some coffee and went to wait on some other guests. The young couple looked around the dining room. There were linen tablecloths and ruffled curtains on the tall windows, set against walls with floral wallpaper. The floors were polished hardwood covered with large, thick rugs and the meals were served on real china.

Half Pint took it all in and then said to Slim, "Isn't this the grandest place you have ever seen?"

He watched her and smiled, "It is nice. I'm glad you like it."

"Oh Slim, it is so lovely. How was the rooming house?"

"Clean and comfortable. It was good."

"I still don't feel right about being in luxury, while you are roughin' it."

Slim laughed "I'm not roughing it. You deserve some nice things."

"I have nice things."

"What do you want to do this morning?"

"Lana asked me to pick up some flannel so she could make diapers for her baby. I thought I might get some material to make her a nice gift. That is all."

"Okay, we can go to the General Store."

"What did you want to do?"

"Be with you."

They ate in silence for a bit and then Half Pint said, "Slim, do you think that Johann ever cared about me?"

Slim studied her a minute and then said thoughtfully, "I think he did. I'm almost certain that something happened that had nothing to do with either of you. I have no idea what, but I guess he was forbidden to marry you, too. That's likely why he left. I think he cared a lot for you. He would have been a fool if he didn't."

"You are always so kind when it comes to me. I'm not so nice, you know."

"Hm. What is it that you do bad?"

She swatted his arm, "I don't do bad. You know what I mean."

84

"No, I don't. I told you once that I love you. I'm willing to wait for you as long as you need. I hope you can care about me."

"Oh Slim, I do. I feel I love you, too. I worry though, because I thought I loved Johann. Maybe I don't know how I feel?"

Slim raised his eyebrow, "Leisel, love grows. It isn't something that is just there. It either will grow if nurtured or die of neglect. I think maybe your love for Johann is dying of neglect."

She reached over and squeezed his hand.

Before they finished eating, Elizabeth came over to their table. "If you don't have pressing things, Angus and I'd like to invite you to dine with us tonight. Do you think you could clear it for us?"

"I would love it," Half Pint answered. "If Slim thinks so."

"Sounds good. What time?"

"We usually eat about six? Will that work?"

"We have to help load supplies, so we should be able to be there about six," Slim answered, "We might be a bit late."

"Let's plan on six-thirty then," Elizabeth smiled. "It'll be so fun to have guests for dinner. Knock on the blue door when you arrive. Okay?"

Half Pint took Slim's hand when Elizabeth walked back to the kitchen, "Oh, isn't this so exciting?"

He smiled, "Yes, it is. We must try to find them a small gift."

Half Pint got serious, "Arthur, I can tell you had a good upbringing. You have good manners. Were they from your Mom?"

"Grandma," Slim chuckled. "She was a gentle lady, who handed out big thumps for ill-manners."

"How old were you when you lived with her?"

"I was just four when I went to her. I lived with her until she returned to her Maker. I was thirteen then. I started on a New England logging crew a few months later. Then I heard about more work out West, and here I am."

"I'm glad you're here."

They walked down the street of the small town. The town was nestled in a wide valley between two tall mountain ranges with the river running right down the middle. A huge tributary from the east merged with the Yaak just above where the lumber mills were located. Down from the tributary were several lumber company yards where they piled the logs until they were cut.

It was a fascinating place. They watched as a herd of horses were brought through town for some auction. They wandered around the assayer's office and learned a bit about the mining business. When the General Store opened, they went in. They must have spent an hour there, looking at everything. Half Pint bought the flannel for Lana and found some fabric so she could make a new nightgown for her. They found some carved candlesticks for Angus and Elizabeth. Then they found a nice snuffbox for Cook and a new handkerchief for Booker. Half Pint was delighted when she found some used books. She bought one to give to Ink Slinger. They carried all their packages back to Campbell's Bed and Breakfast and packed them in the Kennebecker. While Half Pint changed into her wool pants and shirt, Slim said he needed to run an errand and would be back as soon as he could.

She had just read a chapter of Ink Slinger's book, when he knocked. He came in with a grin, carrying a packet from the General Store. He winked, "I got you something."

Half Pint frowned, "Why did you do that? You know I didn't get anything for you."

"Too bad," Slim thrust the packet toward her, "Open it."

She opened the package and found a pretty, new shirt. "Slim, this is magnificent. Why did you spend money on me?"

"I thought you could wear it tonight at dinner, instead of your blood-stained shirt."

She gave him a big hug which ended in a real kiss. The kiss started to become quite passionate before Slim pulled back. "Come on, girl. We have supplies to load."

She smoothed her hair and put on her jacket. As they went out the door, she said, "Slim, I love you."

He never answered.

After loading the trailer with piles of supplies, Cat Skinner was taking off to the saloon. "Have any plans for tonight, you two?" he teased.

"Dinner with friends," Slim answered.

Cat Skinner stopped and gave an odd look, before he said, "That is a mighty fine thing."

They just barely had time to change from their work clothes and make it to the Campbell's blue door by six-thirty. Angus opened the door for the couple and said, "Very punctual."

Slim handed Elizabeth the candles and she was so pleased, "Look Angus! These are the candles I admired last week. How did you know?"

"Half Pint chose them for you," Slim said with pride.

Dinner conversation was filled with laughter. It was delightful. Angus asked Slim if he cared to share a cognac while the ladies did up the dishes. He looked at Half Pint and she smiled, so he said yes.

In the kitchen, Elizabeth observed, "Your young man is a fine soul, Leisel. How do you feel toward him? I believe he is looking to nest with you. Are you of a like mind? Please don't tell Angus I pried, he'd have my hide."

Half Pint giggled, "I won't tell. I'm glad you mentioned it. I'm bothered over it and need some advice."

Then she explained briefly about Johann, her father and now the feelings that she and Slim shared. "What if I don't know how I feel, Elizabeth? Should I be waiting on Johann? I did promise to marry him."

"Yes, you did, but Slim is correct when he said that love needs to be nurtured. I cipher from the note he sent your brother that he does not intend to marry you. That doesn't mean that he never cared about you, or that you never cared about him. You must realize, that there are things in life you cannot change. You should be very careful to not to hold on to a lost chance, while passing up another. You can't live for yesterday. You need to realize that probably yesterday isn't the plan. Maybe now is."

"What are you telling me?"

"I think that you do love Slim, but you are holding on to something that can never exist. You can always have a special place in your heart for Johann, but that doesn't mean that you can't love Slim with all your being. He seems a fine lad, much different from many of the rowdies around these parts. If I was you, I wouldn't wait much longer. I would marry him and be the best wife I could for him. I think he would treat you right."

"Elizabeth, he is so good to me and I have never seen him get mean with anyone, even if he doesn't like them. He told me he'd wait until I decided about Johann."

"He may do that, but will time? Things in this life are not a certainty. Life is precarious and we need to make our choices accordingly," Elizabeth took the young girl's hand.

"Why Miss Elizabeth, I do believe you want me to marry Arthur."

"Arthur? No! I want you to marry Slim!" the round lady giggled.

"That is his given name," Leisel added.

"I figured. I was teasing you." Elizabeth winked. "Now if you do decide, you get a message to me. I'd love to help you with your dress. The Lord never saw fit for Angus and I to have a family, so I'd love nothing better than to help you with your wedding."

Leisel didn't know what to say. The young girl put her arms around her and hugged this kind lady. Through tears she said, "That is a promise. I'd love your help. I mean if Slim wants to get married."

"I have no doubt about that, my girl. None at all. I think he wants to make certain that you can marry him without a lingering question. Now, let's go see what the menfolk are up to."

16

The trip back to Yaak Camp was cold and took forever. Whenever they crossed a trestle bridge, it was tedious. The amount of weight any trestle could bear was by-guess and by-gosh. At a trestle crossing, the tractor would cross first, leaving the loaded trailer behind. Then a long extension of chain connected the tractor and the trailer. The tractor's weight would be completely off the bridge before the trailer would move out on the trestle. It was a slow, nerve-wracking process, but everyone knew a trestle could not hold both.

At every trestle, Cat Skinner and Half Pint would across on the tractor. Once safely on the other side, Cat Skinner would wave and Slim hooked up the chain and rode the load across, helping steer the unwieldy trailer. Half Pint almost threw up when one of the trestles began to sway while the trailer was creeping across. When it was safely on the other side, she ran to Slim and gave him a huge embrace. "I was so terrified!"

Slim chuckled, "I was okay. I'd have jumped to safety."

Half Pint swatted him, "You dumbbell. You would have fallen to your death and I would've had to watch!"

He looked at her with great gravity, "Then you shall never watch a crossing again. You hear?"

The men hooked the trailer up closely behind the tractor. The rest of the way back to camp, Slim kept his arm around her waist while they rode on the back of the tractor. Just before they made the last turn into the camp, he gave her a sweet kiss.

Time passed with great speed. Timber was stacking and the ice was still holding. But there were some signs that spring was coming. Everyone was getting anxious for the summer break.

It was early June when another letter arrived from Cap. It was the news that Leisel had been waiting for. He had heard from Johann. He wrote he was in Georgia and wouldn't be back. He and his father had a frightful falling out and he was bound not to explain. However, he worried for Leisel, and asked Cap to let her know that even though that is what he had wanted, they could never marry. It simply could not be. He was releasing her from her promise. He wished her happiness and a good life. He said he was so very sorry, but it was very much out of his hands. If she wanted to know more, she would have to find out from his father.

Leisel didn't know what to think and couldn't wait for Slim to come in for dinner. They had never spoke privately during any regular meal, but this time she waited for him. When he was leaned over the washbasin by the door, she whispered to him, "I need to talk to you."

Slim stood up holding the towel up to his wet face and said, "Right after dinner."

She waited to hear him come to the cookhouse and then ran out to meet him. "Can you come to my room? I need to speak to you."

Slim went right to her room, closed the door and asked with concern, "What is it, Half Pint?"

She collapsed in tears into his arms and blurted out the whole thing. He just let her ramble for a while. When the tears began to subside, he said, "Want to go for a walk?"

She sniffled, "Yes, I really do."

They walked through the damp forest. Slim was wearing his tin pants, the name loggers gave their waterproof pants. They were made of a stiff fabric to begin with and the pine sap made them even more so, but those pants and the tin coats kept them dry. After a short time, tin pants could literally stand alone.

It was so muddy and soggy, Half Pint's boots sucked into the soil beneath. They didn't talk, but Slim did chuckle a few times when he had to tug her out of the mud.

When they got to the pond, they found a nice place to sit. "Now, you tell me about it. Okay?"

She explained the letter and then said, "I'm not so much sad that Johann doesn't intend to marry me. I already figured that. I was very grateful that he released me from my promise, so now I can go on with my life without a lingering thought. But Slim, what could it be? If his father knows, why didn't my father tell me? He certainly must know. Apparently, Johann was told. What could it be?"

Slim put his arm around her neck and pulled her toward him. Then he kissed her forehead, "I have no idea. Do you think you father would tell Cap? Or you? I can go with you to Dahlgren on break if you want. Or should I go and ask him myself?"

"I doubt he would tell anyone and I wouldn't want Father to be so violent to anyone else. I guess even if I never find out, it probably wouldn't change today. We should just leave it. I have never seen a man so filled with rage as Father was that night, even when that short-staker came to the cookhouse."

"Yah, he was drunk, but I'm certainly glad that the man who murdered Pendergast was caught and hanged. Pendergast was a good-hearted soul and did not deserve to die that way. I still miss him."

"Me, too. I think of him every night when I crawl into bed. I remember that feeling of security I had when he carried me out of the forest. Of course, he would have never done that if you hadn't found me."

"I always knew someday I'd find a treasure in the forest."

They shared a long kiss and then Half Pint said, "If you still want, I'd be honored to be your wife."

Slim looked at her, "Are you very sure? Is it just because things are over with Johann or because you want to be with me?"

"Arthur, I decided it a while ago, but I wanted to wait to see if I had any lingering questions. You told me to not say yes until I could. Now, I can feel I'm not breaking my word. I love you, and I've grown to love you more each day."

Slim broke into a huge grin, "Good! How soon can we get married?"

"How about over summer break?"

"That would be perfect. I'll talk to Boss Rudner and see if he will let me build a cabin in the 'village'. Unless you don't want to live here?"

"Of course I do. This is our home. Oh, I sort of promised Elizabeth she could help me with my wedding."

"Elizabeth? How long ago did you talk to her?"

"When we were in Yaak. See, I really have loved you a while."

Slim gave her a big hug, "You are my girl, alright! I love you, Half Pint! How are we going to do that? You'll need to write to Elizabeth right away! We have to get married before Booker goes to Yakima or on his way back! I know he won't want to wait around."

She had never seen him so happy and that made her happy. However, there was still a big ache in her heart as she wondered what on earth her father wouldn't tell her.

She did write to Elizabeth that very night. She was so excited. The next day, Booker, Cook and Ink Slinger gave the couple a toast with their coffee mugs after dinner. Everyone clapped and hooted. It was a lot of fun.

Rudner said he was glad to give permission for Slim to build his cabin. Several of the loggers volunteered time on their Sunday to help put it up. It would be twelve feet wide and fourteen feet long, like the others. They had a step to the door; a porch would come later. They could either build their own outhouse, or share with the 'village'. They decided to share until they had time to build their own.

There was a chimney, but they had to provide the stove. They planned to buy a Ben Franklin stove in Yaak on their summer break, along with a set of springs for the log bed Booker was crafting as his gift to the newlyweds.

The following week, Lana had a fine baby girl. Everyone was happy with the dainty, little thing. They named her Sarah Leisel. Leisel was thrilled. Because of their new baby, the couple decided to stay in camp over summer and keep watch over the place until Cook's return. However, that meant Lana would not be able to be at Half Pint's wedding, but she lent her the veil she wore when she married.

Before the big thaw, Ink Slinger asked Half Pint to come see him in his office. She was nervous, worrying that she might lose her job. "Sit down," he smiled. "Why are you so pale?"

"I'm worried about what you want with me," Half Pint answered.

Ink Slinger chuckled, "You dumbbell. You're one of my best friends. I only wanted to say that I noticed your boots are getting too small. You have grown at least another inch taller since you arrived. I want to measure your feet for new boots and take the old ones in trade."

"I don't know if I can afford new boots now. We are saving for the stove, you know."

Ink Slinger grinned, "I do know. Cook and I decided to buy the springs for your bed. So, you have some money to spend on boots. You won't be a happy wife if your feet pinch!"

"That's too much."

The dark-haired Ink Slinger frowned over his bi-focals, "You don't have the right to tell us what you think is too much. That is for us to decide. Got it?"

"Yes sir, but you are way too kind."

"Yah, yah. Now put your foot out for me to measure. I want you to know that Slim is a fine man. You two should have a great life if you stick to it. I haven't many friends in my life, but Slim always treated me square."

A frown flashed across her eyes, "I thought you'd have a pile of friends. You are one of the best guys around."

Ink Slinger grinned, "That's why I love you. You have lit up this camp like no one else. So, my special present to you is a fine pair of these walking shoes. They are dressy. Something a lady would wear to her wedding. They will be at the Yaak office waiting for you when you get there. Wear them in good health. No girl should have to get married with the spikes of her calks ripping up the aisle floor! Logging boots don't fit well under a wedding dress."

She giggled, "I love you. Why you would be a fine husband for any girl!"

Ink Slinger looked at her seriously, "I'll tell you a secret. Slim and Cook know, but no one else. If you tell, I could be totally ruined. I'm trusting you. Have I got your solemn word?"

Leisel looked at him with great gravity, "You do."

"I have never had any interest in the ladies. Since polite society doesn't approve, I live here. I sleep on the bunk in my office and keep to myself. The loggers wouldn't approve either. I have a few very good friends. This is the best life for me."

Leisel didn't really understand, but knew it meant a lot to him. She gave him a hug, "I will keep your secret. You can trust that."

"I thought so," he smiled. "Now about those walking shoes, black or cream-colored?"

"But I need to know something."

"What is it?"

"What is your given name?"

"Joshua Jacob Rosenberg from upstate New York. I am thirty-six years old and had been an accountant for most of those years."

Before she left, Half Pint gave him a hug, "You forgot one thing, Joshua Jacob Rosenberg. You forgot that you are a fine person and a great friend."

"Well thank you, Half Pint. That means a lot."

That evening when the boys came in from the mountains, the word was out. The ice was breaking and they could 'bring her in' within a week. Everyone was anxious and eagerly looking forward to the drive. It had been a long winter.

Half Pint and Cook worked hard to get the van loaded with the help of some of the men who were finished with their strips and waiting to drag up.

Then Boss Rudner appointed the River Boss. This man was a logger who also worked as a River Hog, but was in charge. He organized and orchestrated the drive. He placed men along both sides of the river where the logs might jam up, so they could keep them flowing. It was his job to break apart the log jams. It was dangerous and often deadly work.

Booker and Slim both worked as river hogs. Their regular work was done when the drive started, so they 'rode' the logs to their destination. Armed with their peaveys, (cant dogs which were long rods with hooks on the end for moving timber) that every logger carried and gin sticks (longer rods with hooks, specifically for river drives) for breaking up jams, the River Boss spread his crew out along both sides of the river.

Cook and Half Pint headed off to set up camp at the first stop. They tried to keep ahead of the log movement. Once it was started, the logs didn't stop for nightfall, weather or meals. It was non-stop until they had brought her in.

C ook and Half Pint left before the great celebration at the landing when the first pile of logs rolled into the raging river, to great cheers and whoops! The celebration was short-lived because the work started immediately. There were great splashes and much groaning from the stacks of timber moving now toward the water from the long stationary positions. Teams and the cat skinners worked incessantly to keep moving the huge stacks of forty-foot long logs to the river.

Cook and Half Pint did not travel on the corduroy road, but on the skid roads and back trails that followed the river. Their teamster was an older man with a sullen demeanor. He rarely said more than a word, but he knew his team and was not afraid of work. They got to the first camp site and started to get set up for the night. Some of the men had been stocked with nosebags until they could get into van camp.

"How long will it take us to get to Yaak?" Half Pint asked as she dug a bean hole to fit the bean pot.

Cook answered, "If we don't have too many jams, about six days."

"Gee, camp isn't that far out. Why so long?"

"See Half Pint, the river follows is own trail. It has more turns than you can imagine. It doesn't care if it goes to Yaak or Canada. It is all the same to it. If we plan on using the river, we have to follow it. The first logs should be catching up with us by early tomorrow. Pray there are few jams, Girl. They can be costly in time, coin and life."

Half Pint gave him a worried nod, "Cook, is it really dangerous what Slim is doing?"

"Yes'm, it is, but so is his full job. Logging is dangerous. No candy coat for it. But he isn't a rowdy or a show-off, does good work and is as safe as can be. Don't worry or you'll be gray by dawn." Then he handed her a huge bowl, "Now mix up those biscuits, or your job will get very dangerous fast!"

The logs didn't come through that night or even at sunrise. Everyone was keeping a one eye on the river while they ate. By the time they were beginning to put breakfast away, someone let go with a holler, "They're bringing her in!"

Half Pint had never felt such pride or welled up with such a thrill! Everyone cheered as the logs began to litter the river with their axe brands of Yaak Camp proudly displayed on their ends. By the time camp broke up, the river was almost bank to bank with fast running logs. Everyone was grinning from ear to ear, even the old teamster.

The next two days were a blur of campfires, loading and unloading the wagons, feeding men over the campfires and watching the logs race by. Things were moving smoothly and everyone was optimistic. Half Pint didn't even think that in a few days she would be married. She was too busy.

The third day they woke early to a heavy downpour. It was raining so hard they couldn't even keep a fire lit. They resorted to nosebags and everyone was rather grumpy! Around ten in the morning, however, the van skirted Slim's pup tent. He was standing out on the riverbank holding his long gin stick. He waved with a big smile to the van and his Half Pint. Booker waved his ratty hat at the van from across the river. He was grinning like a crazy man, a look he had since he made his plans for summer break.

The van made up its camp and expected the logs to catch up with them in a few hours. It was still raining hard, but Cook and the Teamster had rigged something up so they could have a fire.

Men showed up and before dark were becoming nervous at the few logs that were coming down the river. A couple men on horseback were going to head upstream to see where the jam was. Fishhook Canyon was notorious for jamming. It was steep and rocky, with many crooked jags and boulders jutting from the riverbed. Forty-foot timbers fought the curve and piled up there on nearly every drive.

Before long, some men came to the van and said that sure enough, the jam was at Fishhook, and it was a doozey. The River Hog Boss was going to blast as soon as he could get the charge set.

Half Pint had a huge pit in her stomach and finally had to talk to Cook. "Where is Slim from Fishhook?"

"He is on this side. The jam is above him. Keep calm, girl. It isn't in your hands and you can do nothing but make things worse if you fall apart. That's an order!"

"But Cook, I'm worried!"

"You're not alone in that. Now where's the stuff you were made of?"

"Okay, I will try."

"That's all I want. After dishes, you can have a shot of my brandy, go in the wagon bunk and have a good cry. But in the morning, I want it over."

"Yes sir."

That is exactly what she did. By the time the dishes were cleared away and the campsite readied for morning, there were still only a few logs drifting by. Everyone was on edge. The rain was still pelting and there was a low fog. Visibility as only a few feet. She came to Cook and said, "I'm ready for my shot now."

"Reckon you are," he said seriously. "So am I."

He poured them each a shot and they downed them. "Now get some shut eye and I'll cry out if the logs start flowing!"

She had a terrible time getting to sleep. Half Pint kept trying to recapture the security she'd felt in Pendergast's arms. She tossed and turned, but eventually, she managed to drift off before the sun began to lighten the rainy sky.

She stepped out of the wagon into the continuing rain. Now it was a bit windy and felt chilly. Half Pint looked up when riders came into camp at a full gallop. They had come from upstream to report the news. The logs should be flowing by any minute.

The River Boss had blown the jam at Fishhook and logs flew all over creation. It was difficult to see because of the overcast rain clouds. The logs tore loose and became projectiles shooting downstream. It was dark when they came past the turn at Elk Meadow, where Slim and Booker were posted, they hit the opposite bank at such great speed and force, the first ones jammed in to the side of the bank. Slim worked frantically to break them loose but managed to only free a few. The first logs were embedded in the side of the bank and the mass of timber piled up behind them.

Booker worked like a demon on his side to turn the logs that he could. He had to reach out as far as his gin stick allowed to capture the tall timbers and turn them before they became caught up in the jam. He wanted to keep as many flowing as possible, at least until River Boss could get there to blow the embedded logs. He and Slim yelled back and forth across the river and tried to communicate over the noise of banging logs, rushing torrents of water and down-pouring rain. Only a few indistinguishable cries carried to across the commotion.

The crew from above was having difficulty getting through the mud on the way down to Elk Meadow to help. Slim and Booker worked at full bore for at least five hours on their own. Adrenaline was pumping. Experience and skill kept them going. Slim was calling out but it had been sometime since he had heard Booker.

It was not daylight yet, when the crews from above joined up at Elk Meadow. When they arrived, it was still over an hour before they could see well enough to fix the jam. It had to be blown again on Slim's side of Elk Meadow.

As the charge was set, they took a headcount. It was then they realized that Booker was missing. He was nowhere around, but his gin stick was flopping among the timbers. He had been lost. No one knew for certain when, where, or how, but he was gone.

If a man fell into that jumble of logs, he would be crushed, drowned or both. If he wasn't smashed between the tons of logs, he would have been forced under them. There he could not resurface and would drown. There would be little chance of survival. Since his gin pole was still flopping, obviously attached to a timber, they guessed that he had somehow become inextricably hooked on a log. In daylight, a man had a chance to get it free, but in the dark, it was almost impossible. In this case, it was impossible. The gin stick was still there, but Booker was gone.

The men didn't want to blow that jam if there was an outside chance he was somehow still afloat, but the jam was building with great force. Finally, with no sign of him, they had no choice. They blew the charge.

When they blew the embedded logs, the rest gave lose. The jam freed and the men worked feverishly to get the backed up timber flowing again.

One of the men found part of Booker's arm that had blown across the river. Apparently, his body was wedged under the logs. When it was blown, so was he. They found his ratty old hat on the bank of the river and one of the men brought it to Slim. Everyone knew they were best friends. Booker's body was never found and no service was held. Booker had gone to his watery grave on Elk Meadow that night.

The next night, those men finally caught up with the van camp. Slim just cried his heart out to Half Pint when they were alone. He handed her Booker's hat and said, "We must put it on Pendergast's tree. Okay?"

She nodded and held him until he fell asleep. When he woke in the morning, he was covered with a blanket in the wagon and Half Pint was cooking breakfast over a campfire. He came out of the wagon and she smiled at him, "You're a muddy mess!"

He looked at her and laughed, "Cook, can you straighten her out?"

"She might be wrong or then again, she might not be," Cook answered. "You better grab a cup of coffee. The others are getting ready to move out."

When Cook handed him his cup, he put his hand on his arm, "Sorry Slim. I'm really sorry. Booker was a fine man."

Slim nodded and went over to grab a plate from Half Pint to gobble it down so he could leave with the others. He gave her a quick peck on the cheek and whispered, "Love you."

She looked at him and said, "Me, too"

The rest of the drive was hateful to Leisel. She hated the weather, the logs and the job. She didn't even like men who could care about someone, but not take time to mourn their passing.

Cook let her grump around for two days and then he took her by the arm and sat her down. "Look here, I know you don't like it. None of us do. We can't stop those logs once they're in the water. Booker knew that and we know that! Girl, you know that! I know you want to cry, but what would that solve? Would it bring Booker back? If it would, I'd cry with you. Otherwise, knock it off. We have work to do and I'm not giving you anymore of my brandy until we hit Yaak."

Leisel glared and him a minute, and then shrugged, "Yes sir."

I t was four days later when the van made it into Yaak. There was great deal of commotion. Men were getting paid out and heading off for their summer breaks. The van was parked behind the Yaak office and the horses were put out in a nice, lush pasture. Slim joined Half Pint by the van and they told Cook goodbye. Ink Slinger came around from the office to join up with Cook.

He shook Slim's hand, "I was very sorry to hear about Booker. He was a good man. I know I'll miss him greatly and I'm sure you will. If you give me the name of his lady friend in Yakima, I'll send her a wire so she knows why he didn't show up." Slim nodded.

"I have it in his things. I'll go get it."

After he left, Ink Slinger put his arm around Half Pint's shoulder, "Slim will be broken for a while, but he'll get over it. You can help him. It is a gift from God that burning loss lessens over time. We'll all get together again someday, I just know it. And Old Booker and Pendergast will be there, ready to give us a bad time!"

Half Pint smiled at him, "Thank you, Ink Slinger. Cook wouldn't let me cry."

"And he shouldn't have. Booker would have kicked your hinder if you gave in. I know that Cook was close to Booker, so he was hurting, too. Bawling doesn't mean you cared more. It only means you bawled. Now, you go get your new shoes. They are in the office and I'm anxious for you to try them on. Slim might need to stretch them for you before you go down that aisle. Oh, Cook and I will be in town at the Rooming House for a few days. We'll check the desk to find out where the wedding is. If you tell us where you're getting hitched. I might even get Cook to wear a necktie!"

Half Pint giggled, "That would never, ever happen."

"Might not, but then again, it might," Ink Slinger chuckled.

Slim came back with the address. "She is Estelle Latimer at The Curly Cue Gentlemen's Parlor. Here, keep the note. You know, I think he was really sweet on her."

"I might tell her that."

"That would be good," Slim said. "Thank you. You know he lost his wife and all four children to whooping cough about five years ago. I think he had given up hope, until he found her."

"Speaking of sweethearts, when are you and Half Pint tying the knot? I was just telling her if it is in the next few days, Cook and I want to be there. We are bunking at the Rooming House, so let us know."

"I will do that. In fact, since Booker was going to be my best man, maybe I could talk you into doing the job."

"I'd be honored. Let me know the details."

Half Pint got a silly grin, "Hold up here, will you? I need to talk to Cook a minute. Wait here."

The two guys watched her run off and shook their heads to each other.

"I wonder what she is up to now!" Slim grinned.

"I think you have a fine girl there, Slim. Take care of her," Ink Slinger said. "She is one of the best little gals I've ever met."

Slim smiled proudly, "I think so, too."

She came back and held out the Kennebecker to Slim, grinning like crazy. He looked at her and said, "Apparently, Cook did what you wanted."

"Not yet," she just about burst, "He said he might not, but most likely he will!"

"That's as close as you'll get to a yes from him!" Ink Slinger laughed. "Well, see you later."

The sun was just beginning to go down, when the couple knocked at the blue door. It was a few minutes before Angus opened the door with a big grin. He opened the door and motioned for them to come in. "Elizabeth, come see what the cat drug in."

Elizabeth came in and ran to give them both an embrace, "Have you eaten yet? Do you have a place to sleep?"

Slim smiled, "I was going to check in right after we said hello."

"No need to check in, Laddie." Angus said. "Family is on the house! And the wedding suite is waiting for you."

"Oh, I'm so excited," Elizabeth said. "I can't wait to show you all the things I have assembled. It will be so grand! But Angus, get a bowl of stew for these young folks. Here, sit. Take a load off and tell us all your news."

It was the closest to home that Leisel had felt since she had left home. She had some wonderful times since she left, but this felt like home. They talked late into the night. They talked about Booker and Pendergast, and the letter Half Pint had received from Cap. Leisel noticed that Slim was the most relaxed she had ever seen him. He seemed to feel comfortable, too and that made her glad.

Finally, the yawns were creeping in and Angus looked at the kitchen clock, "My word Elizabeth, it is almost morning! We'd better get to bed before we meet ourselves at the door. I'll have Sam bring you some water for baths tonight and you guys sleep late tomorrow."

"Yes, and we have plans to make!" Elizabeth giggled.

"Lordie be, Slim. You should be glad you were in the woods! This woman has been so busy pecking and scratching over this wedding, it'd have put a nest of hens to shame."

"Oh, we have to find a justice of the peace," Slim exclaimed.

"Don't know why? You have been yakking at one for a couple hours! I would be pleased to officiate! Angus Campbell, Minister and Justice of the Peace, at your service!"

Slim grinned, "I would be pleased. How about you, Half Pint?"

"It would be wonderful!"

"Okay, off to Sam. He'll have your rooms ready."

That night as Leisel lay in the clean bed with fluffy pillows, she felt like a princess. The last seven months had been a great change for her. She had been more afraid, more proud, more sad and more in love than ever before in her life. But mostly, she felt she had grown up.

The next morning, Half Pint was up before six. She wore her dress and her old shoes, even though they no longer fit. She didn't want to mess up Campbell's floor. She came downstairs and went into the dining room. She thought maybe she would find Slim there, but he was not. Elizabeth however, greeted her with a big smile.

"You need to go into the kitchen, you won't believe it! I've seen it with my own eyes, and I don't."

Half Pint gave her a curious grin and went through the door to the kitchen. As soon as she saw the men, she started to laugh. Slim was wearing one of Angus' large aprons and flipping pancakes. Angus was telling him the difference between beating and stirring. They looked up and both asked, "What?"

"You guys! I didn't know you knew how to cook?" she said as she gave Slim a quick hug.

"Slim didn't know either, but now he does!" Angus boasted. "He may be a chef one day!"

"Just because you know how to flip a pancake, doesn't make the taste good," Half Pint retorted.

Angus said, "Well little Lassie, you set yourself down to a big old stack and let us know what you think!"

He pulled up a chair and pointed to it. Then he set a plate of pancakes that Slim had just taken off the stove in front of her with a dish of butter.

She looked at him, "No syrup or jelly?"

"Good pancakes taste good without, like a good steak tastes good without catsup!"

"Maybe," she nodded. "I still think they might be better with!"

"You're a tough one!" he laughed. "Taste first and then you can have some syrup."

Slim set a cup of coffee down for her and watched her as she while she put the forkful of pancake in her mouth, "What do you think?"

She grinned, "You better not tell Cook your recipe or he'll be jealous! They are really good. In fact, I think they are so good I might marry the cook."

Elizabeth had come into the kitchen, "Oh my, you have fallen in league with them!"

"No, but I wanted to show them I appreciate their efforts!"

The ladies both laughed and the guys grimaced at each other. Angus then said, "Well what are your plans? When are you getting married?"

Elizabeth said, "Today, Half Pint and I have work to do, shopping and stitching. You leave us be on our own. We can be ready tomorrow or the next day. What do you say Leisel?"

"I guess it is really up to Arthur, because he will be the one taking a wife."

"Let's do it the next day, in case we have to get some things sorted out we haven't thought of now. Sound good?"

"Okay," Angus said with authority, "June 28! Thursday at one in the afternoon. We can finish serving breakfast and have time to spit polish the sitting room. Will that be okay for your wedding? We thought that Elizabeth could play the piano if you wed in the parlor."

"It would be really nice," Half Pint said. "I love the sitting room."

The day was busy. Elizabeth took Leisel under her wing and they spent the day working on her wedding dress. She had sewn one, but hadn't finish it because she wanted to fit it to her. She was able to fix Lana's veil so that it fit her well. They fiddled around with her hair and tried it several ways. All the while, Elizabeth gave Leisel good motherly advice about being a wife. She also spoke to her about faith and put real life words to the Testament she had read. It was a great day.

Slim and Angus spent the morning in the kitchen and then they went off to the bank, barber, mercantile and the county clerk's office. All the while, he too was giving Slim fatherly advice about being a good husband. He was glad to discover that Slim had gone to church when he was a boy and helped him realize that the tools he learned there could help him and his new wife build a good life.

That evening after dinner, the young couple went for a walk. They stopped at the Rooming House and left messages for Cook and Ink Slinger. Then they walked almost the entire length of Yaak.

For a long time, they didn't talk. They just walked, holding hands. Then as they stopped on a short bank near the river, Slim slipped his arm around her waist. They leaned on the fence there and watched the water flow by.

"I hope that Booker didn't suffer," Slim said quietly. "He was a good friend."

"I doubt he did. Those logs were moving fast. It couldn't have been more than a minute."

"Half Pint, I was thinking. If we work a few more years, maybe I should quit logging and move to town. I'm not afraid for me, but I don't want you to worry. I saw the fear in your eyes. I don't want you to have to feel like that."

"What would you do?"

"Don't know yet. I'll think of something to look after you. We can't keep living up there when we have little ones. Look how hard it is for Lana and Bert. I know Cat Skinner is planning to move to town as soon as he can."

"Lana mentioned that. We can do that. I love the camp, you know that. You are right. It isn't the best place for families and schools and I do worry about you."

"Okay, we'll plan on that then. By the way, I bought the Ben Franklin while I was out with Angus. It will be delivered to the Yaak camp. I sure like that guy."

"I like Elizabeth, too. You know she sewed the prettiest dress for me from just her memory of my size! I think you will like it!"

Slim gave her a sweet kiss, "I know I will. We'd better head back. I promised Angus I would help him cook breakfast tomorrow!"

"Just think, in two days we'll be married. I can't wait."

The Mercury came to rest on the highway. A uniformed highway patrol man waved them to stop. Jeff tried to roll down the electric window, but it was frozen shut. He got out of the car. "How bad is it?"

"The plow will get this cleared, but where you headed?"

Sister came around the car and joined them, "We were hoping to get to Dahlgren, west of Eureka."

The patrol man thought and then said, "Won't make it. You can't make it through Kalispell today, but the weather is supposed to let up tomorrow. Then you might get to Dahlgren by going around through Libby. They had a big snow slide outside Eureka blocking the road. It will take a while to clear it. Your best bet would be sitting in West Glacier a day and seeing how much the weather cooperates. The road is closed outside West Glacier right now, so you will be stuck there for a while anyway. If I was you, I would put my feet up for a day and then see what I could do."

"That is disappointing," Sister said. "My mother is critically ill."

"Sorry, but you still can't get there unless you go around. I'm sure it will make you anxious, but getting stuck in a snow slide, won't fix it. We'll be hung up here for about an hour. Then you can follow the lead car through."

"I understand," Sister nodded. "Thank you. That is what we will do."

Back in the car, Jeff turned to her, "I'm so sorry. I hope you get to there in time."

"Jeff, we left as early as we could. That is the best we can do. If they had called earlier, we might have missed the storm."

Jeff nodded slowly, "What would you say about dipping into one of our many nosebags and finding a sandwich?"

Sister turned and leaned over the seat with a giggle, "My thoughts exactly. I noticed that Nora had some ham and cheese sandwiches near the top. How does that sound?"

"Good," Jeff said as he put his seat back and moved the steering wheel up, "There are some chips in Mo's basket, too. Would it be okay if I turned the car off for a bit? I don't want us to get too cold, but I don't want to waste gas. I'd never hear the end of it, if we ran out of gas!"

Sister handed him a sandwich and the potato chip bag, "That wouldn't be pleasant. Could you pour some coffee? We'll have a fine picnic."

As they ate their lunch and watched the snowplow slowly make it's way toward them, Jeff said, "Campbells seemed like really good folks."

"They were like parents to Slim and I."

"What did Half Pint ask Cook? I'm curious."

"Yes, you are," Sister giggled. "I have talked more this trip than I have for years! I can't believe you haven't bailed out of the car by now!"

"Look out there! It is colder than the North Pole! Besides, I like Half Pint and her friends."

Well, the morning of the 20th, Half Pint got dressed and went down to the kitchen. She and Slim were family now, and family ate in the kitchen. She came in and Angus immediately handed her a frying pan. "It's breeding customers in the dining room! Could I ask you to fry up some eggs? I need to help Elizabeth. Slim is flipping cakes as fast as he can!"

"Of course," she giggled.

The next couple of hours, they must have served breakfast to every person on the Yaak River. Folks were coming in by the droves for the Fourth of July celebration. Yaak had even ordered some fireworks and they would be set off after the rodeo at the fairgrounds. Loggers, miners, rodeo cowboys and families were in town. Both cafés in town, the hotel dining room and the Bed and Breakfast were jammed. Some very industrious citizens were selling ham and biscuit sandwiches on the street corner.

At ten, the crowd thinned and Angus put the closed sign out. Slim said, "Angus, you will be losing a lot of business if you close today."

"My boy, there are times when coins don't jingle loud enough. We will work like beavers in a vat of coffee tomorrow and stay open all day, but this day, we are closed. We have more important fish to fry!"

"I'm mighty obliged. What could I ever do to repay you?"

"Be a good husband to Half Pint."

Slim shook his head and Angus slapped him on the back, "Now, get to Sam! He has a bath set up for you in the back. You have to look dapper for the big doin's!"

About noon, Cook and Ink Slinger arrived at the Bed and Breakfast. Cook was wearing a tie and one look would tell any observer, it was against his will. He even wore a suit. Ink Slinger looked very neat, but he usually did. Cook still looked like a lumberjack cook, even in his new suit. But he had it on and didn't make a fuss about it, and didn't fidget or scratch too much.

A few minutes to one, the group gathered in the sitting room and Elizabeth came down the stairs and went to the piano. She whispered to Cook and then started playing the wedding march.

Half Pint appeared at the top of the stairs and she was beautiful. She wore a white cotton muslin, ankle length dress. The sleeves were gathered at the elbow and finished off with a ruffle. The skirt also was hemmed with a ruffle. There were creamy beige bows on the bodice and sleeves. The full gathered skirt was tied at the waist with a wide creamy beige bow. Lana's veil was cream-colored and the ladies had found ribbon that matched the color nicely. She carried a small bouquet of wildflowers tied with white and cream-colored bows. Of course, she wore new cream-colored shoes.

When she got the bottom of the steps, Cook held out his arm. He walked her up the 'aisle' and then stood beside her as her attendant. Slim and Ink Slinger shared a wink and both grinned as the watched Cook try to hold back his tears.

Angus began, "Dearly Beloved—," only to be interrupted by Cook's stifled sobs. Elizabeth came up beside him and handed him her lace handkerchief. Everyone waited patiently while the mound of a man blew his nose and pulled himself together. After a couple minutes, he nodded and said, "Carry on."

After the vows, Slim kissed his Half Pint and they were pronounced man and wife, Mr. and Mrs. Arthur Peterson. There were congratulations all around. Everyone praised Cook and told him he did a great job both giving away the bride and being the bridesmaid, too!

"Ah, it was nothing," the big man blustered. "I knew I could handle it in my sleep, or maybe not."

They laughed and Angus handed out glasses of wine. Ink Slinger proposed a toast to the young couple and everyone drank to them. Then Elizabeth ordered Angus to seat everyone in the dining room while she kidnapped Ink Slinger. They came from the kitchen with a platter of sandwiches and a huge bowl of potato salad.

After lunch, Angus rolled the rug back in the sitting room and asked Ink Slinger to find a station on his new-fangled radio. Cook was pressed into helping Elizabeth clear the table and serve lemonade to everyone. Then they danced.

Before sunset, Slim and Half Pint walked along the river, holding hands. Half Pint could feel the ring on her finger. She twisted it around with her thumb and then smiled, "I am so glad that yesterday was like it was. I would have never had such a wonderful today otherwise. I love you and this was more wonderful than I could imagine."

"Did you miss your family?"

"Cap maybe, but not really. I had family here." Then she giggled, "Wasn't Cook a sweetheart?"

Slim chuckled, "He is quite the Cook! He made us all promise we'd never tell a soul what he did today!"

"He didn't ask me!" Half Pint laughed. "But I would never tell. It was so very sweet of him to do it."

They stopped by a bench under a tree and sat to watch the river go by. "Did you miss your family?"

Slim answered, "No, this is my family."

The young couple kissed tenderly and Slim asked his new bride if they should head back to their room.

When they arrived at the Bed and Breakfast, Sam handed them a key. "We took the liberty of moving your things to the wedding suite. There is water in there for the tub, if you want. Congratulations and have a good evening."

Slim took the key and when he unlocked the door, he carried his bride across the threshold. The young couple made love, clumsily at first, but later with more confidence and tenderness. They were truly happy.

The patrolman knocked on Jeff's window and motioned him to get behind the lead car. They quickly put their picnic away and were back on the road. It was scary to see the steep drop-offs beside the road, especially since there was still some snow rolling down across the remainder of the road. Neither said more than a word the whole way into West Glacier. When they finally got to the edge of town, they both gave a big sigh of relief.

Sister said, "I was more worried than I thought I was. I think I only inhaled twice on the whole way!"

"Me too," Jeff chuckled. "I chewed the inside of my cheek so much, it feels like hamburger!"

"Too bad!" Sister laughed, "Here I was planning to buy you a big old steak."

"I can still eat steak. Just watch!"

"Okay, let's find rooms and maybe call home. Then let's find a good steak."

They found a small motel that still had a vacancy and they checked in. Jeff carried Sister's bag from the car and set it inside her door. "Here is your Kennebecker. See you in a few minutes for dinner."

Sister smiled at him, "Make it ten minutes. I have to decide what to wear!"

He laughed and shook his head, "You do that."

Over dinner, she shared that she had called Swan. She said her mother was still holding her own and the family knew the weather was atrocious. "The patrol man was right. You can't come by way of Eureka. You will have to go around. Even if they cleared the snow slide, you wouldn't be able to cross the river."

"Good to know," Jeff nodded. "I talked to Vicaro and he was going to pass the word on to everyone in Merton. They know we are safe and sound—and I've been filling gas at every pump!"

Before the steaks came, Jeff asked, "What did you ever know about Cook?"

"Never even knew his real name or where he was from. Don't really know anything at all except he was a gem. The older I get, the more I appreciate him and all that I learned from him."

"What became of him?"

"He stayed with Yaak Camp until it closed and then moved to Colorado to be near Ink Slinger. He was killed in a car accident one day on his way to visit him at the sanatorium. Ink slinger and I kept in touch by mail until he died from consumption about seven years later. He was probably the most supportive, non-judgmental friend I've ever had. No matter how grim things got or down I was, he was always there to bolster me up. I still miss him."

"Why was he in a sanatorium?"

"He developed a cough when they returned from that very summer break. Cook always blamed it on a man who had a terrible cough in one of the rooming houses they stayed at a couple nights. They were really more like the ram pastures than anything. The man had the bunk next to Slinger's and hacked throughout the night. I don't know if that was it or not. Cook took him to the doctor in Kalispell who eventually sent him to a sanatorium in Colorado. He and I corresponded until he passed. I was able to go to his service. I was surprised to find that he was Jewish. That is the only Jewish funeral I've ever attended. He left me a Star of David pendant and I still have it. I put it on a chain and use it as a bookmark in my Testament from Elizabeth."

Jeff stirred his coffee, "He was a wonderful friend. When did Yaak Camp close?"

Sister continued.

The newlyweds spent the Fourth of July with the Campbells. They attended the rodeo and watched the fireworks, but mostly they helped the older couple with the Bed and Breakfast while the crowd was in town.

Ink Slinger and Cook stopped by to tell them goodbye before the left for Kalispell. The night of the fifth, they went for a walk down by the river. Slim had been rather quiet and Half Pint was worried he wasn't happy.

When they sat on their favorite bench, Half Pint took his hand, "Are you unhappy about something? Tell me if I'm not pleasing you. You are so quiet, I know there is something eating you?"

Slim put his arm around her waist, "You have pleased me in every way, but you are right. Something is eating me. I was wondering if you'd like to go to Dahlgren to see if Cap is there, or maybe talk to Johann's father?"

She started shaking her head no before he even finished, "I will not. My family told me to leave and they have not invited me back. I see no reason to go. Cap didn't say that he wanted to see me. No, I'm very happy here with my new husband. This is my life; Dahlgren is theirs."

"You certain?"

"Yes, very much so. Do you not like being here with Campbells?"

"I love it here. I really do, but I don't want you to feel that you have to put any part of your life on the back of the stove. You and I are a team now; your concerns are mine. If I miss one, you need to tell me."

"I'm not the one that keeps things to himself! I'm always blabbering," Half Pint said. "You however, tend to keep mum."

Slim turned to her in surprise, "You have told me that before. I do that. No doubt. I give you my word, I will try to do better. Have you been happy?"

"Yes, very much so. I was thinking of what we need to do at the cabin before Camp gets back into swing. When do you think we need to go back?"

"Next week? Then we'll have a week to get the stove hooked up and our bed set up. That was really something for Cook and Ink Slinger to get us the springs."

"Yes. I'm anxious to set up my own house, even if I don't have to worry for cooking or that."

"You're so sweet. I am the luckiest guy in these mountains."

"Is that all? Here I was thinking I was the luckiest gal in the world!"

He shook his head, "Whatever, Half Pint. Let's head back. I might help Angus fix his roof tomorrow. He said it needed repair and he was going to wait until fall before he fixed it. Since I'm here, I thought I could help him."

Half Pint kissed him, "You're a nice guy."

They returned to Yaak Camp at the end of the next week. They set up their cabin and were all settled before Cook and Ink Slinger got back. They brought a young fellow about thirteen with them. He had applied at the office and was hired to help Cook. The freckled-faced Elias Madison moved into Half Pint's old room. He was a fun kid and really liked hanging around Slim. They became great pals.

Those were fine times. Baby Sarah watched while the meals were served, from her playpen in back of the cookhouse kitchen. Blacky moved his wife Maybell in, but she spent most of her time at Boss Rudner's house and had little time for Lana or Half Pint. However, a new mechanic Cecil brought his wife Rosa! They built the cabin on the other side of Lana and Cat Skinner. It was becoming a real village. Cecil was a jolly man and Rosa was a crazy, fun girl. She was fiery and enjoyed most everything. No one had more energy than Rosa! Half Pint loved her because she made her laugh, but Lana was still her best friend. They had shared so much.

In November, Lana and Cat Skinner got the word that he could transfer to the Yaak Lumber Mill. Plans were made for them to move over the Christmas break. Cecil and Rosa were going to stay in camp and shooed Cook out the door. He and Ink Slinger decided to help Bert and Lana move and then go to

Kalispell, so Ink Slinger could see the doctor. Elias had no plans and seemed in the dumps.

The week before the winter break, Slim asked Half Pint how she would feel about taking Elias with them to Yaak to see Campbells over Christmas. She thought it was a grand idea. Elias didn't know about it, but Cook told him to go.

Of course, Angus and Elizabeth were excited when the couple came to the blue door with their new friend in tow. Angus insisted they not pay for their rooms, but Slim insisted back they pay their way. A deal was struck. The three would help out at the Bed and Breakfast, so Sam and his wife could travel to her family for Christmas.

The young folks were given a quick course about signing in the guests and caring for the rooms. Elias loved it. Cook had told Slim that the boy was an orphan who had lived with his grandmother until she passed. Slim strongly identified with that and was very glad when the lad was soon calling Campbells, Grandpa Angus and Grandma Elizabeth. The Campbells were very happy about it, too.

They all went to church together on that Christmas Eve and then came home to decorate their tree. The next day, they all opened their gifts. Elizabeth and Angus had sweaters for their guests, Slim and Half Pint gave everyone some good winter socks and Elias gave them all the best batch of fudge anyone had ever eaten. But Half Pint had the best gift of all. She shared the news with a delighted Slim on Christmas Eve and then the whole group on Christmas. She was in a family way. She and Lana figured the baby would arrive sometime in late May or early June.

As they celebrated New Year's, all felt it would be the most wonderful year yet.

When everyone returned to Yaak Camp, things started out as usual. Half Pint really missed Lana, but enjoyed Rosa. Elias was doing well and decided to practice his reading after a lecture from Angus. Everyone worried about Ink Slinger. His cough was worsening and even though he had seen a doctor in Kalispell, he was not getting better.

It was a dry winter by comparison to the norm. Slim mentioned the concern about fires was extremely high for that time of year. He told Half Pint he wanted to move her and their baby to Yaak on summer break. He felt his wife and child would do better there. Half Pint said she would think about it, but she didn't want to be away from him.

She even worried that he might not want her anymore or their new baby, but he told her she was being a dumbbell. "It is because I love you that I want you to be safe. I don't want to be away from you either, but if I work until the winter break, we can buy a place. I really want you to have a home, Half Pint."

She promised to think it over, but she couldn't any see any good reason why she should be away from Slim. Lana and Sarah stayed with Cat Skinner until they could all move together. That was the way it should be.

In February, she received two letters from Cap. She opened the first distressing letter. Her father was very ill. He had fallen from the back of wagon he was repairing and landed on a sharp piece of metal. It penetrated his abdomen. He was probably not going to survive and while he was seldom awake, he had asked repeatedly for Leisel. Cap and his mother thought she should come. She broke into tears, "Slim, what am I to do? He sent me away! Now he wants to see me! What should I do?"

"My girl, I'll talk to Boss Rudner and see if he'll let Cat Skinner take us to Yaak. We can hire a team there and get to Dahlgren in no time."

"But what if Father changes his mind again?"

Slim took his wife in his arms, "Sweetheart, you should do this. Even if he changes his mind, your mother has asked you to come. I'll be with you. Maybe you will be able to find out what he didn't tell you."

"But—"

"First, read the next letter. If he changed his mind in that one, then I would say we don't go, Sound reasonable?"

"Yes. Okay, will you sit with me while I read it?"

"Of course."

Dear Leisel,

I am sorry to write to say that Father died in his sleep the early hours of this morning. Yesterday, when he seemed to know

115

he was becoming weaker, he asked for paper and pen. He made me promise to send you this letter and not read it. I hope it brings you the answers you need.

All my love,
Cap

Half Pint cried so hard she shook. Slim held her in his arms until she calmed down. "Read it, Half Pint. You have waited a long time to know, you deserve to know and obviously, your father thought you should know. I will be right here beside you."

Trembling she nodded and wiped her tears, "Even if it tells something bad about me?"

"I know you. There isn't anything that he could say that would make me think you were bad."

"Okay," she sniffed. She opened the letter,

"Leisel,

I hoped that I could hold on long enough to see you again. I know I wronged you when I sent you away, and when I refused to try to see you again. My worst sin to you however, I committed years ago. I made a horrible mistake. I bedded with a woman other than Mother. Johann is my own son—your brother. I could not allow you to marry and did not have the courage to tell you. I was afraid you would run off to marry him, so I promised you to Otto. Please forgive me. I have always loved my little Leisel.

Father"

Leisel broke down in tears and her understanding Slim held her in his arms until she could get to rest. "There, there my little Half Pint. See, it was never your fault. Now you know why Johann said he couldn't marry you. I'm so sorry that it happened this way, but at least you have the knowledge you were seeking. I hope it brings you some peace. If you want, we can still go to Dahlgren. You think about it and let me know. I'll do whatever you want."

That night, Half Pint fell asleep in the arms of her wonderful husband. She loved him so and was in a way, thankful things turned out as they had. She whispered to him, "Are you still awake?"

"Yes, I am."

"Slim, there was a yesterday when it probably would've mattered to me. But it doesn't now. You have given me a good life and I love it. I don't want to go to Dahlgren and I don't want to move to Yaak. I'm your wife. My place is with you. That is where I'm the happiest and where I belong, if you want me."

The young husband embraced her, "I don't want you to be away from me either and I want to be with my child. A father should never be away from his child. We'll stay together as long as the Lord permits."

"Good." She said as she kissed him.

They made love and probably were closer than they had ever been.

I n late April, Half Pint began having problems with her pregnancy. Mrs. Rudner, who rarely took an interest in the camp, insisted a doctor be summoned to check on her because she was spotting and cramping. No one thought she could make the trip to Yaak to stay with Mrs. Campbell. The doctor said that she would likely give birth sooner than anticipated; but said she was doing fine considering she was carrying twins. He insisted that she take it easy and made her promise to keep her feet up and not be too active.

Rosa and Ink Slinger made it their mission to enforce his policy. Rosa had delivered babies before so she knew she could do it as long as the doctor said they were healthy and in position for their birth.

Every morning, Ink Slinger would wait for Rosa to walk with Half Pint to his cabin. There she knitted, read and sewed while he did his bookwork. Elias brought them lunch and then he later would walk her back to her cabin to nap while she waited for Slim to get home. Elias brought their dinner over so they could eat together in their home.

Half Pint hated being a bother, but loved the extra time with Slim. They played checkers and he started teaching her chess. She crocheted things for the babies while he worked on the second cradle.

The second week in May, a man on horseback came to where Slim was working. He shouted up the tree, "Better get home. It's the wife's time!"

Slim scurried down the tree and changed places with the rider. At the cabin, Rosa was organizing the troops. Elias, Cook and Ink Slinger were given assignments. Ink Slinger was to help Rosa, Cook was to calm Slim (or vice versa) and Elias carried water. The crew ate sandwiches for dinner that night without complaint, and cheered when they heard two new boys had been added to Yaak Camp!

The first was born with a strong set of lungs, yelling his head off! The next boy was very quiet and much smaller. He hardly made a noise when he cried, but was a sweet little boy. Slim named his sons. The first was Joshua Booker Peterson and the second, the quiet one, was Pendergast Arthur Peterson.

Baby Penn lived three weeks but never was able to flourish. The camp even tried bringing up goat's milk for him but the little boy didn't survive. By the end of May, Half Pint and Slim buried their infant son next to his namesake in Yaak Camp's cemetery. He was buried beneath Booker's hat. They both felt the gentle giant would care for their son in the hereafter. Half Pint was deeply saddened by the loss. With the help of her mourning husband, she tried to focus on her gifts, rather than the loss.

The summer came early. It was hot and tinder dry. This year, the drive started in mid-June. Slim still worked the river, but Rosa and Elias rode in the van with Cook. Half Pint and Joshua went down to Yaak to wait for them to 'bring her in' with Campbells.

The wait was horrible. There wasn't a night that Half Pint didn't cry herself to sleep with worry about Slim. Angus and Elizabeth let her worry a couple days, and then Angus read her the riot act! "There will be no dripping around here, Girl! You don't control life and death, that is God's work! All of us have to live until He calls us home. The rest of us, need to accept that. When our work on earth is done and then He will call us home. That is the way of it."

"Just what is this work God wants us to do, anyway?"

"Help each other. Slim knows is, Cook and Ink Slinger know it. Don't tell me you don't."

She glared at him, but nodded, "Yes sir."

She knew he was right. She had a fine son and a wonderful husband. She should be grateful, but she still worried. Every day, she would put Josh in the pram Campbells had borrowed, and walk to the office to see if the logs were coming in yet.

Ink Slinger, of course, came down to the office to help the clerk there with the final pay outs. He loved playing with his namesake, but worried about holding him because of his terrible cough. He had to content himself, like he had done so much of his life, by sharing from a distance. He was certain Little Josh was the brightest child in the world! He knew he could be a scientist or a President, anything he wanted. Mostly, though he knew he would be a good kid with a loving heart.

There were worries with the drive because the water levels were low, but on the seventh day, timber bearing the Yaak brand began to flow toward the mill. No longer could Half Pint contain herself. Except for feeding Josh, she paced back and forth in the office waiting for the first man to arrive. Actually, for a certain man to arrive!

She greeted the van and was delighted to hear that there had been only minor jams, mostly when logs got high-centered on new sandbars. Cook announced he had seen Slim the night before and he was well and anxious to see his Half Pint.

Elias ran to pick up Josh and gave him a big squeeze. He loved that little kid. Then he put him back in his pram and told Half Pint. "Cook said as soon as I clean out the spittoons in the office, I can go see Grandma and Grandpa! Slim told me he won't be in until tomorrow, so I should make you go back to the Bed and Breakfast."

Half Pint was puzzled, "How did he know I would be waiting here?"

Elias laughed, "Half Pint, everybody knows you are waiting on Slim!"

"Very funny, Elias. Go clean out the spittoons. I will walk back with you, but not on the same side of the street!"

Ink Slinger looked up from his ledger with a smirk, "Kid knows of what he speaks."

"Don't you have columns to add? I think I will go talk to Cook."

Even the clerk chuckled, "Like he would take your side."

Elias ran the last block to the Bed and Breakfast and knocked on his way through the blue door, shouting "Hello? I'm here!"

When Half Pint arrived, Elias was already halfway through his first cookie! She came in laughing, "He couldn't wait to see you. I bet he didn't even wipe his boots!"

"No need," Angus sprung to his defense. "He came to see his Granddad. Leave the boy be."

Half Pint smiled as Angus tousled Elias's straw-colored hair. "We may have to think about seeing a barber, huh boy?"

"Yes sir. Josh needs his haircut too. It is all straggly in back."

"I think his Mom and Elizabeth will do that. You, however, need a sheep shears!"

The next morning, Elias watched Josh while Half Pint went down to the office. She was there about an hour before a crew of boys arrived. She noticed Slim right away and ran out to meet him. He jumped off the wagon and swirled her around in a big hug. Then they walked to the office together.

"I missed you so much, I don't ever want to be away from you," Half Pint said as she gave him a big kiss.

"I missed you, too. What did you do with Joshie?"

"He is at the Bed and Breakfast, being spoiled beyond reason. Slim, Campbells have been holding him almost non-stop. The child will never want to sit alone again! They are so proud!"

Slim laughed, "I was thinking, if we keep our noses to the grindstone, we should be able to get a place by Christmas. We might not be able to buy, but we can rent. I want to look now over summer break. What do you say?"

"I say yes! This is so exciting! I love you."

"I love you, Half Pint."

They stopped at the office so Slim could collect his pay out, told Ink Slinger and Cook to have a nice trip to Kalispell and waved goodbye to the crew. Then they walked to the B&B, with Slim carrying his bindle over his back and holding his wife's hand.

The summer break was a happy time. Elias had decided that he would move to Yaak when Half Pint and Slim did, but he wanted to work at the Bed and Breakfast with Angus. Campbells approved but informed him he would have to go back to school. He frowned, but decided that wouldn't be too bad.

The next day, Angus went with Slim to look over real estate and job opportunities. They found two places that they could rent by Christmas and Slim was going to take Half Pint out to look at them.

That night on their walk, Slim told his wife he had talked to the men at the livery and the mill. The timber was so dry that summer that they didn't know if they would have work for their crew all winter, but he should check back. If work was available, he'd have first choice because he already worked with Yaak Lumber. The livery said they used few men over the winter, but when many of the normal residents went south for the winter. Chances were good he could have work. He was not very encouraged, but not discouraged either. Then he said that Angus would like to have him help over winter, so Sam and his wife could vacation and maybe he could take Elizabeth to the coast.

Slim was worried, "Do you think we should try for it? What if I can't make enough to take care of you and the baby?"

"Slim, you have always taken care of us. I know you will. Don't worry. You always tell me not to worry. Now, you don't."

"Okay, but I would feel better if I knew what to plan on."

"This is only the first day of summer break! I just know you will find something," the she kissed him.

He took her in his arms, "I love you."

The next day, the couple went to look at the houses. One was way too big and more expensive. The next one was a small bungalow two blocks from the Bed and Breakfast. It had a precious yard, two bedrooms and and nice-sized kitchen. Mostly, she fell in love the sitting room. It was small but had two bay windows with a window seat. Slim teased that she wanted the window seat and the house was an add-on. The following day, they went back and Slim signed an agreement on the small rental with the sitting room. Half Pint was on cloud nine.

Half Pint received a letter from Cap. He said he and Virginia had married and moved into their cabin in the clearing. He said he was disappointed that she had not brought her new husband to meet the family, but didn't invite them either. It was obvious that her Father had never told his family that it was not in any way Leisel's fault that he made her leave or what the reason was! So, while her father had apologized to her, he still fully expected her to keep quiet and live under the dubious cloud he had dispersed. He left her in a less than good situation and she resented it.

Mrs. Haldoran knew that Cap had Leisel's address and she could have written. Slim was curious why her mother never made an effort to bring her daughter back into the fold, but she never did. When they talked it over, Half Pint pointed out that she knew she herself was being stubborn about it, too. Slim wondered if they should just rent a team and go up to Dahlgren, Half Pint said she wanted to think about it.

T hey stayed in Yaak to help with over the Fourth of July. It was very busy in town and Elias just loved the rodeo. They didn't have very many fireworks that year, because it was so dry. Slim and Elias helped Angus with his yard and then painted the outside of the Bed and Breakfast, while Half Pint helped Elizabeth can vegetables, sew and care for the baby. Dahlgren was never mentioned again.

The summer break flew by and before long, everyone was back in Yaak Camp. Joshua was now the one in the playpen in the cookhouse, watching the workings of the kitchen. He was a favorite of most of the men. Before long, would pull himself around to watch while they were eating.

While Cook was pouting that Elias was going to move to Yaak, he was glad for him. He made him promise he would study hard in school. Cook said if he got good grades, he would give him money to go to university, because he wanted his Elias to amount to something. Just what he wanted him to amount to, he never said.

The Rudner women returned from California in late-August, and Maybell, Blacky's wife, started teaching their little girl. It was a couple weeks later, however, Mrs. Rudner became ill. She had a high fever, cough and later developed a rash. Maybell knew it was difficult for her to care for the little girl, so she brought Lilly down to stay at the village. Rudners did not want her to be around the cookhouse, but she did play with baby Josh and Elias. After a week, Mrs. Rudner began to regain her strength and by the first week in September, Lilly returned to the big house.

Baby Josh was beginning to sit up and could move himself around. Everyone thought he would be crawling soon, although none of the rough, wooden floors, pocked by the calks, would have made a decent place to crawl. He was five months old and smiled a lot. He would acknowledge it when the men hailed him before they went back to work.

Mostly, he loved his daddy. When Slim came in the cookhouse, always at the second sitting, Josh would wiggle and coo. After dinner, Slim would pick the boy out of his playpen and take him back to the cabin. They would play together while Half Pint helped clean up after supper. There was never a prouder daddy anywhere.

Often when she got back to the cabin, Josh would be asleep in his father's arms in the rocking chair Cook and Slim had fashioned. Then she would move the child to his crib and take his place in Slim's arms.

It was an almost idyllic time. Sundays, Ink Slinger and Cook would spend some time with their godson, since Angus had baptized him on summer break and those two were his sponsors. Ink Slinger, of course, always kept his distance, but Josh seemed to recognize him. Ink Slinger would wave wildly at the boy, and the second week in September, he sort of waved back. Ink Slinger just knew the child was a genius!

The following week, Lilly and Maybell came down with the same fever and rash that Mrs. Rudner had previously. Mrs. Rudner explained that several of her family members in California had it while she and Lilly were visiting. Most became quite sick, but all had recovered. Maybell and Lilly had a tough time with it, but in about ten days were on the mend.

The forest was so dry, the men were on constant watch for fires. They had put out several small ones. All were anxious for the fall rains. This necessitated avoiding sparks, so they had quit using the caterpillar tractors and went back only to hand tools and teams as much as possible. It made the work more difficult and nerve-racking.

The men also talked about the extensive number of widow-makers; that is, dead trees that would fall partially but become entangled in another tree and then crash to the ground with a little wind or movement. No one knew what would set them lose. That fall, one of the men had been working in an area for a couple days with no problem. The next afternoon, a gust of wind swung the dead tree loose and it crashed on top of him and pinning him under a ton of rough timber.

"It was quick," Cook said. "That is about the only good of it. Damned shame he never got a chance to know he was dragging up."

Slim hated them. It was one of the few things in the forest that he was very afraid of. "I don't mind being high up and dangling off something, because I have never thought I would fall. But having something fall on me out of nowhere scares the bejesus out of me! At least, it would be quick."

Half Pint frowned, "Maybe we should go to Yaak sooner. We can find work there."

"Ah my girl," Slim assured her. "We can't run off anytime we are a little afraid of something. Neither of us have done that and we won't start now. I want to have a fine home for my family."

"I know, but I want you in it."

Slim hugged her and after their boy was asleep, they made tender, passionate love. "This has been the happiest time of my life, Half Pint. I always knew I would find a treasure in the forest. I just didn't know it would be a little girl."

"I'm not a little girl."

Slim chuckled, "Oh yes. You are my little girl."

A couple days later, Josh started to run a fever and got a runny nose. Half Pint and Rosa thought he might be starting to teethe. By the next day, however, he had started to cough. Ink Slinger was worried sick he had passed his consumption along to his godson. Slim assured him that was not the case. "You have always kept a safe distance from Josh. I just know it isn't from you. I think it is more likely the thing the Rudner's had."

Sure enough, it was. The following morning, Josh was covered in a rash. The young couple stayed with him constantly and Slim didn't go out to the strip. He held, rocked and cared for his son in any way he could. When his fever got worse, the couple carried cool water from the well and tried to bring it down. It did little good.

Boss Rudner was worried by the sixth day, "I'm sending Bert with the tractor into Yaak. We will have the office bring a doctor there and then bring him back to camp to care for the boy. I believe we are responsible for bringing this sickness into camp."

"You didn't do it on purpose," Slim said. "But I would be glad if a doctor could see him."

"I'll send Cat Skinner today."

When Cat Skinner got to Yaak, the office sent a telegram to the nearest doctor. He said he would be there the next morning. Cat Skinner walked over to the Bed and Breakfast and told Campbells. They decided immediately to go back with him to see the boy. "His folks might be in need of a helping hand," Angus said.

Cat Skinner nodded, "That they might."

That next evening, the tractor arrived in Yaak Camp with its precious cargo. Half Pint and Slim were shocked but delighted to see Campbells. Angus took Slim for a long walk and let him unload all his concerns he had been worried to share with Half Pint.

Elias, of course, was thrilled to show Angus and Elizabeth his home and where he worked. He let them use 'his room' and he made out a bedroll in the cookhouse. Cook was tickled to show Angus how to 'really' cook and Angus helped him while the ladies stayed with Joshua.

The doctor had bad news and said he didn't think there was anything that anyone could do. He was likely to succumb. The rash was deadly for babies and old folks, because they hadn't enough stamina to fight it off. Then Boss Rudner had a cat skinner take him back to Yaak, but Campbells stayed.

The next day, they still hoped the boy would somehow find the strength. By that evening, they all knew that he wouldn't make it. Half Pint and Slim were devastated, but after a good cry, everyone bolstered them up. "Don't be giving in yet," Angus demanded. "That is not what you will do! Hear me?"

"He's right," Cook said. "We at Yaak Camp are stronger than that!"

Ink Slinger just turned and walked back to his cabin, his small frame jolted by every deep cough. Maybe he wasn't stronger.

Slim embraced Half Pint and then whispered in her ear, "I have something I have to do. I'll be right back."

Half Pint nodded, "Make it quick."

Slim knocked on Ink Slinger's door and waited until a bout of coughing ceased and the door opened. Ink Slinger was shocked to see him there. "Come in," he said wondering what would have taken this man from his son.

"I came to ask you if you would like to hold your godson. Your cough won't make a difference to him now, but I think holding him will. Half Pint and I would be obliged if you could rock the boy."

Ink Slinger stepped back and was lost in thought for a minute. Then he let his tears fall, "I would be proud to, but don't you want to be with him now?"

"We'll be right beside you, but I think he wants to meet his godfather up close."

"Let me wash up and I'll be right there."

A minute after Slim returned to the cabin, Ink Slinger arrived. He had washed up, combed his hair and changed his shirt. Slim ushered him in and sat him in the rocking chair. Then he had Half Pint put their son into his arms.

The little boy was very sick, but he did grab onto Ink Slinger's finger and everyone told him that they knew he recognized him. The frail accountant rocked the boy until he no longer could keep his eyes open. The little boy's breathing was becoming very labored. Ink Slinger looked up to Half Pint and said, "I believe he wants his mommy now."

Half Pint took her son. She and Slim were holding him when he died a little later. When the boy was gone, Angus said a prayer and he was placed in his cradle. Cook and Elias carried him to the cookhouse. Some men had fashioned a lid-like top for the cradle, as they had done for Baby Penn. That night, they closed it and in the morning, Angus held a service for the child. He was buried next to his twin brother under that old lonely pine. Angus and Elizabeth asked Half Pint if she wanted to come to the Bed and Breakfast with them, but she didn't. She wanted to stay there with her Slim.

Sister and Jeff were sitting in a café in West Glacier when Sister told about that. Jeff knew it was very emotional for her and said, "How about we walk back to the motel? Your St. John's boys sent something for you that you might want tonight."

Sister looked at him quizzically, "Whatever would that be?"

"Come, I'll show you," Jeff said.

They walked back to his room and he found two glasses. Then he rummaged through his bag and found the bottle of sipping rye and poured them each some in a glass. He handed it to her.

She smiled and said, "My boys always keep watch on me, don't they?"

"Indeed they do." Jeff nodded, "If you don't want to talk more tonight, I understand. Looks like we'll have all day tomorrow to hang around here."

"Yes, but I think, since we are comfortable, I might as well tell you more."

The next couple weeks, Half Pint became more and more discouraged and withdrawn. She would spend every free minute standing over her babies' graves. She never cried, but just stood there. Everyone tried to snap her out of it, but neither cajoling nor criticizing seemed to make a difference. By the end of those weeks, she had begun to isolate herself more and rarely even talked to Slim.

One afternoon, Ink Slinger, who rarely criticized anyone, saw her standing by the grave and walked up to her. "I never imagined I could be so disappointed in you!"

She turned abruptly and snapped, "How can you say that?"

"Look Half Pint, I know it's been horrible for you. I can't imagine how you must feel, but you've forgotten one very important thing."

"What's that?"

"Slim feels every bit as bad as you do. He loved his children, too. Don't be so selfish and stop pushing him away! He doesn't deserve it. He is the best person I know. I won't stand by and let you hurt him. Now, you made a promise to him. I remember. I was there! You said you would be with him through everything, and this is part of everything. Now I expect you to do it."

Half Pint frowned, "You don't even begin to understand."

He looked straight into her eyes and asked, "Don't I?"

129

That conversation made Half Pint furious. She hated this stupid place, these stupid trees and every stupid person she had met here! There was no one who could begin to know how she felt, not even Slim. He went out every day and climbed up those stupid trees like always. His life wasn't different.

She never said a word to anyone that night at dinner, and only snarled when asked a question. After things were cleaned up, she walked back over to the cabin. Slim was already fallen asleep in bed. She looked at him, "I know he can't feel as bad as I do! He can fall asleep at the drop of a hat!"

She changed her clothes and crawled into bed. Slim stirred and woke up a little. He reached out to put his arm around her and she turned over, facing away from him. She was so angry. They both lay there, not saying a word. Before long, Slim got out of bed and pulled his clothes on. She never moved. He put on his mackinaw and went out the door.

First she thought, 'Good! Just go! See if I care!'

After a few minutes however, she began to think, 'What in the world am I doing? Ink Slinger was right. I'm being selfish and horrible.'

She got out of bed and dressed. She went out the door and looked around. There was only a little light and nearly no moon. Her eyes searched for Slim, but didn't see him. She walked a ways toward the cookhouse before she noticed him over at the cemetery. She quietly went over to stand beside him.

He never looked up or made a motion toward her when she came up. He just stood there staring at those graves that held most of the folks dearest to him. There were tears silently rolling down his cheeks.

She reached over and took his hand. He squeezed it, but never made a move or said anything. She felt so bad and realized how much she had hurt him. He had never been anything but good to her. What was the matter with her? She turned to him and leaned on his arm, "I'm sorry I treated you so horribly. I had no right to be this selfish."

He didn't look at her, but put his arm around her. After a few minutes, he hugged her, "I don't like it. I know I don't understand God's reasoning. These folks all *had* to leave; they had no choice. But you don't have to turn away from me. You have a choice. You've never done that before."

Half Pint put her arms around his neck, "I'll never do that again. I promise. I was so busy feeling sorry for myself; I neglected to see what I was doing for you. Will you ever forgive me?"

He hugged her and then kissed her forehead, "Want to walk over to the pond? We haven't been there in some time. There is hardly any water in it, but maybe we can still find a mosquito to swat."

She nodded and took his hand. "I never told you how I depended on your strength all this while. And you have always been there for me and our family."

Slim helped her over some fallen debris, and said, "Everyone was so nice to us. I can't believe that Campbells came up, and Boss Rudner couldn't have done any more than he did. You know, Half Pint, I used to wonder how my dad could just walk away from me like he did. I understand it now. It was probably just too painful for him to stay. He was always good to me and made sure Grandma could care for me. He just couldn't be around because of all the pain. Do you think that was it?"

"I'm sure it was. Then I almost did the same thing to you," she sat on a log and pulled him down next to her. "I made such a mistake."

"We all make mistakes, Half Pint, but you owned up to it. That is the important thing." Slim kissed her cheek and then slapped a mosquito. "By jiminy, there are mosquitoes in this bog!"

She giggled, "That is what you said there'd be. Why are you surprised?"

He shook his head, "Let's go back, they are attacking me. They must not like you as much as me."

"They know who tastes good!" She giggled as she took his hand.

The couple walked back to the edge of camp and as they passed the cemetery, Slim said, "Do you think we will really get to see them again? You know in the hereafter, like folks say?"

"I don't know Slim, but I hate to think we won't. You know, we don't even have a picture of any of them."

"We do in our hearts," Slim nodded. "That I do believe. Would you be afraid to have another baby?"

She turned to him, "Not at all. I would like for us to have children. You are the finest papa I have ever seen."

"My sons never lived long enough to call me Papa," then he started to weep.

That night, she held him while he mourned.

Things improved dramatically for the couple. They developed a deeper bond than ever and started to have fun again. They worked hard and were closer than ever. They made plans for their future and even thought about starting to build a family again.

The weather did not let up. The wild animals in the forest were not doing well and many of the bears had not put on enough weight for their winter hibernation. Fires were more frequent and many areas were abandoned because of the fire threat.

Ink Slinger was not tolerating the smoky air well, and Cook was taking him to the doctor in Kalispell on break. Few thought he would be able to return to the mountains. Rosa and Cecil decided to move to Eureka after the winter drive. It was doubtful the camp would be working at full juice after winter break if the winter rains didn't start soon.

It seemed a chapter of their lives was closing. The timber business was changing and so was the weather. Many forests had been harvested and it would take time for the regrowth. Of course, it was still rugged, mostly untamed country, but it was changing. Slim wondered if that was how the first mountain men must have felt when the wagons began to appear loaded with settlers.

He was convinced it was time to move to Yaak. If he didn't find work there, he would find it somewhere. He was strong and willing, so he could find something. He often told Half Pint he was sorry he hadn't quit before the twins were born, but both decided that it must have been the way it was to be.

By mid-November, the forest was a pile of kindling. Rudner had made a trip to the owners and told them it was too dangerous to continue, if they didn't get rain. They were aware of the number of fires and gave permission to close down for the winter break early, if it didn't rain in two weeks. They would put off the start until it rained again. No one would be allowed to stay in camp.

On the Monday night of the last week of camp, the young couple received a visitor. It was Boss Rudner. They welcomed him into their cabin and he sat in the rocking chair. "I can never tell you how badly I feel about your loss. This has been a torturous year for you. The sawmill will be laying off men, so there will be no work there when you get to Yaak. I have a few letters for you. The first off, here is a job offer for the mill. When work opens up again, you have a job. Until then, I took the liberty of writing you both letters of recommendation. If at any time, I can help you get a job, please feel free to ask. I would be proud to brag on you."

With that, the man handed over the letters and rose to his feet before they could say a word. As he went out the door, he said, "It has been a fine pleasure knowing you both."

They fell asleep that night in each other's arms after making passionate love. As they lay there, Slim said, "Half Pint, even though we have had some hard times, you will always be my treasure. I'm so thankful I found you in my forest."

The morning was windy, with clouds over the ridge. Everyone was optimistic that the rains would finally come. Before Slim left for the strip, he ran back to the cookhouse. He grabbed Half Pint and swung her around in an enormous embrace. She giggled, "What are you doing? You need to get to work!"

"I'm telling my girl how much I love her!" he gave her a huge kiss and then ran off to catch up with the guys.

She stood there shaking her head. Cook came up beside her and put his hands on hips, "Good thing work is closing down. That boy might just have to pay out if he keeps dallying with the help!"

The boss decided to move into the last strip that morning, on a higher plateau of the mountain which hadn't been cleared yet. It would be their last chance to get that tall timber. The drought was hurting the tall trees. Rudner thought that clearing out some of old timber, would save more moisture for the newer growth. There was a lot of deadfall and many dry branches everywhere, in many cases clinging onto other deadfall.

Elias and one of the bullwhackers (men who drove the oxen teams) came to the cookhouse after early lunch and reported they would need a nosebag show for the second lunch. Boss had also said they should go out and clear as much dry timber as they could from the perimeter around the camp. He had put ten men on it and wanted them to help.

Before they headed back out for the second lunch, it had started to storm. It was extremely warm and still for November. The sky was black with undulating clouds and then the thunder and lightning came, but no rain. Boss told them to forget the nosebags and instead to hurry out and call the men back. It was too dangerous out there with all the lightning.

Half Pint was helping clear dead grass from the village, when she noticed the smoke. It was up on the plateau. Her heart sank. The wind was coming up. The dry lightning was so loud and frequent the air filled with incessant cracks that could be felt.

The electricity in the air was palpable. It made the earth tremble as each bolt penetrated the earth or split trees like a banana. The thunder was unremitting and so loud ones chest vibrated with each peal. It was like the deafening roar of a locomotive.

Explosive infernos were breaking out everywhere with a rush of forced hot wind clearing its path. That with the wind from the storm generated a reverberation.

In the yard of Yaak Camp, the air was filled with smoke, debris, dust and pits of ash. Some pits of smoldering debris fell on the ground and would start to burn wherever it found enough fuel.

She ran to the cookhouse to find Cook and Ink Slinger staring at what they could see of the sky. "Is that the plateau where the boys are?"

"Most likely, Half Pint," Ink Slinger hacked. "But we can't be certain from this standpoint. If not there yet, it is nearby. This looks very worrisome. I'm going to go over and put the ledgers in the safe."

"I'll help," Half Pint said and she went beside him to the clerk cabin. Once inside, she said, "You know, Slim is hardly ever afraid of anything, but he is worried about this forest."

"I know, many of the men are. I wish they had shut down last week. I know everyone will need whatever logs they can get for pay."

She helped him as he carefully put the important papers in the safe, "Do you think the camp will burn?"

"Don't know, but we need to be ready. They are hitching a team to get us out if need be. The Rudner ladies left half an hour ago. The horses are nervous and didn't want to be hitched, likely because of the thunder and smoke. We don't have control over the weather. Our job is only to do our part. Hear me?"

"Yes. Before I forget, I want to thank you for getting my head on straight after Josh died. I needed it."

Ink Slinger grinned and patted her on the back, "I might have laid it on a little thick. You didn't disappoint me that bad!"

Sister fidgeted, "May I ask you to replenish my sipping rye while I use your bathroom?"

"I was thinking more rye sounded good. I will go over to the motel office and get some ice, okay?"

A few minutes later, the pair were settled again. Sister took a sip and started again.

On their way back to the cookhouse, Ink Slinger and Half Pint heard a very loud crack of lightning. They stopped to stomp out several small burning patches in the yard.

The thunder and lightning strikes were so close together, it was difficult to tell when one ended and another started. Frequently, one could hear a tree split from the lightning and crash to the forest floor. On the steps of the cookhouse, they looked over to the plateau. It was now ablaze.

The winds were ferocious and the fire had crowned. Crowning is when it exploded across the tops of the sappy pines, and then leaves the trees to burn from the top down. In minutes, the fire spread over acres. New lightning strikes were causing trees to split in half or burst into flames everywhere.

Half Pint froze and stared at the blaze. It took a minute before Cook joined them on the porch. He looked at the inferno and put his hand on her shoulder, "The men know what to do. If it is possible to survive, they will."

The three stood motionless until they heard the wagon tear into the camp. It was the one bearing the Rudner ladies. The teamster shouted, "The trestle bridge by Pine Creek has burned! It's gone! The only way out is down the back road and I couldn't trust it. The forest floor is covered with burning widow makers. We need to hole up here!"

"Come inside. No point in watching it burn."

But they did. They all stood watching the nightmare unfold before them, unable to do a thing about it. As others that had been clearing the camp arrived, they joined them in spellbound terror. The sound was overpowering, but no one could hear human voices. They were too small to be heard over the power of the fire and the storm.

It was almost an hour later, before the first men began to straggle into camp. None of them had an easy time of it. They had lost contact with each other, many horses had fled off without their riders, and they all knew of men who had been lost, although few knew who they were. One man reported a flaming branch fell on his friend's back and knock him to the ground while they were running from the fire. He pulled it off, but his friend was unable to move his legs. While he worked trying to help him, another widow maker crashed. It was only by luck, the survivor saw it coming. His friend was lost. Another reported he saw the outlines of two men silhouetted against the background of golden flames gasping for air. The fire had sucked all the oxygen in its ravenous hunger and left them to suffocate. He did not know who they were. Two men reported they saw a man surrounded by flames. They were close enough to hear the shot when used his pistol before he burned to death. Animals were wild with terror and ran frantically to find salvation. Even the best trained could not be counted on in the panic.

It was a while before Elias and the bullwhacker arrived. One of his steers had become crazed and broke loose in a frenzy. They rode back on the other, having passed the carcass of the crazed animal on the way. It had fallen into a rocky ravine and broken its neck. It was beginning to burn as they passed by.

Elias went over and sat quietly by Half Pint and once in a while, had a few tears. Cook asked around for news on Slim, but there was little. One of the men said that he was working to the west and they saw it crown around that area but they didn't know if Slim had made it out beneath before the oxygen was gone.

Half Pint hardly heard a word. She just sat with her arm around Elias and stared at the floor. She knew. No one had to tell her. She knew in her heart that her beloved Slim was gone. She was so deeply sad should couldn't even cry. She knew she had lost her beloved Slim.

The fire skirted the camp and for a while, looked like it would devour it. The work to clear around camp had paid off and the voracious fire decided to greedily move on to more voluminous fodder to the north. It fringed Rudner's summer garden and burned one of the out buildings, but everything else escaped although the wood of some buildings were dried to powder from the horrific heat. Everything was covered in ash and char, but it still stood. The heat from the fire was unbelievable. It was as if a furnace of molten lava had been dumped on them. It was so hot, breathing was almost impossible. The acrid debris and suppressing ash clung on everything.

After the fire raged for four or five hours, the rains started. The sky finally released its store of healing waters. While it would not put all the smolders out, it stopped the high winds and the no new fires were starting. Now, all the folks at Yaak Camp could do was wait. Wait for men to return so they could find out who was missing. It would be dawn before they could go out to look for the missing and there were a lot.

Cook finally summoned the folks to have sandwiches and then ordered them to get some rest. Rosa, Maybell and Mrs. Rudner helped tend the injured while Ink Slinger began to make a head count.

By ten that night, they knew that eighty-two men had not returned. They also knew that there were many lost, because some of the loggers in camp had seen bodies. Boss Rudner worked with Ink Slinger to get the area plotted out and organize a search for the morning.

Cook insisted Half Pint get some sleep and sent Elias off to his room. "I'll need you both in the morning, and you have to be ready to work."

Half Pint went to the cabin and crawled in her bed. She was moving out of habit, not by any conscious thought. She curled around Slim's pillow and cried herself to sleep.

It was still raining when Elias rang the Gut Hammer. The cookhouse was bustling. The teamsters had brought their teams and oxen to be used as riding horses. There was no trail open for a wagon. Crews were sent to clear the road to Yaak and rebuild the burnt-out trestle. The others were divided into sectors to search areas to bring back the wounded or dead. It was a grim and grisly task ahead, but no one shirked. There was time for few tears because there was too much work. No one could justify taking time out to mourn, when there were still folks who could be rescued.

By nine, a rider told those at the cookhouse a crew from Yaak had moved up the road as far as they could to help. Some were from the Yaak mill, but others were from the town. Later, a group of eleven men straggled into camp on their own. Ink Slinger was delighted to check their names off the list of missing. Sadly, they notified him of two men who were certainly lost. He put their names another list.

Afternoon brought more news. Five more dead were identified and fourteen more found alive. Some were injured, often quite seriously; many were able to go back out to help with the search after a rest and some food.

That evening, two riders came back from the area Slim had been working. Two were sharing one horse and carrying a body over the other. Ink Slinger had his arm around Half Pint while the men explained what they found, "Seems he was on foot. The fire had crowned and he was surrounded. Though oxygen was sparse, no doubt, his neck was broken when a huge widow maker fell on him. He never knew what hit him. It was probably quick, Miss Half Pint."

Ink Slinger asked, "How did you know it was deadfall that hit him?"

"It's roots were in the air. It was burnt, either before or after, but his neck was broken beyond a doubt. We found that when we moved the trunk off his body. Where should we put him, Ma'am? He is burnt pretty bad, but that happened after he died."

Ink Slinger answered, "We are putting the deceased in Bunkhouse Three. Slim will go there, too."

The men nodded and rode off. Half Pint turned to Ink Slinger's arms, "I knew it, you know. I knew yesterday. In fact, I believe Slim had a foreboding. Do you think he can rest with his twins? I mean when this is all sorted out. I believe he would want that."

"I will see to it. Half Pint, my heart is broken. He was like a brother to me. Promise you will live bravely to make him proud. He loved you so."

Half Pint cried, "Yes sir, I will try."

Jeff and Sister were both crying, and then she looked at them. "My word, what folks would think if they saw us now?"

"Well, they won't see us. If they knew, they'd be crying with us. One more shot of sipping rye before we give it up for tonight. Sister, how many men died in that fire?" Jeff said as he poured them another drink.

"When the tally was made, eighteen men died. Mostly, it seemed when the fire crowned, it trapped many of them. In the end, I was thankful that the tree hit Slim and took him fast. I don't know if I could have made it knowing he suffocated or died in the blaze. At least, it was quick."

"You were a brave lady," Jeff said with some conviction.

"Jeff, it isn't brave to learn the one you love died. Platitudes and verses can get you through that. The bravery is needed when you get up day after day and have to face life without your partner. I have to admit, I still wake sometimes at night and imagine him walking down the street in Yaak with his bindle over his back. I have never loved anyone so much in my life. I appreciated many others, but Slim was my reason. Between you and me, he still is. There are days when I still want to give up, but I remember what he believed and expected from me. I hope someday I will get to see him again and that he will be proud of me."

"I'm sure he will, Half Pint. I'm certain he will."

Sister smiled at the young man, "Thank you. Now this drunken old nun better stagger back to her room before we create a scandal!"

Jeff walked her to her room and went back to his. As he cleaned up their glasses, he felt he was fortunate that he had come to really know her. Sister Abigail was by far the most amazing person he had ever met.

The pair had breakfast in a diner crowded with stranded truckers. They talked to several and the consensus opinion was that by afternoon they should be able to head out to Kalispell and likely to Libby, about a hundred miles further. There, they needed to check the road reports. One way was further, but better road. The other, was shorter on a worse road. Jeff chuckled, "A coin flipper, then?"

"Could say it that way. But for the morning, you might as well read a book."

Jeff grinned, "Or listen to a story!"

The trucker didn't understand, but smiled, "That would work too, I reckon."

After breakfast, they wandered around a gift shop and then sorted out things in their car. They filled gas and then Jeff went to buy some Coca Cola. Then he looked at her and chuckled, "Your place or mine?"

She laughed, "Since we were at your place last night, what about mine?"

"Sounds good. I have to take this stuff to my room and then I'll be over."

By the time Jeff left his room, it had started snowing. He knocked and she opened the door, "Look what it is doing out here!"

"I just called Albert, Swan's husband. He said to just stay put today. Mother is holding steady and the weather is dreadful there. Trucks can't make it in from Libby, on either road and don't know about tomorrow."

"I'm sorry, Sister."

"Don't be. Like I said before, they could have called me earlier. If I make it—fine, if I don't, then I don't. You know, reminding myself of why they let me be on my own all those years, has made me realize that those things have not changed. What could they possibly say now that would change a single thing?"

"Not much, but on the other hand, understanding is usually a good thing."

"Usually. After Father told me why he did what he did, I understood. But what did it accomplish?"

"I think it did do some good. It helped you realize that Slim was right and it wasn't your fault. There was a serious reason that Johann didn't come searching for you. Think if he had not been told! You may have married him, or worse, not married Slim."

"Yes, I have thought about that. Believe me, I have. However, I still wasn't eighteen years old yet and a widow who had lost her two children. When I wrote and told Cap, he wrote back that they were saddened by the news. However, they did not ask me to come home or say they would come see me. They didn't know if I was all alone. But of course, you know, I also had many things to hold on to."

"Your friends?"

"Yes, the Campbells, Cook, Ink Slinger and all of them. But I had more than that. I had the lessons of those who had passed on ahead of me. I had shared strong friendships and a love that few have the opportunity to share. I was blessed. Those were my angels, no doubt."

"I believe that," Jeff smiled, "So, was Slim buried under the lone pine?"

"Yes, he was."

After Ink Slinger talked to Boss Rudner; the foreman made a decision. He decided to enlarge Pendergast's cemetery to make room for the men who were lost in the fire. Everyone thought it was a good idea because there would be little chance of transporting them anywhere until the trestle bridge was repaired.

Men worked all night, building caskets. The next day, the victims were all laid to rest. Some men, known to be religious, had a cross with their boots nailed below their name. Others had a rough log post with their charred boots nailed below their names. Slim, like his sons, had a cross, but his boots had burnt off, so he had none to hang. The day after finding his body, Slim was laid to rest on the other side of his twin boys.

Half Pint was stoic throughout the ceremony that Boss Rudner conducted. The harmonica player had died in the fire, so one of the loggers simply led them in a chorus of *The Old Rugged Cross*. After the ceremony, she walked to back to the cookhouse with Elias, who was having quite a struggle.

"Miss Half Pint, I don't think a person shouldn't care about anyone, do you? Cause it seems to me that when you do, you just end up crying," the young lad asked seriously.

"No, Elias. I don't believe that."

"I loved my parents and grandmother, and they died. Then Josh and Slim and now they are gone. It seems that way to me."

"I see that, but Elias if you had quit caring about people after your grandmother, you would have never met up with Josh or Slim. I know you enjoyed being with them and they both thought the world of you. Right?"

"I guess. I guess I still have Grandma and Grandpa Campbell, Cook, Ink Slinger and even you."

Half Pint giggled, "Thanks for including me! You dumbbell! You can't close yourself off at any time, because you might miss out on something good. I'm very glad that I kept going and met my Slim. I will always be grateful for my time with him. I'm extremely sad it was so short, and I miss him terribly, but he'd be upset if either of us gave up. He wasn't that way and wouldn't be happy if we were."

They walked a ways before he asked, "What are you going to do now?"

"I don't know. Of course, we'll close up Yaak Camp and then you and I will go to Campbells. I'll decide there what to do. I know what you will do, though. You're going to start school there and accomplish great things, like Slim and Cook wanted. Does that sound good?"

"It would've been a better idea, if you and Slim would be living down the road."

"We can't bring Slim back, but you know what he hoped you would do. Am I right about that?"

"Yah, I do. It just would be easier if he hadn't died."

"I agree. I wholeheartedly agree." Half Pint went up the steps to the cookhouse. "I'm going to see if Cook has a shot of brandy he will spare. Think you might want one, too?"

"Could I?"

"I think you have behaved like an adult, so I see no reason why not. That is, if Cook will share."

A small group shared a shot and then Elias went off to bed. Cook looked to Half Pint, "The kid is having a hard time."

"Yes, he is," Half Pint agreed. "But he'll do okay. Well, Ink Slinger, would you be of a mind to accompany me to my cabin?"

"I would."

The camp didn't close for another two weeks, but no one could have left because the trestle wasn't finished. The day that Cecil loaded her things on the trailer, Half Pint had the hardest time of her life. Pulling the door closed on the cabin Slim had built was the hardest thing she ever did. Then she walked over to the cemetery. So much of her life was buried there. Now that part of her life would be left to the care of the mountains. She knew what she had told Elias was right, but she missed her Slim, so much. She could no longer hold her little babies, or—. She collapsed in tears.

Cook came over and picked her up off the ground, "I know, Half Pint. I do know."

"I want to just die too, Cook. Why can't I just die, too?"

"Because there is some work for you to do before the Big Boss calls you home. Then you can go. You know, we can't leave until the work is done. Remember, Booker kept on after losing his wife and all four of his babies. You aren't the only one who has ever lost someone. Slim would tell you to get up off the ground. He stood you up once and watched over you until you could stand on your own. I expect he would want you to stay up, now."

Half Pint wiped her eyes, got up and then nodded, "Yes sir."

Jeff watched her as she sat quietly wiping her tears away. "Have you ever gone back to visit their graves?"

"No. By the time I could, I knew Yaak Lumber Company had closed and didn't know if the cemetery was even there. Besides, I think I was afraid. I didn't even want to talk about it. You know when you mentioned going to see Pendergast's grave, I started to wonder why I never made the trip back. It might be a good trip, although the weather now isn't conducive to a journey there. I would like to plan to do that one day while I still can make the trip."

"You have my word, Sister," Jeff made an oath, "I'll accompany you there. If not now, as soon as we can."

"I might want to hold you to that."

Half Pint and Elias told Cook and Ink Slinger goodbye at the Yaak office and then rode with Rosa and Cecil to the Bed and Breakfast. There Angus and Sam helped Elias and Cecil to unload their things.

That evening, there were many hugs, tears and remembrances in the kitchen of the Bed and Breakfast. "When we heard of the fire, we wanted to come right up. As you know, there was no road, so we had to wait. When the rider brought your letter, our hearts were torn. We loved Slim like a son, but we are blessed that we still have our Half Pint and Elias. You are our family and we'll help you get through this. We know that Slim would have wanted that."

The next day however, they focused on the future. Angus had talked to Cecil about the house that Slim and Half Pint had signed on to rent. Since they needed a home, Angus went with him to the owners about letting them take over the lease. They were agreeable. Then they helped them move in.

On the walk back to the Bed and Breakfast, Half Pint said, "At first, I was jealous that Rosa was moving into 'my' house. Then I realized that it wasn't 'my' house anyway and while probably yesterday I would have loved living there, my every dream of it had Slim in it. I would have hated being there without him."

"I know," Angus said. "It will be a nice home for them. And you can visit."

The next morning the weather surprised everyone. There was a slightly balmy breeze blowing out the remaining clouds. Calls to the weather bureau and the highway patrol revealed the highway to Libby would be opened and in rather good condition by noon. With the thawing trend, it should be possible to make it to Dahlgren, the long way around, by the following evening. Over breakfast, Sister Abigail decided they should at least try to make it. They would leave for Libby after breakfast. The next morning, they would make the decision about traveling into Dahlgren.

As they were packing the Mercury, Jeff watched his new friend, and then said, sternly, "You and I are heading to the coffee shop. We can fill the thermos, and I want to talk to you."

As they sat in the booth, Sister asked, "Did I do something wrong—offend you?"

"Not at all," Jeff smiled and then put his hand over hers. "I think you are hiding from yourself."

Sitting across from him, she frowned, "Whatever are you taking about?"

"The closer we get to Dahlgren, the heavier your shoes are becoming. I'm not certain you want to see your mother, or the rest of your family for that matter. I would like you to be square with yourself about it and if you feel you can, be square with me."

The waitress took their order and left with their humongous thermos. Sister read the menu, even though they only had coffee. After the waitress brought their coffee, Jeff took the menu from her and replaced it behind the napkin canister. "Would you prefer talking in a room, we haven't checked out yet."

Sister shook her head, "No, it would be better if I said it here. Otherwise, I will probably just lose it."

"If you want to lose it, I can handle that. I was a priest long enough that I'll extend to you the strictest confidence. I think you have worked in a bottling plant long enough—and now you need to spill it. I have to tell you, if it was me, I would probably have told the whole schmoley to go fly a kite. But," he chuckled, "We know me!"

"You are a dear. That Bishop in Boston must have had rocks in his head to let you and Matt go. You're right. I'm having a terrible argument with myself. Frank knew it and that's why he insisted that I go and not by myself."

"What does Father Vicaro say?"

"Over the years, Frank has learned about my life and my family. He understands my point of view and agrees. But he still thinks I need to be forgiving and give them a chance. Somehow, he seems to think that seeing them will be good for me. From my point of view, I think it just dredges up old hurts and I can't see anything to be gained. Probably yesterday, I cared if they would accept me back into the family. They never did. Now, for them to ask me to come see them, I find it almost insulting. Although I don't know why I should be insulted."

"My guess is that you feel that it is for them, and not really for you to make the effort. I know that's the way I would feel." Jeff patted her hand again, "I think Frank is right. Don't sink to their level. Don't give them that. You and I both know the Lord would likely want us to extend a hand. I'll make you a deal, if you want to hear it."

Sister smiled, "I would love to hear it!"

"I'll be right beside you. If they push you too far, you give me the high sign. I'm no longer a priest, so I can tell them to take a hike! I won't punch them out because I flunked Boxing 101, but I can yell with the best of them!"

Sister laughed, "That is the best deal I've ever been offered! Come Sir Lancelot, Queen Guinevere is honored to be protected by such a fine knight."

Jeff got out of the booth and held out his arm, "Our mighty steed the Marquis de Mercury awaits."

"I think we better get our thermos and pay our bill of fare, or the Sheriff of Nottingham will have a time.

"Was that even the same era?"

"Who cares?"

Once on their way, they faced slippery roads, but could see the sun beginning to dry off the roads. They felt things would be better in a couple hours.

"Will we need a motel in Dahlgren?" Jeff asked.

"I haven't been invited to stay with any of the family."

"Okay, I think you might not want to anyway. I will take the liberty of finding us rooms so you have a place to hide out if you need it. We still have some sipping rye, too!"

"You must be on the Devil's payroll!"

Jeff chuckled, "Yah, but the last check bounced! It sounded like Slim didn't drink."

"Oh, he did, but not a lot. His Grandmother said it was silly to drink something that made you unable to walk straight!"

"She's right!" Jeff drove a ways, "May I ask, how did you get from Yaak to Merton. That is still quite a leap."

Half Pint and Elias stayed with Campbells. He started school and worked diligently on his studies. Half Pint was very helpful around the Bed and Breakfast and and they loved having her there. In the evenings, however, she would walk down to the river and sit on the bench that was Slim's favorite. There she would stare at the fire-scarred mountains until it was dark.

Campbells became more and more worried about her. She never said anything to anyone. When asked, she would say there is nothing to do but accept it. Elizabeth and Angus were unable to find something to snap her out of it, even though they prayed fervently about it.

In mid-April, a letter arrived from Boss Rudner. Yaak Lumber had sold the Yaak Lumber Camp and would be closing the sawmill as soon as the last of the timber was used. He had taken a job with the Black Hills Mining Company out of Deadwood, South Dakota. The mining company had a great deal of timber on their mining leases and thought it might be worthwhile to harvest it, rather than waiting for it to turn into deadfall.

He was assembling a crew to take with him. He had contacted Cecil, Blacky and Bert to join him. He had hired many of his 'old guard' whom he knew he could trust. He had contacted Cook, but he decided he was needed more by Ink Slinger. Besides, he was too old to start again. Boss Rudner explained that the bunkhouse would be in Deadwood, and not up in the hills. Family men could have their own homes but the rest would live in the bunkhouse. It would be more like a rooming house than the old bunkhouse. He wondered if Half Pint would run it for him. He knew she could do it. Where Yaak Camp had between two and three hundred men, this bunkhouse would only be forty or fifty men. He would also hire her helpers.

That was the first time Half Pint had an interest in anything. She ran over to Lana's and they both thought it would a good new beginning. Campbells also thought it could be, but warned her this would be different. There would be no Pendergast, Cook or Slim. However, they thought she should try it.

Elias was less than thrilled until Angus promised him they would go see Mt. Rushmore in the summer after the Fourth of July celebration. Then they could visit with Half Pint. After looking up Wild Bill Hickok in the encyclopedia, he couldn't wait for her to leave. "We will get to see his grave and Calamity Jane's and all that! It will be so good."

"You will get to see me, too."

"Oh yah, Miss Half Pint. I will see you. Maybe you could take me to see their graves!"

Half Pint tousled his hair, "If I didn't know you better, I could get my feelings hurt."

"No, I will miss you. Do you want me to help you pack?"

Before the beginning of May, a small convoy of trucks left Yaak, Montana. Half Pint was riding in one of them. After a morning prayer, Angus presented her with a box of his precious recipes and told her to remember she was never alone. The good Lord was with her and she needed to rely on that. All of her friends were hoping she would make them proud.

The trip was amazing to Half Pint. She had never seen prairies before, treeless prairies. She had never seen the horizon clearly, unhampered by hills or vegetation. At first, she wondered if there were any animals on this barren land, but before long was noticing antelope and deer. Their first night on the road, she went outside for a walk. It was the most amazing panorama of stars she had ever imagined. She wondered what Johann thought when he first saw the 'big sky'. Surely, he had to think about their imaginary Mars.

The next day, they saw the Black Hills off in the distance, and understood immediately why the Indians called them the Black Hills. They stood stately and tall, black with trees against the golden browns of the barren prairie. When the convoy made its way into them, it was a lovely return to the forest. The best part, it was a forest, but not the Purcells. Somehow, to Half Pint, that made a difference.

They headed into the isolated little town of Deadwood, South Dakota. The little village was unpretentious and seemed to care much less about its colorful history than the tourists did. It didn't take them long to find the bunkhouse where they would all stay the first night. The next afternoon, Boss Rudner was coming by to sign them up and then take them all out on a tour of the property where they would be working.

That afternoon, they unloaded the kitchen supplies and Half Pint's few things. The other furniture was already in place, though not set up. Lana, Maybell and Rosa were going to stay at the bunkhouse until they found homes and would help Half Pint get organized. The rest of the crew would begin arriving within the week. By late May, Rudner hoped to be ready to start. There was a sense of adventure and excitement. Even Half Pint was excited.

When she moved into her room off the kitchen, she laughed. There was a single bed, a chair and a four-drawer dresser. The only difference between there and her room at Yaak Camp was this place had a closet and a modern bathroom off to the side. This window looked out about four feet before a huge tree obliterated the view. At Yaak Camp, the tree was only a foot away.

26

The next afternoon, the group all dressed in their work camp clothes, even the ladies, and headed to the timberland. The area was dotted with mineshafts; some abandoned, some active. Boss Rudner explained that the entire mountainside was littered with tunnels and shafts underground. It would present a danger for the lumbermen. A crew from the mines was actively working to try to map the first area, so that it would be safe from collapses and cave-ins. It would not be an exact map, because in the past, men dug everywhere and seldom bothered to document it. Rudner's crew were brave men and careful. That is about all one could expect.

The group wandered around for a couple hours. The mining fascinated Half Pint. There was some blasting going on off to the east, but Boss Rudner said he had been assured that it wouldn't affect the area where they were.

The folks broke up into smaller groups, visiting and looking at things that were interesting. Half Pint was with five men looking at the cracks in the ground. They had decided they must be from a tunnel below and were just moving away, when they heard another distant blast.

Half Pint woke up in pain; not a little pain, but horrendous pain, all over! She was only awake a minute, but heard a man say, "She's alive."

She tried to wake up, but couldn't. She fell into a deep dream. Slim was there holding her in his arms. "I'll be waiting for you, don't worry. But you have to go back and finish your work. I'm proud of you. Be my girl and be strong. Help others and be their angel. I will be here waiting here with all my love." Then he kissed her warmly and said, "I love you."

He faded away and she cried. First, she was so inconsolably sad; but soon that was replaced with anger. She didn't want to finish her job! She wanted to be with him. She was tired of being strong. Half Pint wanted to curl up in his arms and feel safe again. She hated this.

The next time she opened her eyes, there was a kindly lady sitting beside her bed. When she noticed the girl was awake, she smiled, "Good afternoon, Leisel. I'm Sister Anne. I've been waiting with you to wake up. I imagine you have many questions."

Half Pint tried to talk, but was unable to move her mouth. She frowned at this lady and wondered who she was.

Sister Anne seemed to understand her questions and said calmly, "You were in a cave-in of a mine in the Black Hills. You were fortunate to be pulled out of the rubble and saved. The mining company sent you here because your injuries were so numerous. You have several broken bones. There are many cuts and bruises, but nothing that isn't healing. It was a miracle that you were saved. God must have something very special for you to do."

Half Pint frowned at her and thought, 'He wasn't listening to what I want! I don't want to be here. I want to be dead. He can find someone else to do whatever this job is.'

Tears began rolling down her cheeks and Sister Anne wiped her face gently. "We are glad you are alive, Leisel."

Half Pint groaned, "Die."

"No, little one," Sister smiled, "You have a broken jaw that is wired and that is why you can't talk well now. You won't die from these injuries. It will take time for a full recovery, but you should be back to normal. You will have difficulty bearing children because of your pelvis, but you still can."

Half Pint glared at her, "Dead."

Sister didn't understand and answered, "Two of the men you were standing with died at the scene and one the next day, but two others survived."

"Slim?" Half Pint asked hopefully.

"I don't know anyone's name but yours. I'm sorry. I can try to find out for you. Was Slim with your when it happened?"

Half Pint answered, "Gone."

Sister Anne didn't understand, which made Half Pint very frustrated. She just closed her eyes and went back to sleep.

151

It seemed that life became an endless round of waking in pain, seeing either Sister Anne or a minister of some kind, not being able to communicate with them, and becoming frustrated. They both seemed like nice folks, but Half Pint didn't care to see them. She wanted Slim, Cook or Campbells. Why didn't they come? If she couldn't die, she wanted to see them!

Sometimes nurses or doctors would move her about, ask her if she hurt this place or that and then leave. She didn't know any of them. The only person whose name she knew was Sister Anne.

One day, she opened her eyes and saw that minister. He looked at her and smiled, "Hello Leisel. If you can stay awake for me, I have some news for you."

She turned her head toward him with great difficulty. He told her to lay still and he would talk to her. "My name is Father Benedict."

She tried to say Benedict, but couldn't. It came out more like Ben.

He chuckled, "You can call me Ben."

She was relieved to hear that.

"May I call you Leisel?"

She emphatically answered very slowly, "No. Half Pint."

"Okay, we won't call you Leisel. I got that, but I don't understand what you want to be called. But please let me know if your real name is Leisel Peterson?"

Half Pint finally got a yes out. Father Benedict thanked her and asked, "Now, let me try to figure out what we should call you? Could you say it again, very slowly?"

"Haffff."

"Half?" he asked with a grin.

"Yes."

"Okay, the rest?"

"Pint."

"Pine?" then he chuckled, "I know, Half Pint! Is that it?"

"Yes."

"Okay, I think you make a good Half Pint. We have some things we need to sort out, if you could help me. Okay? Was your husband with you when the ground caved in? We have been unable to locate him."

"Die."

"Did he die in the cave-in?"

"Fire."

"I don't understand. There was no fire. We were told there was a cave-in. No one mentioned a fire. I'm going to look into this more. Okay?"

"Yes."

"You did work for Black Hills Mining Company?"

"Yes."

"I will contact them, Half Pint. We'll find out all about you. Okay?"

"Yes."

"Could you try to tell me the name of someone to talk to who knew you? That might be helpful. I know it is hard work for you, but could you try?"

"Ruddd."

"Rud?"

"Nerrr," she said as clearly as she could.

"Rudner?"

"Yes. Boss."

"I will try to talk to him. You did a good job, Half Pint. Now do you want to take a nap?"

"Die," she said pleading with her eyes.

He smiled compassionately, "No. You can't die yet. It isn't time."

Then she cried. He tried to comfort her as best he could and before long she fell asleep.

The next time she woke up, Sister Anne was there. Half Pint looked at her and smiled, "Hi."

"Hello yourself," Sister said. "Are you feeling a bit better today?"

"No."

"That was a silly thing for me to ask. I meant are you feeling more awake?"

"Yes."

"Father Benedict has been very busy trying to find out as much as he can for you. He told me that you want to be called Half Pint. That is a fun name."

"My name."

"I have a little good news for you. The doctor said your ribs are vastly improved and so is your collarbone. Your hand is healing but it will be a while."

"Hand?"

"It was smashed in the debris," Sister Anne explained. "You broke so many bones, but things are beginning to heal. The doctors are hoping that your jaw should tolerate more movement very soon. Then we will be able to visit. Won't that be nice?"

"Eat?"

"You won't get real food for a while, but soon. I bet you are looking forward to that."

"Yes."

Half Pint didn't understand why they were talking about a cave-in. She also had no idea where she was or how she got there. They all seemed to know more than her. She really didn't care. She just wanted to sleep. Maybe Slim would come to see her again.

Things made no sense to her and she hated not being able to move. She had to admit that she did like seeing Sister Anne and Father Benedict when she woke up, but she still desperately wanted to see Cook, Campbells and Elias. She thought about Ink Slinger a lot. She was glad that Cook was there with him. No one should be alone, like she was.

One morning, Father Benedict called her name, "Half Pint, can you wake up for me? I have some news. I really want to talk to you. Open your eyes."

Half Pint opened her eyes and saw the priest peering over her. It made her smile and sort of giggle.

"I do believe you are laughing at me, Miss Half Pint! I have half a mind not to tell you what I found out!" he teased.

"Please."

"Okay, but only because I had quite a time making contact with Boss Rudner! He seems like a fine fellow and he sure thinks a lot of you. He said to tell you that he sends his best wishes. He seems like a good friend."

"Yes."

"So, I will tell you what he said and if you disagree, say no. Okay?"

"Yes."

"He said you came to work at Yaak Camp. He said that you married a young logger named Arthur Peterson. You and he had twin sons. They both died before their first birthday and the following year, Arthur died in a forest

154

fire. He said he would contact the Campbells who are dear friends of yours, and maybe they would get in touch with Mr. Cook. I contacted your family, and they said they wished you a speedy recovery.

"It was only minutes later, when Mr. Campbell called me. We were unable to talk very much, but he said to let you know they love you and will come to see you as soon as they can."

"When?" Half Pint was flooded in tears by now.

"He said right after the Fourth of July."

"Now?"

"It is the second week in June, so in a few weeks. They are coming by train."

Half Pint frowned, "Where?"

"You are in St. Paul, Minnesota. You were standing with some men when a tunnel to an old gold mine caved in. Others dug you out and took you to Rapid City. Your body was so badly broken and they felt you would be cared for better here in St. Paul. You are here at St. Mary's Hospital. Your employer had you sent here by train and are paying for the best care we can provide."

"Minnn?"

"Minnesota. That's right. And Sister Anne and I have adopted you," he grinned. "We want to be help you with your long recovery. Since you decided to break every bone you had, you are rather incapacitated. So we want to help you."

"Good."

"Well, thank you. I will tell Sister Anne."

"Good."

"Is there anything I can do to help you? I would be willing to do most anything."

"Die. Me die," she said slowly and ardently.

Father Benedict patted her head and said, "No, my girl. That I will not do. I won't interfere with God's plan. You know, we are all on the planet to love and help each other. I can try to help you feel better about living. It seems to me that you have lost so much. I understand that you probably feel rather forsaken. Things will get better, I promise. Life will look more appealing when you can get around and see your loved ones. We have to work on getting you repaired before your friends come to visit. Will you help us help you?"

She didn't answer.

"Okay, Sister Anne and I'll do it without your help, but it'd be more fun if you would help too. Think about it?" He started to get up to leave.

"Ben?"

He stopped and turned, "What is it, Half Pint?"

"Ring?"

"Ring? Whose ring?"

"My."

The priest looked in the bin at her bedside stand, "There is no ring here. I'll ask and see if anyone saw a ring. Is it your wedding ring?"

"Yes."

"Did it have a stone?"

"No."

"You have my word, I'll try to find your wedding band. Now you rest."

T he doctors and nurses seemed to be moving her around more and making her sit up. Others came in and forced her limbs to move and exercise. It was very painful and she hated it, but they didn't stop. Sister Anne patiently stayed by her side as much as she could, and encouraged her to keep moving.

"I know it is difficult, Half Pint. Remember, we want you to be able to stand up and walk a little when your friends come to visit. Wouldn't that be nice? It would make them very happy."

"Sleep."

Sister Anne smiled, "As soon as we do these exercises, you can take a nap. I promise."

"Why?"

"Why what?" Sister asked.

"You help me?"

Sister smiled, "Because you need help and we are all here to help each other. I am fortunate because I am a nun and I can spend all day helping you. Isn't that nice?"

"Yes."

The following week, Half Pint was finally able to move enough to notice her casts. It made her laugh. A mass of bandages covered her left hand with a cast from her armpit to her wrist. Her left leg was in a cast over her knee and to her toes. Her ribs were wrapped and her lower jaw was fixed into a contraption to keep it from moving. Mostly however, the worst pain was from her hips and pelvis. Sister Anne explained that she had part of her pelvis crushed by a beam and the rock from the cave-in. It made it impossible for her to sit easily and standing was extremely painful. Because of the broken ribs, crutches were torture.

Half Pint looked at her casts and then at Sister. "Mess."

Sister smiled, "You are a mess; but you are less of a mess than you were when you got here! Why I think you have at least seven bandages less and one cast off!"

Half Pint crossed her eyes, "Yeah."

"You seem very perky today."

"Yes."

"Anything I can get for you?"

"Ben."

Sister said, "Father Benedict couldn't be here the last few days because he was very busy. He will be here tomorrow. Is there something you would like me to tell him?"

"Hi."

Sister smiled, "I will do that. It will please him."

"Good."

The next day, as promised, Father Benedict came in and tapped her on the shoulder. She opened her eyes and smiled, "Hi."

"I want to thank you for the message. That was very kind of you to tell me you were thinking of me. I wanted to be here, but I had some things that I had to get finished."

"Done?"

"Yes," he smiled. "I got them all done. Now I can spend more time with you. We have twenty-three days before your friends will be here. If I could count on you helping us, we would like to get you moving by then."

"Try."

The middle-aged priest's dark blue eyes sparkled, "That is wonderful! I'm so glad you said that. I was worried you were going to be troublesome."

"No bad."

"You aren't bad. You know what. I've been talking to folks who knew you. No one has said you are bad. In fact, they all think a lot of you!"

Half Pint smiled, "Dumb."

He laughed, "They didn't say you were dumb either!"

"They."

"Now, that was bad." He chuckled and then got serious, "I found out about your ring. I'm sorry but it was lost in the rubble. Two men named Cecil and Bert got some fellows to help them dig through it, but they were unable to find it. They will try again, if you like."

Half Pint's tears ran down her cheeks, but she answered slowly and with great effort, "No. Thank. Love them."

"I will tell them," Father Benedict said. "I know it must break your heart. You can still love Arthur without a ring."

"Slim."

"I'm sorry, I forgot you called him Slim." Then his face brightened, "I almost forgot the best news! I got a couple letters for you! Would you like me to read them?"

"Yes!"

"Okay, relax and I'll start with the first one. Okay? This is from Angus Campbell."

Half Pint grinned as big as she could and the tears started rolling down her cheeks. The priest wiped her eyes, "Let's start. 'Dear little Half Pint, Elizabeth and I were devastated to hear the news. You have had to handle so much, but we have every confidence that only means God has great plans for you. I can imagine that made you mad, but you know how we feel about that. We have to carry on. Slim would be the first one to tell you to be brave and strong. Elias said you told him that a guy should never give up, so you better not. He is studying very hard to learn his mathematics so he can come see you. We wrote to Ink Slinger and he is going to write to you. We are taking care of things at this end and now you do your part there. We will see you soon. Make Slim proud. God's blessings, the Campbells.'"

Half Pint was very quiet but had stopped crying. Father Benedict watched her a minute, "They seem like wonderful people."

"Yes."

"I can write to them for you, if you would like."

"Yes."

"Should we do that now, or should I read the next letter?"

"Next."

"Okay, the next is from someone named J.J. Rosenbaum."

"Good," Half Pint smiled.

"Dearest Half Pint, Cook and I heard the news! Girl, I'm the one in the hospital, not you! Cook said if he had been there, he would have pulled you out before you got hurt. He is very upset that he can't take care of you. If you want him to come there, he will. I will share him for a while. He has a room not far from here and comes to visit me every day. My cough is about the same, but I have a pile of books to read! Boss Rudner sends me a new one every month. He is a fine man. I think of Yaak Camp every day and what a dear friend Slim was. (And Pendergast and Booker!) You and I were very lucky. Many people never have as many dear friends as we did. Don't cry, we should be feel very fortunate. You and I know how important it can be to have folks to depend on. They were there for us, now we need to be there for others. I have even found a few folks here who need to have a shoulder now and again. It also gives you less time to whine about yourself. Oh, oh. I think I just gave you the business again. Now, I fully expect that you will be up and wearing your fancy shoes again soon! Then you can come see Cook and me! Cook says to tell you he found a place that serves flapjacks here, but he wants you to taste them. They say they have the best in the west, but he is sure his were better. Know you will always have a special place our hearts, Ink Slinger and Cook."

Half Pint smiled, "Love."

Father Benedict agreed, "They seem like very good guys. Is his name Ink Slinger?"

"Yes," she smiled.

"He seems very educated."

"Yes."

"That is all I have today, but I want you to know that Boss Rudner has called me twice to check on you. He said to tell you that Lana and Cat Skinner, Blacky and Rosa are doing well, as is his family. May I ask where does everyone get their names?"

"Yaak Camp," Half Pint struggled to get out.

"Do you want me to write to them now, or do you need to rest?"

"Nap. Thanks."

Over the next couple weeks, Sister Anne and Father Benedict were with her except when she was sleeping. They worked with her, exercised her limbs, wrote letters and visited with her. She came to really like both of them.

Father Benedict wrote her letters, which was very difficult, since she couldn't say more than one syllable at a time. Before long, they developed a sort of sign language and shared a lot of jokes. He got to know her very well from the letters she received in return.

One day, he brought another letter from Ink Slinger and as he sat down next to Half Pint's bed. Before he read it, he looked at her very seriously. "You haven't heard from your family." Then he asked, "Did you want me to write to your family?"

"No."

"Did you hear from them?"

"No."

"Don't you think you should let them know you are recovering?"

"No."

"Don't you think they are worried?"

"No."

"Okay, but when you can talk better, maybe we can talk more about it. Oh, and on that subject, the doctor said that you will get your jaw out of that contraption day after tomorrow! Won't that be exciting?"

"Eat?"

Father laughed, "Next week, if all goes well."

S hortly after her jaw was unwired, Half Pint and Father Benedict had a long talk. It started about her family. He suggested that simply because they were not making an effort to rebuild their relationship, didn't give her an easy out. He thought she should still make an effort.

"Why does it always have to be me that does it?" Half Pint grumped. "Cap didn't even write. What is wrong with them?"

"I don't know and you don't know. If you want to know, you should write and ask. Maybe there is something that happened so he can't write. You didn't ask him, now did you?"

"Sometimes I like you better when I'm asleep!"

Father Benedict chuckled, "I imagine you do. What do you say? Should we write a letter?"

"Can't we write to Ink Slinger instead?"

"We wrote yesterday, right after we wrote to Campbells."

"Okay, but it better be short."

Half Pint also began visiting with Sister Anne about what a nun was and why she became one. "Does that habit thing itch?"

Sister laughed, "No. I imagine it would if you were allergic to the fabric."

"Yah. Why do you want to be a nun?"

"This way I can devote my life to doing God's work, without being distracted by other things. I can work for Him full time."

"I don't know if I believe in God that much. I mean, I believe in Him, but I am really angry with Him."

"You have said that often. You know, He loves you. I think that you just don't understand His plan, so you are unhappy with Him."

"Sister, He let my husband, my children and my best friends die! I think that was His plan! I don't like it even a little bit! There is no reason good enough."

"He allowed you to meet your friends and your Slim in the first place. He didn't have to do that."

"No, but it isn't very nice to let me love them and then steal them from me! I don't care! I'm mad at Him! If I was in charge, I wouldn't let stuff like that happen to anybody!"

"He didn't have to steal them. They were already His. He let you borrow them." Sister Anne smiled as she helped her get ready for her nap, "But I will look forward to you being in charge."

"I bet Father Benedict would agree with me."

Sister winked, "Why don't you ask him?"

So, she did and much to her dismay, he didn't agree with her. He did agree that she was angry with Him and that it seemed unfair to her. That question was the beginning of a long discussion. They both read, looked things up and talked about God. Half Pint began to really like their discussions and looked forward to them, but she was still unhappy that she couldn't find anything to change Father's mind. "I will, you just wait!"

"I have plenty of time. You just keep looking."

"You just think He is always right."

"I have to believe He is. I have full faith in Him. I have lived long enough to know that many times, things I thought were outrageous at the time, made sense later. I still get frustrated and often don't understand His reasons. Few do because many of His decisions are not the same ones we would make."

"It gives me a headache," Half Pint grumped.

"That's why I love visiting with you! You want to know a secret? It gives me a headache too, sometimes."

Half Pint smiled, "Thank you."

"Oh, I got a letter from a Brigit Haldoran. Would you like me to read it to you or do you want to read it yourself?"

"Could you please?"

"Dear Leisel, I'm so glad you wrote again because we had lost your address. There was a big accident. The rock ledge above the house gave way after a huge rain. The house was destroyed in the rock slide. Everyone is safe, but it was a terrible loss. We moved into Dahlgren and live in a small house behind Swans. Birger is in the Army now, so he wasn't home to rebuild. I have sent him your address and he'll be writing to you. Cap and I looked all over and were unable to find the letter that said where you were. Mom and the others are well. Cap and his wife are expecting a baby soon. I think of you often and still miss you. Your sister, Brigit."

Half Pint was lost in thought for some time. Then she smiled, "You were right. They did have a reason, uh? I guess I was being hot-headed."

"I'm glad that you decided to write. I could have been wrong, too. It is usually wise to give others a chance."

"How many chances?"

"Oh, very many."

"Father, what do you think our job is? You know, everyone says my work isn't finished so it isn't my time to die. What work is it?"

"I imagine we each have specific things we must learn or do. I don't know for certain what mine are, let alone yours. The Bible tells us to love one another and help each other. That is usually a good place to start. If your job is to help just one other person, that is important."

"Slim used to say that. In fact, Ink Slinger says that, too. But I don't have anyone to help; everyone is helping me! I feel worthless!"

"Maybe you help more than you know. When I was gone those days, I had a lot of work to do, but I was also having a struggle with myself. I felt very down and lonely. When Sister came to me and told me you said Hi, it meant so much to me. It brightened my whole day."

Half Pint frowned, "That was no big deal."

"Most of the time, folks don't need a big deal, Half Pint. They just need a little smile or a bit of encouragement."

"I've been pretty grumpy, so I don't think I encourage anyone."

"You know, even when you were hurting very bad, you still managed to smile. That helps others find strength."

Jeff asked for some coffee from the thermos. Sister Abigail poured it for him, "I feel badly that I haven't driven an inch! You have done all the work."

"I wouldn't look at it like that. I have enjoyed this trip, very much. Except following that lead car! Wow! How would you like to do that for a living?"

"I wouldn't. You know, I have enjoyed this trip too, and having the chance to get to know you."

"Ditto. We are coming into Troy and the day is still young. Do you want to try for Dahlgren today?"

"Not that far, but how about eating in Troy? We can check on the roads and then go to Yaak. I would like to spend the night there. We could get into Dahlgren early the next day. I don't know if there is a place to stay there, so we could get back to Yaak for the night, if we need to."

"Don't you think your family would put you up? I can see where they might not want to put me up. You could stay and I can go back."

"No way. I need you to stay with me, Jeff. Please don't leave me. Promise?"

Jeff saw the expression which made him think very much of little Half Pint. "I will stay with you. You can count on it."

"I'm sorry. I'm being a big baby."

"I don't think so. This could be traumatic and I should have thought about that."

"You know," Sister said thoughtfully, "Maybe it is just the silliness of an insecure little girl. It will likely amount to nothing. Mother will say goodbye and that will be it."

"If that is the case, then we can both be on our way in no time. I will be with you. Think of me as Pendergast."

"Sort of a petite version, but the heart is as big."

"Thanks." Jeff grinned, "How long was it before you got out of the hospital?"

Half Pint was walking with aid by the time her visitors came. She was delighted when Angus, Elizabeth and Elias arrived. The best news was the surprise they brought with them! The bearded Cook was dressed in his blue jeans with suspenders, his red plaid flannel shirt and his boots! They were logging boots, but without the calks. He met her with tears and a great hug. "I don't want to hurt you, Half Pint. So I can't squeeze you hard!"

He had met the others in Missoula and traveled with them by train to St. Paul. She could only have been happier if Ink Slinger had been able to come too, but he sent a message, "I am only sharing Cook for a bit, so send him back! I wish I could come see you. My heart is there with you always, Ink Slinger."

She was very excited to introduce them to her new friends. They could only stay a couple days, but Father Benedict arranged a fine dinner in her hospital room for them all on the last night. It was great fun.

By the end of August, the doctors said she could leave the hospital, but was still unable to travel anywhere. Father Benedict and Sister Anne arranged for her to stay at the convent. They didn't spend as much time with her as before because they had other patients to care for, but they had become her friends. They visited with her at least every other day.

Sister smiled at Jeff, "And as they say, the rest is history."

Jeff grinned, "They got to you, huh? When did you convert and then join the convent?"

"Later that fall. Father got me out of my funk and got me busy. He took me to visit with folks who were facing medical problems and told me to just listen and try to help them. One day, I asked him why he did that and he grinned, 'You need to think of something else and you are very good at encouraging others. I need help and you looked like a good candidate. Remember, I heard what Ink Slinger told you. He was right. You didn't whine as much!'"

"Sister, how did you ever get over being mad at God?"

"I gradually just got over it. I still don't like it. I still have questions about why things happen, but I guess I take His word for it that He knows what He is doing. I have lived long enough now to understand that I don't understand everything. And also, to see that things do sort out. One day I look at something and say, 'Oh, now I get it.' And this sounds pessimistic and I don't mean it that way, but sometimes I think that by taking my loved ones home so early, He allowed them to avoid a lot of the pain of this old world dishes out. They really are in a better place. I'm just jealous I didn't get to go, too!"

"You couldn't go! Who would take care of that mob at St. Johns? You wouldn't have been here for me!"

"That's very nice of you to say. I know you have some doubts about what happened in Boston, but I do believe there was a reason. You got to be here with me! I guess we have to realize that God does have His reasons. Jeff, were you asking for me or for you?"

"Both of us. I know there are things I'd like to understand, but I do know that this is His world. For the most part, He has been good to me."

"You mean, after adding up all the good and bad?" Sister laughed.

"Something like that. I've let Him down big time on a regular basis, so I guess I should cut Him some slack!" Jeff laughed.

"Big of you!"

"I know, huh? Do you know of a place to stay in Yaak?"

"I do. The B&B Motel."

"As in Bed and Breakfast?" Jeff asked with a sly grin.

"Yes. After Angus died, Elias helped Elizabeth run the Bed and Breakfast. The Yaak River flooded about fifteen years ago, and caused a lot of damage. Elias made the decision to tear it down and rebuild."

"Is Elizabeth still with us?"

"She passed away about ten years ago. Even though I wasn't able to stay for her funeral, Elias and I were both with her when she died peacefully. She said we were children." Sister had tears, "I couldn't have found a better family than I had with them."

"Is Elias Catholic?"

"No, he is Methodist like Angus and Elizabeth. He is a fine man. You will like him. He knows we are coming. He said he will have a room for us."

"I'm anxious to meet him. This is exciting!"

It was nearly dark when they drove down the street following the Yaak River. It was a beautiful place. Steep, rugged evergreen mountains graced both sides of swift, clear, cold stream. They turned onto River Avenue. Sister pointed toward the river, "That is where the Yaak Office used to sit. Over there is the bridge. That used to be the ferry dock. The B&B is just down two streets."

They turned into the parking lot of the B&B and stopped at the office. Jeff came around the car and opened the door for Sister. The blue door of the office opened before they got to it. A tall, middle-aged man engulfed sister in a huge embrace. He reached over and shook Jeff's hand, "I'm Elias. You must be Jeff. I'm so pleased to make your acquaintance! I was worried about the roads, but Father Vicaro said Half Pint, er. I mean Sister, was good hands."

Jeff liked this man with the frosty-colored hair and big grin, "I was in good hands with Half Pint!"

"She is very capable, no doubt. I have your keys here. Let's go get you settled and then we can have dinner. I hope you are hungry. The wife has been cooking up a storm!"

Dinner with Elias and his wife Betty was fun and delicious. She had made pot roast, potatoes, carrots and apple pie. The conversation started on the weather, but soon moved to their times at Yaak Camp.

"Sister and I were wondering if it is possible to get up to the cemetery?" Jeff asked.

"It is. I may not have explained it all to you Sister, but it was never neglected. Cook, Ink Slinger, Campbells and Rudners all felt it necessary to preserve it. When Yaak Lumber sold out, Rudner bought the acreage around the cemetery. When he passed away, he transferred it to me. The rest had all left me money for my schooling and such, but I didn't need most of it. So, I put it in a trust for the operation and maintenance of the site. They were all buried there except Rudners. The road used to be nightmare, but last year, we put in better road."

Jeff asked, "Could we make it up there now?"

"It would be muddy, but yes. I have the Jeep. We can do it in the morning, but I thought you were going to Dahlgren?"

"We are, but on the way home, we would love to go up there. Right, Sister?"

Sister bit her bottom lip, "I think I really would. I've never been back there. I would love to pay my respects."

"We will plan on it." Elias stated, "You just let me know when you want to do it."

"You are a saint," Sister smiled.

"Don't say that in front of Betty. She might have a few things to say!"

After a nice breakfast at the dining room of the B&B, Elias filled their thermos. "I have never seen a thermos so big!"

Jeff laughed, "You have to come out to visit in Merton, then you would understand. Those people really love their coffee!"

"We would like to do that. We almost made it last summer, but you know our season is very short here. We get a lot of hunters in the fall, but after that the weather is ugly!"

"Christmas there was wonderful. I was there last year and it was a lot of fun. We had an igloo and all kinds of stuff! I hope you can try to make it."

"Thanks Jeff, we will try."

It was cloudy and blustery when they headed north to Dahlgren. Sister had barely said a word since they got in the car. When they passed a sign saying 'Dahlgren—2 miles', Jeff pulled over on a turnout. Sister gave him a funny look. "Is there something wrong?"

"I don't know. Is there? Sister, I'm going to give you the what for. You aren't allowed to do this! First, you are a Sister and you know your Lord better than most. If you have faith in Him, show it! You know the saying, 'If He be for you, who can be against you?' You can't be a wimp. And second, you owe it to Half Pint to show your grit. If you start to act like you are afraid, I'll whop you! You have nothing to be ashamed of, you live a good life and you are going to see your dying mother. Don't crawl into a shell. Now, do you understand me?"

Sister gave him a dirty look. Then she shrugged, "You are right. Would you mind having a word of prayer with me?"

The two sat in the Mercury on a turnout of a mountain road saying a prayer. When they were finished, Sister nodded, "Thank you, Jeff. I needed that."

Jeff smiled as he turned on the blinker, "The threat or the prayer?"

Sister laughed, "I think those two go hand in hand more often than we acknowledge."

"I believe you're right."

They drove down the main thoroughfare of Dahlgren. It was a tiny village, about a third the size of small Yaak. They easily found the Nystrom Trucking Company owned by Swan's husband. Jeff ran into the shop and asked where to find the family.

He returned to the car. About a block further, he pulled up in front of a tall, home with a verandah across the front surrounded by massive willows and a weathered picket fence. He looked at Sister and grabbed her hand. "This is for Half Pint. Let's go."

They walked up the steps and as they got on the verandah, the door opened. There stood a beautiful young woman. She had bright blue eyes, pink cheeks and white-cream colored hair. Jeff quit breathing and Sister gave him a grin. He looked at her and cleared his throat, as the young lady said, "Welcome. I'm Kathleen, Brigit's daughter. You must be my aunt, Sister Abigail."

Sister smiled and introduced Jeff, "Hello Kathleen, this is my dear friend, Jeff Wilson."

"Are you a priest? Father Wilson?"

"No, I'm just a Jeff."

A voice from behind the girl, said, "Invite them in, Kathleen."

"Oh, I'm sorry. Come in," she backed and ushered them in. "The family is gathered in the dining room. Can I get you some coffee?"

The couple sat at the dining room table and were introduced all around. Then Sister asked, "How is Mother doing?"

"She is slowly failing a bit more every day," Albert Nystrom answered. "The doctor was worried if she could hang on until you arrived. We told her you were coming, and she seemed determined to see you. Do you want to see her now?"

"Let her finish her coffee, Albert," Swan said. Then she frowned, "I didn't know that nuns could drive around the country with men who weren't priests."

"This is special circumstances," Jeff answered thinking that her question was a bit strange.

"Oh. I thought they were supposed to be above reproach."

Jeff responded, "I don't know what you do when you travel to see an ailing relative, but I assure you, our trip was above reproach."

Kathleen frowned at Swan and then Brigit, Kathleen's mother, said, "Well, I'm glad you didn't have to travel alone."

"Thank you, Brigit. Jeff was a dear to drive me."

Swan rolled her eyes and Albert almost snorted.

Kathleen intervened, "Cap and Virginia are coming in when they get their chores done. They should be here soon. My dad had to take a load of hay into the valley, but he will be back. Uncle Ollie will be here by noon."

"How is Oliver?"

"He is good, and anxious to see you."

"Well, I have finished this coffee, so if you show me the way, I'll go visit Mother."

Albert stood, "She is at the top of the stairs, first door to the right. I will go in with you."

Sister turned to Albert and said definitely, "Jeff will come with me."

Albert frowned, "Mother doesn't even know him."

"No," Sister smiled, "But I do."

Jeff and Sister went up the wide staircase. The house was an older, but well-built home. It was gorgeous and the furnishings were lavish.

At the door, they hesitated before opening the door. There was a man in his early forties sitting by the elderly patient. He stood and extended his hand to Sister, "Hello. I'm Swan's son, Christopher."

"Hello Christopher. I've met you before, but you were just a baby then."

"And this is?"

"My friend, Jeff Wilson."

"Hello Jeff," he shook his hand and then said to Sister, "Grandmother is sleeping, but I'm sure she'd like you to wake her. Her vision is terrible, but she can hear well. I'll let you be alone. Need anything, I'll be right outside."

He went out of the room and carefully closed the door behind him. Jeff asked Sister, "Would you like me to leave?"

"No, please stay."

Jeff stood at the end of the bed. Sister sat down and leaned ahead. She took her mother's hand and said, "Mother, it is me. Leisel."

The lady's eyebrows slightly flinched and then Sister repeated her statement. This time, her mother opened her eyes and looked at Sister in doubt.

Sister explained, "You may have forgotten that I became a nun. I am Leisel. Your daughter."

"I can't see very well. I'm waiting for my daughter, Leisel." The elderly lady squinted at her, "I don't know you."

Sister looked to Jeff, "I don't think she'll recognize me with my veil."

Jeff thought, "Take it off, Sister. I can hold it for you and you can put it back on before we leave the room."

Sister took it off and Jeff held it. Jeff lent her his comb and she combed her short hair. She sat down again. "Now do you recognize me, Mother?"

"You look like my Leisel. You have that cowlick in your bangs like my Leisel. Are you her?"

"Yes. I am, Mother. I'm Leisel. Swan said that you wanted to see me, so I came."

"I waited for you. Leisel, I have something extremely important to tell you. I should have done it years ago, and I was afraid. I worried I wouldn't have time. I should have stood up for you when Father made you leave. I was wrong. We should've never made you leave," her mother said between tears and heavy breaths.

"That is long over, Mother. No need to worry. I understand you not wanting to stand up to Father."

"No, you don't. You don't know. You see, I didn't want you to marry Otto, but Father couldn't go back on his word to him."

"I know, Mother."

"I couldn't let you marry Johann either! You see long ago, Father and I were having troubles. We didn't get along at all. Father was cavorting around and I was very angry."

"Don't worry, Mother. There is nothing for you to apologize over."

"But there is. I never knew who Father was running with, but I wanted to hurt him. I decided to make him jealous with a married man. Leif Lohgren, Johann's father. After I did it, I became frightened, especially when I discovered I was in a family way. You couldn't marry Johann. Don't you see? He was your brother! If I had told you, Father would have killed me. I was a coward."

Sister didn't move but was transfixed. After a pause, Jeff came beside her and took her arm. "Can you say something to your mother? She apologized to you."

"Ah, do you think she knows what she is saying?"

"Who is that?" Mother asked.

"Hello, I am Leisel's friend, Jeff. I didn't mean to intrude, but I brought her here. She is quite stunned by the news you gave her. Are you certain of it?"

"I am. Father was not her father. Leif Lohgren was."

Sister asked, "Mother, did Father know?"

"No, never! He'd have killed me. After I did it, I was afraid. I purposely slept with Father so he wouldn't know. When I was pregnant, I guess he decided to be a family man. He never strayed again."

Then the patient was crying and began to cough, Jeff helped her sit up and handed the veil, coif and bandeau back to Sister. "You might want to replace them before the others come in."

Sister did while Jeff talked to her mother. "Leisel has to fix her hair. You know, she wears a veil as part of her religious faith."

"What is that?" he mother frowned.

"She is a Catholic," Jeff answered. "Her name in Sister Abigail now."

"Her name is Leisel. It is a good name," the lady repeated and then began to cough again.

Sister was just finishing with her veil, when Jeff went to the door. He turned to Sister, "You okay? Can I call Christopher?"

"Yes," Sister said as she sat down by her mother, trying to help her control her cough.

Jeff went to the hall and motioned for Christopher, "I tried to get her readjusted to help her stop coughing, but it didn't work."

"I'll help you."

The two men got the patient settled down. Then Sister took her mother's hand again. "Mother, I'm glad you told me. Don't worry about it at all. I'll never tell anyone and I do not hold any of it against you."

"Thank you. I'm so sorry I never told you that Father wasn't your real father. No one can ever know that Leif Lohgren was your real father. Will you forgive me?"

"Of course. You are forgiven," Sister hugged her mother, and held her while they both cried.

The elderly lady was soon able to pull herself together, "Thank you so much, my Leisel. I must rest now."

Christopher listened to his grandmother and then gave Jeff a quizzical look and a thoughtful grimace. When her mother closed her eyes, Sister stood and said, "Jeff, I really think I'd like to go for a walk. Christopher, could you stay with her?"

"Of course. Is everything okay?" he said as he walked them to the door. "Look, I know there was a scandal, but I never heard what it was. If you want a place to talk in private away from prying ears, go to my camper. It isn't much, but it is nearby. Here are the keys. It is the one behind the green Chevrolet. There might be some soda in the fridge. Help yourself."

Jeff smiled, "Thank you Christopher. We will take you up on that."

"Call me Chris."

"Thanks, Chris. I think Sister could use a break."

Chris nodded, "I would think so."

The two went down the steps and at the bottom, Jeff said, "Do you want to tell them we are going for a walk?"

"Not really," Sister said.

"Don't blame you," Kathleen smiled as she came up behind them. "These guys tend to be a bit stiff about things. I'll tell them you needed some fresh air. Want your jacket, Jeff?"

"Thank you, Kathleen."

Outside, they walked over to the camper without a word. Jeff unlocked the door and folded down the steps. Then he helped Sister up the narrow little steps. Inside, she sat down and he went to the fridge, "He has some Cola and Seven Up in here. Which would you like?"

"Either." Sister said, "Do you think she knows what she was talking about?"

Jeff returned with the sodas, "Yes. She seems weak but very lucid. I think she knew exactly what she was saying."

"You know what that means, don't you?"

"That your parents were both philandering?"

"No,—well, yes; but it means that Johann wasn't my brother. If the man who was my father was not his father but my father, then we weren't related."

Jeff sat down across from her with an odd look on his face. He couldn't help it and started to chuckle, "I think that is right! He wasn't your brother!"

Sister wasn't laughing, "That means we could have married! Probably if everyone had known this on that long ago yesterday, it would have made a difference. It really doesn't now."

Jeff took her hand, "Honestly Sister, I'm glad you didn't marry him. Even if each of your parent's think the other is or isn't the other parent, it would be difficult for any of them to really know. It sounds like they were pretty busy!"

"That is true. I wonder which story Johann heard? That I was his sister by his mother or by his father?" then she started to giggle. "This is horrid!"

She sat quietly a minute before she said, "Jeff, you know they were both willing to let me suffer for their bad behavior. Not very commendable. I feel I was summoned more for their sake than mine."

"Look, that doesn't matter. She wanted to come clean and she did. Unless you can explain to me otherwise, it is up to you to forgive her."

Sister wagged her head, "I know. I can forgive her. My goodness, she has had to live with it for a long time, as did Father. Those two were more alike than even they realized. What a crazy situation."

"If I may ask, what is with Albert and Swan? Everyone else seems nice, but they are a bit standoffish."

"Swan has always felt that it was something that I did when I was told to leave. After I was gone, she felt sorry for Mother and Father for all I put them

175

through. She always thought she was superior and that confirmed it in her mind. Albert just goes along with her. Of course, from what Cap says, once he started making a lot of money, it went to his head."

"What faith are they?"

"I never heard. I expected them to be that way, however. Chris was nice and I saw you quit breathing when you saw Kathleen. I thought I might have to resuscitate you!"

"She is beautiful," Jeff agreed. "And she seems nice, too. I quite liked Brigit."

They both nearly jumped out of their skin when there was a knock at the camper door. Jeff opened it to a shivering Kathleen, "May I disturb you? Chris told me where you were."

"Sure," Jeff said as he took her hand to boost her up the step. He scanned the weather, "Is it snowing?"

"Sleet. Wet and cold," Kathleen said as she gave Sister a hug. "Chris told me that he offered you a place to regroup after seeing Grandmother. He said it was quite traumatic but he was also very cryptic. All he would say is that all these years, his Mom had been all wet! Most of us knew that, years ago! I'm sorry, that wasn't very nice. I'm rather frustrated because I have been trying to keep Mom from plucking Swan's tail feathers! After this last go round, I decided to let her have at it."

"What happened, if I may ask?" Jeff said as he sat next to her.

"Oh, Albert made some crack about leaving you two with Mother because you might upset her. Then when you went outside, I went up to check on Chris. He and I were visiting and Grandmother woke with one of her coughing attacks, no more than she has done before. He sent me down to get some hot tea for her, and Albert and Swan immediately were convinced you went in to start a row with her! They both charged upstairs like the Light Brigade! Chris told them that was nonsense. He said that if anyone upset anyone, it was the other way around. Then Aunt Swan went into a total nosedive because you weren't there. I told her you just stepped outside to get some fresh air and I'd come get you. So, here I am."

Sister smiled, "Oh my, it looks like there's a bridge in need of repair! I'll go in."

Jeff started to get up and Sister winked, "No. You young folks sit and let us work this out. It's our mess, we should fix it."

Jeff smiled and opened the door for Sister. "If you need me, say the word."

He went back and sat across from Kathleen, "I can offer you one of Christopher's sodas. He has Seven Up or Coke."

"Thank you. I'd like a Seven Up. I'll thank Chris later." Then she looked toward the house, "Whatever could that generation have going on that is such a mystery."

Jeff had a real big laugh, "Kathleen, sin hasn't changed since the beginning of time. No matter where, when or how; humans manage to foul things up. Then the very next thing they do is try to cover it up! It is amazing. I will tell you this; your aunt is one fine person."

"I can tell you really like her."

"I have a lot of respect for her. She is a good soul and a lot of fun besides."

"Sounds like a fine recommendation." Then she studied him a minute, "So, what does 'a Jeff' do when he isn't driving folks to see their dying relatives?"

Jeff chuckled, "I'm between jobs just now. I start at a state reformatory in North Dakota in a few weeks. I had a job in New Mexico, but I left it earlier than anticipated because the counselor I was filling in for returned from his stint with the National Guard early."

"Lucky for Sister and us," Kathleen smiled. "I imagine your job is quite interesting. I don't know if I could work with juveniles. I have enough problems counseling adults."

"You are a counselor?" Jeff asked, and then crossed his eyes. "Stupid question! Like you just go up to unsuspecting adults in a supermarket!"

"I tried that, but got pelted with tomatoes!" She laughed, "I work with county counseling facility in Kalispell. All my patients are adults."

"Kids are more bendable. Adults have pretty well set their patterns, while there is a better chance with the young ones. I quite like teenagers."

"I bet they like you."

"Well, I was never bombarded with tomatoes! Although, there was a nasty incident with bubble gum once!" Jeff laughed and then looked toward the house. "How long does the doctor think it will be for your Grandmother? Did he say?"

"Any time. She has metastatic cancer in her bones and this pneumonia looks like it will be the exit disease. She waited for Leisel to come. Now, she may feel she can go in peace. I suppose I should go in and pick up the remains of my kin, uh?"

"Are you finished with your soda?"

"Yes, I'm a guzzler," Kathleen smiled displaying her sweet dimples.

Without thinking, Jeff said, "You have a very nice smile."

Kathleen got up and said, "Thank you. You do, too."

Chris was just coming out to get them when they came up the steps. Kathleen asked, "How bad is it?"

"Mom has her ego so blown up, it's a good thing we have a roof on the house! She was all over Sister for upsetting Grandmother. Then I told her that she was wrong. All wrong. She went ballistic. Good thing I work in the mines, because I'm used to that kind of language! Mom's façade of the demure, delicate lady of the manor went right down the old tubes! Then she demanded that Sister or I tell her what Grandmother wanted to talk to her about. Sister wouldn't answer and I didn't feel it was my place. I decided to get the heck out of there while the getting was good. Brigit is up with Grandmother and Sister is trying to calm the others. Jeff, I think Sister should just tell them! That would tip their canoe in deep water!"

Jeff shook his head, "Sister would have my hide!"

"You know, sometimes things need to be out in the open."

"I know, but Sister gave her word to both of her parents. So she won't."

Chris got a quizzical expression, "You mean Grandfather knew?"

"Ah, I said too much. Let's just say there are many ripples in the stream."

"What exactly did happen when Leisel left home?" Chris asked. "All I ever heard is that Leisel was misbehaving."

"I know what happened that day, but obviously not the background details," Kathleen said. "Mom and Uncle Cap told me. I will tell you in the camper, because I'm freezing out here. Are you coming, Jeff?"

"No, I promised Father Vicaro I'd watch out for Sister. I should at least check on her."

Inside the hall, Jeff heard coughing from upstairs and yelling from the kitchen. He said a quick 'Our Father' before he headed down the hallway toward the kitchen. When he came through the archway, Albert glared at him. "This is private, family business. You have no place here."

"It is up to Sister. If she wants me here, I'll stay."

Sister bit her lip and the tears started to fill her eyes, "I think we should leave. I'm sorry we came. This isn't my home."

Jeff was mad, instantly. He turned to Albert, "How can you be so unkind? That woman is her mother! How do you have the right to go against Mrs. Haldoran's very own wishes! She requested that she come."

"Because she upset Mother," Swan said, smugly. "Leisel always was upsetting to Mother. This is just her last chance to get a jab in."

Then Sister started to cry and Jeff put his arms around her. "Okay, we'll go. Do you want to tell your Mother goodbye?"

Albert threw a fit. "She is not allowed to speak anymore to Mother. She has hurt her enough!"

"Like bloody hell," a voice bellowed into the kitchen.

It was Cap. He was livid. He sent his wife, Virginia upstairs and asked that she send Brigit down. He took charge, "We are having a meeting, here and now!"

"This is my house, Cap. You have no right," Albert started to say.

"What are you going to do about it? It is about time this is settled, for once and for all. Chris and Kathleen are on their way in with Oliver. Some of us have things that need to be said, so the whole family hears it. Now, sit down and act like a responsible person."

Albert sat down but never stopped glaring at Cap. A minute later, the others came in and Chris introduced Oliver and Cap to Jeff. There were nods all around and then Cap said, "Okay. This all goes back to when Leisel left. I can tell you that everything was fine, until Leisel said that Johann had asked her to marry him. Father went bezerk and grabbed the whip. He beat Leisel and threw her in the woodshed until she would promise to marry that Otto Amundsen. Isn't that right?"

Sister nodded yes. Then Cap turned to Brigit, "That's what happened, right?"

"Yes."

Swan was very haughty, "Well it was her fault! She should have married Otto!"

"Father and Mother didn't make you marry him! You should have. He wanted to marry you first!" Brigit retorted.

"I would never marry anyone like him!" Swan ruffled indignantly, aghast at the idea. "He was disgusting!"

Oliver shook his head, "But Leisel should have? Listen to yourself, Swan. You don't even make sense."

Then she sat down and frowned, "Well, no. I don't blame her for that. Otto was a horrible person. But she must have been dallying with Johann for Father to be that angry! He always liked Johann."

Sister's tears started again. Chris cleared his throat, "Dammit. I think you should tell them!"

"Maybe she doesn't have to," Cap said. "I have a confession to make. When Father wrote that note to Leisel before he died, he asked me to mail it without reading it. I made it halfway to Dahlgren. But Leisel, Johann and I were best friends and they were both gone. I couldn't stand not knowing why. So, I read it."

Sister turned to him in shock, "You never said anything. No, Cap. Don't repeat it."

Albert was almost in glee, "Yes, do! Now we'll finally find out what exactly Leisel did to cause all this distress in the family."

Chris just rolled his eyes, "You are so impossibly stupid!"

"No, I am going to tell. It is long past time. Father wrote to apologize to Leisel. He said that he couldn't allow her to marry Johann, because Johann was his own son. He had slept with Mrs. Lohgren!"

Swan almost passed out and Albert didn't know what to do. But Chris grabbed his head and yelped, "My god, I can't believe it!"

"Why not?" Cap asked. "Don't you believe me?"

"I heard what Grandmother said to Leisel! She said she never stopped Grandfather from kicking her out because she'd an affair with Leif Lohgren. Leisel is his daughter!"

Oliver rolled his eyes, "Even my wildest shore leave was never this bad! I can't believe that I thought that old couple was so straight-laced! Well, I for one want to tell you Sister, that I always thought you were cool. I'd like to apologize on behalf of this pack of idiots for all the years you suffered for something you had no control over." Then Ollie hugged his sister, "So, that

181

is why Johann took off too, huh? They had a regular little wife-swapping ring going!"

"Oliver, I won't have you speaking that way about our beloved parents," Swan screeched.

Chris turned to her with a frown, "Oh Mom, gag me! We can still love them, but I think you were the only one who thought they walked on water. They were people. Real people. I think you should try being real once in a while!"

"Well, I never!"

"Nope, you sure never did while I was around! Try it once, you might like it."

Chris shook his head, "I'm going out to my camper and have a beer. Anyone care to join me?"

"I don't want a beer, but coffee sounds good," Oliver said.

Albert stood, "No. There is more room in the house. You're all welcome to stay in here, have your beer and relax. In fact, a beer sounds good to me, too. I want to apologize for both us. I guess we just didn't look at things from every angle. Leisel, I'm so sorry."

"I think we should all put this behind us," Cap said. "I have to say I was as bad as the folks. I should have said something years ago, but I didn't want anyone to know I read the letter!"

Before long everyone was visiting and though still strained, the air was beginning to clear. Swan offered sandwiches to everyone, and Jeff volunteered to make them. Chris and Kathleen helped and soon, they had a fine lunch on the table. Everyone ate and then Oliver and Cap did dishes.

Jeff could see that Sister was worn out and asked her if she wanted to go for a walk. "No, I think I'll go sit with Mother so Virginia can have a break. I'm fine, really. Then we should probably be heading back to Yaak for the night."

"Nonsense," Swan said. "We have plenty of room. No need for you to go all the way to Yaak. Brigit's husband should be here soon with their sons. They are staying at Caps, but Kathleen and Oliver can stay here, too."

"Are you certain?" Jeff asked. "I don't want to impose."

"You aren't imposing one bit. You will stay, both of you."

"Thank you," Jeff said. "I need to call Yaak to tell them we won't need the rooms for tonight. Is there a phone at the Mercantile?"

"I'll call," Sister said. "I'd be glad to pay for the call, Albert."

"Don't be silly. Just call from here," Albert stated.

Oliver and Cap went out with Jeff to bring their bags in. Cap smiled at him, "I'm glad you are here for Leisel. This must have been a fright for her."

"She is a strong lady," Jeff said sincerely. "I'm glad it is out in the open. That sort of thing just causes a lot of unnecessary hurt."

After the bags were inside, Jeff was restless. Folks were talking about the prices of timber and ore and he was trying to maintain an interest in the conversation. He felt a tap on his elbow, "Could I talk you into going for a walk with me? I'll give you a tour of our fine city!" Kathleen asked.

"Let me tell Sister and I will be right there."

They headed down the steps of the big verandah and Jeff stopped, "Which way first?"

"Oh, flip a coin. City limits is twenty feet that way or twenty-five feet the other!" Kathleen smiled as she pulled her mittens on. "It is not warm out here."

Jeff folded his jacket collar up around his neck, "No. Maybe we should hail a cab!"

Kathleen laughed, "Good idea! Let's go this way."

They started to walk toward the southwest along the road. There were no sidewalks, or road marks. There was a 'slow' sign when you entered Dahlgren. That was it. The 'city' was built on one bank of the rapidly flowing river. The other side was a sheer drop of mountain down to the water's edge. On the city side were about seven homes and a few businesses along the stretch. One was the Mercantile that Sister had told about where she attended school. Then there was the trucking company, a post office, gas station, school and a taxidermist.

The couple walked the whole distance and was almost back in less than fifteen minutes. In front of the Mercantile, Jeff suggested that he stop and buy some sodas for Chris.

"Good idea, I'll get some too and help you carry it back," Kathleen offered.

They came out of the Mercantile carrying the sodas and passed the taxidermist. Jeff noticed the stuffed heads in the window and commented, "He must stuff game animals."

"Yes, we get a lot of hunter's here in the fall. He butchers, too."

"I've never been in rugged mountains like this before. I spent a lot of time in Boston. Those hills are very tame by comparison."

"Ah, that is the accent I heard. Were you born there?"

"No, I was born in New Mexico," he grinned. "When I got to Boston, I could hardly understand a thing anyone said! You should hear the Mainers. I still have trouble understanding them!"

"Did you go to school out there?"

"Yes." Jeff felt his mouth go dry.

He knew he had to explain his situation, but he was really taken with this girl and didn't want to take a chance she would run like the wind. He debated about whether it was worth saying anything. He may never see her again and it really wouldn't matter. But then, they just went through a big deal about how secrets were not good. As he was cataloging a list of excuses and debunking them one at a time, she had stopped walking. He turned to see what happened and noticed her expression.

"What is it, Jeff? I didn't mean to pry. You certainly owe me no autobiography. I was just talking."

"No, I should tell you. I just haven't had to tell anyone I met socially before. So, I don't know quite how to go about it." He felt sick at how uncool he sounded even to himself.

Kathleen wasn't taken back, however. She gave him a warm smile, "Okay. I'll be your guinea pig. You just blurt it out and we can work on refining it later. That is, unless you are a heinous criminal. Then I think we should just go back to the house without another word."

Jeff could have hugged her; he was so relieved. His deep brown eyes twinkled as he said, "We better get back to the house in short order then!"

"You are a weird one, Mr. Wilson."

"I never learned your last name. Just your first."

"I don't like to give that out to the regular run-of-the-mill heinous criminal."

"Probably a wise plan. Yes, I went to college there. I became a Roman Catholic priest in Boston."

Kathleen was visibly disappointed but said, "Oh, is that how you met Sister?"

"Yes and no. My best friend and I were both priests in Boston. His name is Matthew Harrington. We both had our own parishes and were quite settled

185

in our chosen vocations. Then another priest moved into the diocese. We soon became aware that he was a pedophile. We reported him repeatedly over the next year or so. The Bishop always said he was taking care of it, but very little was ever done. One of the young men he molested committed suicide and I counseled the family. I was livid. I talked to Matt and we went to the Bishop, demanding something conclusive be done. He told us he was handling it and that we needed to accept his direction on the matter. We had become a thorn in his side. He warned us to keep quiet. I went ballistic and told him what I thought of his inaction. Needless to say, Matt and I were both given a suspension to think things over. Matt went to North Dakota for his brother's wedding. He wanted to think it over before he resigned. Me? I just got mad and told them to shove it. That was last summer."

"Oh that sounds awful. So, what happened then?"

"I went to New Mexico and worked there like I told you, while I waited for my petition from the Vatican. Matt stayed in North Dakota and tortured himself with his decision, but he resigned from the priesthood, too. He teaches high school in Merton."

"What happened to that pedophile?"

"He now has Matt's old parish. It still makes my blood boil. I'm not as generous as Matt. When I get mad, I get mad. I went to visit Matt this last Christmas, I heard of the job opening there at the reformatory. So I applied, and got the job. I'll be living with Matt's parents until I get myself grounded. There, now what do you think? How much fine-tuning does it need?"

She stopped walking and turned to him, "None at all. Honest, sincere and to the point. But I have a question?"

"Sure."

"If you are no longer a priest, how did Sister's Father Vicaro ask you to drive my aunt?"

"Because Father Vicaro is a neat human being and he told both Matt and I that he thought the Bishop has rocks in his head. We have become good friends."

"I think that creepy priest should be put away! Just so you know, Jeff Wilson, I am glad that you are with my aunt and also, that you are no longer a priest."

They caught each other's glance and were momentarily motionless, just lost in each other's gaze. Then he said, "So, what is your last name?"

"Finch."

Jeff chuckled and she frowned, "What's so funny about that? I never laughed at your name! I mean, Wilson isn't that special!"

"I apologize. I guess I was just prepared for some very long, difficult to pronounce Scandinavian name and Finch just surprised me. I like it: classical American. Kathleen Finch is a fine, reputable, upstanding name. It is a name you can be proud of."

She shook her head, and he grimaced, "Too much? Think I went a bit overboard?"

She raised her eyebrow and shook her head, "Just a tad."

A truck came down the road and slowed beside them. The driver yelled out, "You some of Nystrom's kin?"

"Yes," Kathleen nodded.

"Let Albert know the road is open to Rexford now. They cleared the bridge this afternoon. I know he was waiting to hear."

"Thank you," Kathleen yelled back. "I will tell him."

The truck drove off and Kathleen said, "That's a relief. Now the doctor can come out and we can get to Rexford if Grandmother passes away. The cemetery is there. Well, should we take the soda in or leave it in Chris' camper?"

"I would like to replace that we used in the camper. He can take it in, if he likes."

Kathleen nodded and set her six packs on the ground so she could knock. A minute later, the door opened. It was Chris. "Come in. I was just washing up."

"We brought you some soda to replace what we drank," Jeff smiled.

Chris looked at their load, "You didn't drink that much."

"We haven't left yet," Kathleen giggled.

"Why don't you leave one six pack of each here and take the rest in? That will give us a small stash of our own."

"How are things going in there?" Kathleen asked.

"They were talking about playing Monopoly when I came out. So, I guess things are pretty good until someone ups the rent on Park Place!"

The young couple left the sodas and took the rest back to the house. On the steps, Jeff said, "Thanks for the walk and for being so nice about my explanation."

"I enjoyed our walk. I would've liked it better if it was warmer out. Don't worry about your explanation. I could think of a lot worse things to learn about someone!"

Jeff squinted, "Have you got a story to tell?"

"Yes. Later, okay?"

"Okay."

Jeff was soon the banker in a hot game of Monopoly. Others took turns playing, watching Grandmother, visiting quietly or preparing food. Albert made arrangements for the doctor to come out from Rexford. He would arrive first thing in the morning.

Later Grant, Brigit's husband, came with his twenty-five year old twin sons, Garry and Larry. Grant said the road from Kalispell was getting slippery with the sleet, but the forecast was for things to clear up. "It will be a relief to not have to worry every time you get in a car. How were things coming out from North Dakota?" he asked Jeff.

They became involved in a conversation about weather, roads and then cars. "So, what do you do out in the Dakotas?"

"I am starting a new job as counselor at the state reformatory in a couple weeks," then Jeff felt his throat dry. He thought and then decided, 'No, I'm not explaining it all to everyone.'

He fidgeted and noticed Kathleen smiling at him. "Dad, he is a counselor, too. Isn't that neat?"

The older man nodded, "I guess it is. Just don't be delving into the crevices of my mind and we'll be okay."

"Deal," Jeff agreed.

Kathleen came over and gave her dad a hug, "No one wants in those ravines, believe me!"

Larry started to laugh, "Not without a safety line!"

"Very funny," Grant said. "I'm going to get some more coffee. Anyone want me to bring the pot?"

They all mumbled no and then Jeff got up and asked Kathleen, "Want some fresh air?"

She nodded yes and they slipped on their jackets. They went out into the yard and Jeff took a deep breath, "I love the smell of the pine. Sister said it is the best."

"I never paid any attention to it. I guess I was around it all my life."

"Did you live your whole life in the mountains?"

"Yes, and the Rockies at that. Not very worldly, huh?"

"Nothing wrong with blooming where you are planted." Jeff opened the picket fence gate, "Where to, Ma'am?"

"I don't know. Where do you want to go? We have seen everything unless you want to go watch Jasper stuff a bear or something?"

"No, I'll pass. Maybe tomorrow though, who knows? Let's go look at the river," he suggested.

"Okay, but we have to be careful. It is very deep as it comes through this narrow canyon and it is running pretty fast now."

"We don't need to look at it," Jeff shrugged. "It was just a suggestion. Do you want to do something else?"

"Like where, the shopping mall or the museum? Okay, the river it is!"

They walked past the Mercantile and turned on an overgrown path toward the river. "There used to be a log bench over by the bank before the last flood. I don't know if it washed away."

"Does it flood here often?"

"Yes, frequently. It depends on the snowmelt. There is no place for the water to go really, but over the bank on this side. Be careful because this path isn't very level."

He followed behind her as she walked through the underbrush, stepping gingerly to find a safe place for her steps. Her delicate frame and nimble steps reminded him of a woodland fairy. He couldn't remember ever being so attracted to someone before. She was lovely and he was mesmerized. He stopped and watched her.

She went ahead a few steps and noticed he wasn't following her. She turned and shook her head, "Are you ogling me?"

He felt his face burn with embarrassment and he gulped, "I didn't mean to. It was so rude. It is just that I think you are beautiful."

The words no more than left his lips and he was totally mortified. He didn't know what to do. "Kathleen, I'm so sorry. I never meant to offend you."

"No problem," she said as she reached out to take his hand. "Let's see if the bench is here, okay?"

They went another ten feet. Last year's dead brush got thicker and the ground was softer. He was about to suggest they just go back, when she said, "Oh, finally. Here it is! A little dirty, but at least it is here! My goodness," she looked around, "Hard to believe this would be anyone's destination. We have arrived."

"It may be a wonderful destination!" Jeff took a branch and used it as a broom to brush off some dust, and they sat down. He looked at the raging river, no more than twenty feet across. They both looked straight ahead at the river a couple minutes, "Yup, it is a raging river, alright."

Kathleen giggled, "It certainly is . . . . Raging."

"Clear, though. I will give it that."

"Yup, you can see the bottom, but don't go look because the bank is so soft it might give way."

After a minute, Jeff cleared his throat, "Kathleen, I want to apologize for—staring."

"Don't worry about it. A girl likes to have a good-looking guy look."

"Ogle?"

"Well no, not ogle, but you weren't ogling. I hope no one can hear us!" she laughed.

He loved her soft laugh, "Me, too. But I think we are safe. There probably aren't too many watching the lights dance across Moon River!"

"No, not likely. This is like a forest from a Grimm Fairy tale, minus the troll under the bridge." She looked around and then sighed, "I grew up in Eureka, east of Rexford, a sprawling metropolitan city with a population of about a thousand if you count the ground squirrels! I graduated and went to college in Bozeman. I got a great job in Missoula. Then I got this job in Kalispell. It is an okay job. That is the exciting story!"

"May ask why you left the job in Missoula if it was great?"

"Oh, there was this coworker. He seemed like a nice man. He was married and had a couple little kids. He asked me out and I turned him down. Then he turned ugly. He started making passes, which before long were grabs. I got mad and told him if he kept it up, I would report him to the boss. He was furious. A couple nights later, I was out with friends, and my apartment was ransacked. I told Dad and he told me to get out of there. So, I moved back home. Then I found the job in Kalispell and I live with Mom and Dad."

"Has he bothered you since? Was he the guy that broke in?"

"I don't know. They police never found out who broke in. Probably it was a coincidence. Anyway, it has been seven months, so I think he has forgotten all about it. I'm glad it is over, but I have to admit, it scared me. Now, I'm twenty-six and live at home with Mommy and Daddy like a big baby."

"I think it was a wise move. You are being careful. That is good," Jeff surmised. "There is nothing wrong with living at home, as long as you are content."

"Oh, don't think that means I'm content. It only means that I'm not very adventurous."

"Not everyone needs to chop their way into the wilderness. It is good that there are folks who keep the old homestead humming."

"I guess that's me. The homestead hummer."

"Hey, why don't you come out to visit in Merton on your next vacation? I know Sister would love it and so would I. I could show you our big city! It takes ten minutes to go through Merton by car!" He pointed out very pompously.

"Oh my! Think I could handle that?"

"I'll go with you so you don't get lost." Then he got more serious, "My friend Matt is getting married this summer. It would be nice if you could come to the wedding. They are having a barn dance afterward. I've never been to one, but I hear they are really fun. If you come, then you could be my date. I mean, if you wanted to go to the dance with me."

She got a playful grin, "Are you asking me on a date in North Dakota?"

"I guess I am. I don't know the wedding date is yet, but I would have Sister let you know."

"Or you could call me and tell me yourself. That would be even easier."

"I guess it would." Then he looked straight at her, "I didn't handle this very well, did I?"

She laughed softly, "Seems to me like you are doing alright."

"Does that mean you will come?"

"It only means that I will try to come. It depends on how long I spend here and then when the wedding is and if I can get the time off. Besides, you might never call me."

"I'm pretty sure I will call."

"Okay, then I'm pretty sure I'll see if I can go to this barn dance!"

"Should I call information and ask for Kathleen Finch?"

"Watch how you say Finch! I will give you my number. I suppose I can find out yours from Sister."

"I'll give it to you when we get back to the house. Thanks, Kathleen."

"You're welcome." She watched his expression, "You haven't asked anyone out in a while, have you?"

"No, does it show?"

"I think you did a wonderful job. It is just that I've never had anyone thank me for saying I would go out with them."

"They should have, you know."

They sat and watched the river for a while and then it started to rain.

Jeff shivered, "It is getting very dark and cold here. Are you sure there are no trolls?"

Kathleen giggled, "Maybe, but did you bring cookie crumbs?"

"No, why?"

"Isn't that what you feed them to make them go away?"

He shook his head, "What kind of fairy tales do you read? The crumbs are so folks can come to the rescue right before the witch throws you in the oven!"

"Huh?" Kathleen laughed, "I take it you are ready to make our way back to humanity. I think Aunt Swan said she had something in the oven for dinner."

Jeff made a face, "Suddenly, I'm not very hungry."

They brushed off the muddy, musty leaves and started back. Jeff took her hand and they almost ran back to the house to get out of the sleet.

32

The evening was quiet. Family came in and out, taking turns visiting with Grandmother. Jeff took a turn sitting with her so the others could have dinner together. When the elderly lady wasn't coughing uncontrollably, she mostly slept, or drifted in and out of consciousness. It was obvious that her cough was no longer clearing out her lungs. When Chris came to relieve him, Jeff talked to him about it.

"It looks to me like it might not be much longer. She is beginning to develop that rattle in her chest. Does she have a minister that she would like called in?"

Chris looked over at his Grandmother, "There is no church in Dahlgren. She never went to church that I knew of, but let me ask my folks. Do you think that Sister could maybe do something?"

Jeff looked at him, "Her own minister would be better. Let me talk to Sister and you talk to your folks."

A few minutes later, Chris came back. "Mom said that Grandmother was baptized Catholic when she was a baby. Then her parents moved here from the old country and as far as anyone knows, they never went to church again. Grandfather had been a Pentecostal before he married Grandmother. So, I don't know what to say. My parents only go to church for weddings and funerals. They have no preference."

"You watch Grandmother and I'll go talk to Sister."

Jeff went down the hall and knocked on Sister's door. It was a few minutes before she answered and asked him in. "I was praying when you knocked. Maybe you were my answer."

"Actually, I came to you with a problem. But first, what can I help you with?"

"I feel so mixed up. I mean, it is good that everyone seems to have put all this business behind them, but honestly Jeff, I don't know if I have. I tried. I did forgive Mother, but you know, why did this happen? Why didn't Cap tell the others years ago so they wouldn't have fostered these feeling toward me all these years? Didn't they realize how hurt I was? I don't know if I should be angry, sad or just forget the whole thing."

Jeff sat on the chair by the dresser and Sister sat on the end of the bed. He thought a minute and said, "You obviously aren't able to forget it. If you could have, you wouldn't be wondering if you should. I guess you have to decide if it is worth spading up the garlic patch to find a sweet potato. What good would you get from hammering it out again? If you think that anyone could say something that would make up for all these years, then do it. If not, then you need to decide if the momentary satisfaction of telling someone they were jerks, is worth it."

Sister's face broke into a devilish grin, "If it was up to Half Pint, she would just sock them and get it over with!"

Jeff laughed, "No way am I going back to tell Father Vicaro I let you whack someone. You have to do that on your own time."

"Could you pray with me?"

"Sure, but before we do, I have something else. Your Mother is beginning to get a death rattle. It isn't going to be very long, I'm afraid. I talked to Chris about calling her minister, but he said that they didn't go to church. He went and talked to his folks and they said that when she was a baby, she was baptized Catholic in the old country. After they came here, they never went to any church."

"That is what I had heard. So, you are concerned because she will pass over without any one?"

"You know, I can still do the last rites in circumstances where there is no other priest available, but I don't know how your family would feel about it. Only Kathleen knows I was a priest. What do you think?"

"If it was up to me, I would just say do it. I do need to talk to them all about it first though."

After prayer, Sister went to talk to her family. Jeff chose to stay out of that discussion, so he sat with Grandmother while they talked. The whole time, the fragile lady slept and coughed.

Sister knocked and motioned for him to come to the door. "We talked and decided that we'd like to have you give her the Last Rites. I told them about that you could still act as a priest in incidents like this."

"How did they take that?"

"Oh, I had to explain everything, but Kathleen was very helpful. Father Vicaro sent his small bag that contains the anointing oil, holy water and communion wine. I'll go get it."

"Let me come with you. I need to pull myself together first. Sister, I haven't done this in a long time."

"Do you think you don't remember how?"

"No, I couldn't forget, but I'm . . . . nervous."

She patted his arm, "Come with, but I know you can do this. Maybe, Jeff, this is 'your reason'."

Jeff looked at her, "I just knew you were going to say that."

He went in alone and quietly gave Frida Haldoran the Last Rites. She did wake up enough to know what was going on and when they were finished, she said, "Thank God you were here. I was so afraid to die. I'm so glad I lived long enough to meet Leisel's son. She must be so proud of you. You are a fine grandson."

Then she fell asleep. Jeff sat there with tears rolling down both his cheeks. It took him more than a little bit to pull himself together before he could leave the room. He opened the door to find the hallway filled with family all looking at him expectantly. He smiled compassionately and said, "She has made her peace and is just waiting. I would like to talk to Sister in private, if I could. Someone should sit with Grandmother."

They walked down the hall and into Sister's room. She looked at him and said, "Why are you so upset, Jeff?"

He started to cry softly, "For that time, I wanted so much to be back to being a priest. I know I can't, but it just about killed me. I really loved it, you know?"

Sister embraced him, "I understand, but Jeff, you need to know that when it was really necessary, you still were. Right?"

"I guess, but it wasn't the same." Then he wiped his tears, "Know what she said when we finished praying?"

"What?"

"She said she was glad that she got to meet your son and that she thought you were proud of me," then he cried again.

This time, she hugged him and gave him a little laugh, "Well, she is right about that. I am very proud of you. Now, let's go see if we can get some tea?"

"Okay, Mom," he nodded. "Do I look like I have been bawling?"

"No. You are okay." Then she stopped and grinned, "Now is it because you wouldn't want Kathleen to think that you had been crying?"

"No, I wouldn't want anyone to think that. What are you getting at?"

"Oh I just happened to notice the spark between you two."

He stopped and turned toward her, "Sister, I have never been so attracted to anyone in my life! Does it show?"

"Not in a bad way. I think she is attracted to you, too. So, it is probably a good thing you are not a priest anymore."

"Sister Abigail! What are you saying?"

"You are such a dumbbell. Figure it out."

Most of the family had coffee or tea and then started heading off to bed, for their home or to the camper. The doctor was going to be there about sun up, but amazingly everyone seemed relieved that Grandmother had time to make peace with the Lord. Jeff noticed that Sister seemed more relaxed after their talk, too. He was glad for that.

Swan asked if he would sit with Mother while she took a bath. Then she would watch her. When she came to sit with her, he took the tea tray back to the kitchen. He set it on the counter without turning the lights on and headed back to the stairs. As he passed the living room, he heard soft crying. He stopped and listened to be certain before he asked, "Is someone there?"

"I am," Kathleen answered from the darkened room. "On the window seat."

Jeff walked over to the window seat. It was about four feet long and the seat part was about two feet wide with a soft cushion made to fit it. There were four arched windows with foot deep sills around them. He got over there but couldn't see her. She said, "I'm over here, on the sill."

He saw her and smiled. She had her hands around her knees and was squished up against the window, facing away from the room. "Tight fit?"

"Yah, tighter than it used to be." She said quietly, "I used to fit in here just right. Of course the last time I sat here, I was only ten."

"That could make a difference," he agreed. "Do you want to be alone?"

"Not really. I'm just feeling melancholy. I know that everyone seems to think that what Grandmother did was wrong. I mean to Leisel. It was, but I really loved Grandmother. I don't think she did the right thing either but I still loved her."

Jeff sat next to her on the window seat, "People we love do bad things. No one is bad all the time, and no one is good all the time. We have to love folks that are both. Loving someone doesn't mean you agree with every single thing they think or do. If we could only love perfect people, we'd all be very lonely."

"Jeff, when I die would I go to heaven? I have never been baptized and have only been inside a church a couple times in my whole life."

"I don't know," Jeff answered quietly. "I know what the churches say, but I don't know if God reads from the same hand book. Have you ever wondered about going to church?"

"Yes, since I have been older." She said still looking out the window, "I would be embarrassed now though because everyone else already knows what they are about. I don't want to feel like an idiot."

"Oh Kathleen, don't let that bother you! Some people don't go to church until they are eighty! There is no age limit. Find a good friend to visit church with, until you get used to it. If any church makes you feel bad because you haven't been there before, don't go back to that one. That is not what Jesus preached. When you come out to the dance, I'll go to church with you. You won't have to feel one bit silly."

"I'll just wait then. Or won't you want to go to the dance with me if I haven't gone to church?"

"Of course I want to go to the dance with you!" Jeff said. "You could pray about it, though."

"I don't know how to do all that gobble-de-gook praying stuff."

"Yes, you do. You just talk to God like if He was sitting here. He knows how you talk and He gets it. If you came at Him with the thous and beseeches, He might think you had been smoking the silly weed." He chuckled. "Just think to Him. I do that a lot."

Kathleen had been watching him with a smile, "You are sweet, you know that?"

Jeff smiled slightly, "May I ask you something?"

"Sure."

"Are those feet in your pajamas?"

She frowned, "Just about the time I think you are so nice, you come up with something like that! Yes, they are feet and they keep me warm! Got a problem with that?"

"No," Jeff laughed. "I guess I better not. I just think of kids having feet in their jammies."

"If you wake up with snow on your bed, you will be glad to have feet in your pajamas," she explained.

"Does that happen often? Waking up with snow on your bed?"

"I'm going to bed. I'm tired of talking to you." She turned to move her legs which were jammed into the window sill frame. "Ah—I think I need a bit of help. My leg is going into spasm and I'm stuck. But you better not laugh or I will sit here until morning."

He helped her twist out of the window sill and didn't laugh. Although, he did smile an awful lot. When she was finally standing up, he said, "Promise me you won't do that again. Okay?"

"I promise." She rubbed her calf muscle. "Now my leg hurts from the Charlie horse. I don't know why I did it. I guess because that is where I used to sit when I came to stay with Grandma. When I was real little, her cat used to sit on the other window sill. Anyway, thanks for helping me."

She looked him directly in the eye and he was captivated. He leaned forward and gave her a gentle kiss on the lips. "My pleasure."

Kathleen smiled and hugged him, "Mine, too."

The doctor rang the bell at five in the morning, but everyone was up. Those that had stayed at Cap's had been summoned and were there also. Grandmother's breathing had become very irregular and she was now

198

unconscious more than awake. He checked her and then came downstairs. "It will probably be within a couple hours."

A few minutes later, she had a very severe coughing attack. Swan was with her and she ran to the door to call everyone. Grandmother was gone by the time the family gathered around her. The doctor checked the time and made the declaration. Jeff led them in the Lord's Prayer. The doctor went down to call the funeral home and make arrangements. He said he would bring her body back to Rexford, if the men would help him put her in his station wagon. They did.

By noon, he had taken Grandmother. The room she used was put back in order. The family had a light lunch and then went to take naps.

Later that afternoon, the funeral home called and spoke to them about arrangements. They had a chaplain that would lead a small service at the funeral home before burial. They could do it the next day. Everyone decided it would the best.

That evening, Kathleen was very quiet while they were doing dishes. Jeff wanted to get outside for a bit because it was so nice out. He asked Kathleen if she would go for a walk with him. A few minutes later, they were closing the gate on the picket fence. "Where do you want to walk to?" she asked.

"Wherever you want to go," Jeff said as he took her hand. "I just had to get out of the house."

"I know people start to make me twitch after a while."

"Exactly." They walked a little way and then he said, "I'm sorry you lost your Grandmother. I'm sure you will miss her."

"Thanks, but I'm glad she doesn't have to be miserable anymore. I hope I die when I'm healthy, so no one is glad I'm gone."

Jeff chuckled, "Why would you die if you were healthy?"

"You know what I mean," Kathleen frowned. "I think you like picking on me."

"I do like teasing you, but I hope you know that I don't mean anything by it."

"I think you do mean something by it. You just like to get me wound up."

Jeff put his arm around her and gave her a hug, "Guilty as charged. I'll be good."

"For about five minutes!" She made a face and then laughed, "When are you heading back?"

"Sister said after the service tomorrow. We will drive back to Yaak for the night and then head home."

"I wish you lived nearer. North Dakota seems so far away and I'll probably never get to see you again."

"Why not? We have each other's phone numbers and addresses. You are going to try to come out for Matt's wedding. If you can't get off, I'll come out to see you. Okay?"

"Really? You would come see me?"

"If you can't bring the mountain to Mohammed, take Mohammed to the mountain." Jeff grinned. "Of course I will, if you want me to. I'm really glad I got to meet you."

"Me, too. I don't feel so bad then. Will Matt get married soon, do you think?"

"He was hoping in June. Is that too soon for you to get off work?"

"I have to check. Maybe I can just take off." Kathleen answered. "I will have to find out the particulars."

"I will call you as soon as I find out."

"Will you call me anyway? I mean, just to talk?"

"If you want me to, I'd really like that."

The next morning was a flurry of activity. Jeff packed their bags in the car and gassed up. Then he dressed in his suit and drove with the family in convoy to Rexford. Sister rode with Oliver and so Jeff would have driven alone, but Kathleen came up to the car. "Mind if I ride with you? I don't think I could take sitting between Garry and Larry all the way to Rexford. They drive me crazy."

"I would like that." Jeff smiled and opened the passenger door for her. He couldn't have been happier. "I was thinking about the barn dance last night after I went to bed. I've never been to one, but Matt said they do all kinds of waltzes, polkas and two steps. I don't know how to do anything but the twist."

Kathleen started to laugh and laughed so hard she got the hiccoughs. "I didn't think it was that funny!" Jeff blustered. "I suppose you know all those dances, huh?"

"Mom and Dad do. I'll have them teach me. Who's going to teach you?" she smirked.

"Don't you worry your pretty little head about it. I will have someone teach me. I will be a regular Fred Astaire when you come out."

"You don't have that much time."

"I have as much time as you do."

"You're right. What do folks wear to a barn dance?"

"I guess regular stuff you would wear to a wedding dance. I mean, they aren't going to be milking cows! I'm wearing a tux or suit, because I am one of the attendants."

Kathleen got very quiet, "Oh."

He looked at her, "Is something wrong?"

"I guess not. I just sort of imagined we would be guests together. I should have realized that you are one of his best friends, so you would be in the wedding party."

"Does it matter?"

"No, I just won't know anyone there."

"You know your aunt! Sister Abigail will be going to the wedding and the dance!"

"Really?"

"Really. And I know that bunch, no one would let you sit alone. In fact, I should worry because you will probably like them better than me."

"Will they make fun of my pajamas with feet in them?"

"Only if you wear them to the wedding!"

The service and burial was just family and a few close friends. There were probably only ten folks there who weren't family. The chaplain did a nice job. Sister sat with Oliver during the service and Jeff sat with Kathleen.

Jeff couldn't get over how he felt sitting next to her. She was beautiful, no doubt. Kathleen had short, thick cream-colored hair with bouncy curls with her true blue eyes and long, dark eyelashes. She was petite, but had a knock out figure. Jeff had never thought of what type of girl he preferred, until he saw her. He instantly decided he preferred her. She wore a navy blue suit with white pearls over a navy blue shell to the funeral. Her navy heels made her tall enough to come just to his chin. She couldn't have been more perfect. Jeff realized though, that it wasn't just that she was beautiful. She made him feel good. She seemed to truly enjoy his company, even when he was being clumsy. He loved that.

After the burial, the family said their goodbyes. Swan took pictures of everyone and they all promised to keep in touch and not let so many years go by before they got together again. Kathleen was going to ride back with Oliver. Jeff went up to her and gave her a hug. He whispered in her ear, "I enjoyed meeting you so much. I'll call when I get home."

"Please do." She gave him a small kiss on the cheek. "I'm looking forward to seeing you soon."

In the car, Sister couldn't wait to ask him, "Did I hear Kathleen say she would see you soon?"

Jeff smiled, "Yes you did, Old Eagle Ears."

"I think eagles have good eyesight. I didn't know they could hear very well." She teased, "Tell me about it."

"I shouldn't you know, but I'm dying to tell someone! I asked Kathleen to go to Matt's wedding dance with me. She said she will see if she can get off work."

"Oh Jeff, that is wonderful! I didn't know Matt and Diane had set a date yet."

"They haven't, but if they don't soon, I will try to get out to Kalispell to see her. Sister, I really am taken with her and I think she likes me, too!"

"I think so," Sister smiled. "The whole family liked you."

"Except maybe Al and Swan," Jeff asserted.

"Oh, they came around by the time we left."

"How are you feeling about things now? I noticed you didn't punch anyone in the nose."

"No, I got over it. I think it turned out pretty well, except for Mother passing away. I want you to know that I really appreciated you doing the Last Rites."

"It felt rather strange, but I think it put some things in perspective for me too. I'm so glad I came on this trip. It has been one of the most moving things I have ever been a part of in my life."

"I'm glad you were with me, too. I feel I have found a very dear friend in you. Maybe we can both put some of our past in the bottom drawer now. I hope we can get up to Yaak Camp."

"Elias seemed sure we could make it. Sister, I hope you think I'm worthy to be your friend."

"I couldn't ask for anyone better."

Jeff smiled, "Then we head home. I have a lot of work to do when I get there!"

"You mean helping Carl with his yard?"

"No, learning how to dance for the wedding! Kathleen said she doesn't think I can do it."

"Just ask Nora. She will gather the clan women and you'll be a dancing idol by sunset." Sister watched him as he drove, "Did you ever have a serious girlfriend?"

"Not really. I dated in high school but there wasn't anyone serious. I liked this one girl, but she liked someone else. Honestly, I have never met someone like Kathleen. I am relaxed around her, even if I am being a dolt. I feel comfortable around her."

"I know what you mean. She does seem like a nice girl"

They got to Yaak before nightfall. Sister insisted she take Elias and Betty out for dinner at the steak house down the street. They had a wonderful meal and Jeff felt very comfortable. Over coffee, Sister brought out some Polaroids that Swan had given her. She passed them around. Jeff hadn't seen them either.

Elias looked through them and stopped at one. His mouth fell open and he exclaimed, "Sister! This looks just like you—Half Pint! The spit and image!"

Sister took the photo and smiled, "I guess a bit."

"A bit? It looks just like you did!" Elias smiled, "Amazing."

"Everyone always said I looked like my Mother."

Jeff reached the picture and he broke into a grin, "This is Kathleen! You never told me she looked like you!"

"I just thought she looked like family."

Elias said, "If this girl was in wool pants, a flannel shirt and logging boots, she would be our Half Pint!"

Jeff beamed, "I always knew I had good taste!"

Sister shook her head, "He is so cupid-bitten over this girl, it is unbelievable!"

Elias chuckled, "I think she is very pretty."

Betty asked, "Is she nice?"

"Yes," Jeff answered. "Very nice. May I have this photo?"

"Yes, you can keep it," Sister smiled.

Jeff put it in his wallet.

The next morning, the four got up early and had blueberry pancakes and sliced ham. Then they loaded into the Jeep and headed off toward Yaak Camp. It was bumpy and a bit chilly, but Sister seemed to relish the drive.

When Elias opened the gate into a heavily wooded area, Sister grabbed Jeff's hand. He gave it a squeeze. Elias drove slowly down a rutted, muddy road canopied by huge pines until he came to a clearing. There were the remains of a few, old log buildings. Some were intact, some had decayed or been partially torn down. Sister's eyes welled with tears. Jeff reached his handkerchief and gave it to her.

Elias pulled into the middle of the clearing and turned the Jeep off. Then he helped Betty while Jeff helped Sister out of the Jeep. Elias picked up a box of plastic flowers that he and Betty had brought.

Sister took a few steps and then asked Elias, "Is that it?"

"Yes," he nodded. "That is your cabin that Slim built. You can go in if you like. It isn't locked or anything."

Sister hesitated and Jeff came up beside her and took her hand. "Let's go look."

He helped her up the steps that were crumbled in disrepair, and they went in. The minute they got inside, tears started to fall. She walked all around the cabin and then went over to the Ben Franklin stove that she and Slim had been so proud of. She patted the side of the old thing and the tears almost overtook her. Jeff came up beside her and put his arm around her.

"Slim built this for us with the help of some friends. He did a good job, don't you think? It is still standing after all these years."

"Yes, he did a very good job."

He stood there with her for a little bit and then asked, "Are you ready to go?"

"Yes," she said. "I still miss him, you know."

"I know. Sister, you loved him very much."

They came out of the cabin and Elias said, "Ink Slinger's cabin is over here. I used it as a place to keep the papers for the cemetery. His old safe is still here. You should come and see it."

They went over and Sister went from crying to smiling when she saw his old desk. "He loved this old thing! It was even old then and all worn. Look," she said as she wiped the dust off the top. "Here are all the old gouges. I never could understand how he could write so neatly with such a chipped desk."

"If you think this is chipped, wait until you see the floor of the dining hall! The ceiling is caved in on side, but you can see in it yet, if you are careful."

"I would love to see it."

They went over to the long, partially caved in building. The long front porch was still up on the end by the door. Next to the door hung the old Gut Hammer. Sister touched it and smiled. They went inside. The floor had deeply worn areas around where every wooden table stood. Many of the deacon seats were still there, though some had been pilfered over the years. Sister shook her head, "Is our old room still here?"

"Yes, come see it. That big old tree by the back window has now finally had its way. It grew through the broken glass into the room."

They looked in and Sister laughed, "You're right, Elias. It finally won. Good for it."

They went back out and Sister turned toward the cemetery. This time, she just reached over and took Jeff's hand. They walked to the cemetery. Before they got there, Jeff recognized the big, lonely pine that Sister had described as Pendergast's tree. The fence around the small cemetery was still standing and in good condition. The graves were all well cared for and Betty was putting flowers on the graves of the loggers killed in the fire.

Sister Abigail stopped in front of the big pine and bowed her head in tears. There, carved on an old wooden cross was the name Pendergast. Beneath it was carved, "Gentle Giant." Sister just sobbed and Jeff put his arms around her. While he was consoling her, he noticed the huge boots, hanging on a rusty nail on the tree. Next to it was an old battered hat, now nearly threadbare. He knew it was Booker's.

On the left side of Pendergast's grave were two smaller ones. One cross read: Joshua Booker Peterson and the other read Pendergast Arthur Peterson. Sister just stared at them as shook her head. Then she bit her lip and looked next to the tiny graves. There was a cross that read: Arthur Peterson, Beloved husband and father.

That was about all Sister could do before she broke down. Jeff let her cry it all out and stood patiently while she did, rubbing her back and consoling her. In a short time, she stopped crying and wiped her tears.

She walked around the three short rows of the graves. She pointed one out to Jeff, "This is the man who played the harmonica."

A few graves later, she said, "This is Top Hat. He spent that first Christmas with us. Oh, look. Someone put that old tin star on his cross!"

Elias came over, "I found it one time when I was cleaning up around here. I thought he would like it."

Sister hugged him, "I'm sure he would love it. And Betty, thank you for putting these wonderful flowers on their graves. They would all be mighty proud that you did that for them. That is so kind."

Betty came up to her, "Here a few bouquets I thought you might want to put on the babies, Pendergast's and Slim's graves if you want. On this side is Ink Slinger, Cook, Angus and Elizabeth."

Sister nodded and walked over to them. She placed the carefully on each grave and stopped at each dear friends grave. Then she asked, "Jeff, could you lead us in a prayer?"

"I would consider it a deep honor."